ALL YOU NEED

ALL YOU NEED

Elaine Feinstein

VIKING

VIKING
Published by the Penguin Group
Viking Penguin, a division of Penguin Books USA Inc.,
375 Hudson Street, New York, New York 10014, U.S.A.
Penguin Books Ltd, 27 Wrights Lane,
London W8 5TZ, England
Penguin Books Australia Ltd, Ringwood,
Victoria, Australia
Penguin Books Canada Ltd, 2801 John Street,
Markham, Ontario, Canada L3R 1B4
Penguin Books (N.Z.) Ltd, 182–190 Wairau Road,
Auckland 10, New Zealand

Penguin Books Ltd, Registered Offices:
Harmondsworth, Middlesex, England

First American Edition
Published in 1991 by Viking Penguin,
a division of Penguin Books USA Inc.

1   3   5   7   9   10   8   6   4   2

LIBRARY OF CONGRESS CATALOGING IN PUBLICATION DATA
Feinstein, Elaine.
All you need/Elaine Feinstein.
p.   cm.
ISBN 0-670-83799-7
I. Title.
PR6056.E38A55   1991
823'.914—dc20   90–50465

Printed in the United States of America
Set in Plantin

For Michael Henshaw

ONE

It was Geoffrey who brought the news, and Nell didn't believe him.

She didn't like Geoffrey.

He had heavy blond hair which fell absolutely straight just in front of his ears, and a red mouth, which showed too much of the inner flesh. It was early September when he first drew up in his bright green Audi outside the house in Plumrose Crescent.

'Your Brian's in a spot of trouble,' he said in his funny looping drawl. 'Shouldn't think there's much to worry about, but he asked me to tell you. He's in gaol.'

And then he laughed at her stunned face.

'I'm standing bail. Don't worry. I should go up at the weekend; he's pretty bewildered. You can both stay at my flat.'

'But how? Why? Whatever has gone wrong?' she managed.

'I shouldn't worry him with too many questions.'

This was the summer of 1987, before the Great Winds uprooted trees all over England, throwing some of them across the roofs of country cottages and others through the fine windows in London squares with impartial violence. The weather was calm; the Stock Market index had not yet entered the news bulletins. No one was talking about 1929 or reading Galbraith anxiously.

From the outside, Nell's house in Plumrose Crescent looked much like the others. Not exactly the same, naturally; every house in the Crescent had different features; but all of them had been built at the same time in the seventies, with Georgian proportions, in bricks of the same tone to make a harmonious precinct of which Nell's house formed a part.

Nell herself was not quite what you would expect to find in the Crescent. There was too much mobility on her mouth. And perhaps there was something even more exotic. For all the bush of

7

fair curly hair, her skin was a pale olive. And her eyes were green as muscat grapes.

Some part of her difference was manifest as soon as she brought you into her house, because Nell's house had books. Fat, heavy books with cut pages. Books in foreign tongues and strange scripts. Nell's main living room was filled with them. And not only on the capacious shelving which covered two walls of the room; but on small tables where only coffee ought to sit, and even on the floor. In contrast, the television set was no larger than the screen of a home computer.

Now the inhabitants of Plumrose Crescent were not more than usually philistine. They were ordinary, decent, eighties people. If Plumrose Crescent preferred to borrow books from libraries, it was because, without question, books make a room untidy. They couldn't see why Nell should want to spend her time grubbing around with print when she could live peaceably in Royston without bothering.

It wasn't as if her husband Brian had unusual demands of any kind. He might have been to Cambridge but he had simple comprehensible interests, like football.

When the residents of Plumrose Crescent saw Geoffrey's Audi parked outside, there was a good deal of interest.

'I think I've seen him on the television. Is that possible?' asked Melanie, the doctor's wife, knocking on the kitchen window to return a videotape quite unnecessarily.

'I don't know what he does,' said Nell shortly. And she wasn't lying, because the truth was she didn't know what Brian did either. Not exactly.

She wasn't yet frightened. She didn't like Plumrose Crescent, but she felt a part of it. Residents of the Crescent were sober, salaried citizens, who had long ago settled for quiet comfort in the market town in East Anglia from which Brian had chosen to commute. Without knowing anything about the Greeks, they suspected that only unhappiness followed from a more glamorous life. Nell found them dull. But then, she found herself dull since she had came down from Cambridge. She could still remember the peculiar sense of satiety that filled her as she looked around her kitchen soon after her child was born, with the smell of good aired

8

laundry in her nose, every cupboard in order, every towel and sheet in its place. She had wondered: What shall I do if there's nothing more than this going to happen to me till I die?

She had not married Brian for adventure, but with a sense of coming home which she had badly needed all her adolescence. It wasn't just her parents' divorce that confused her; it was being left with a needy, miserable mother, unable to hate her father as she was required to do, and then, after his death, unable to mourn him.

What she mainly disliked about Geoffrey was his knowingness, as if everything was easy for those who understood the workings of the world. Even Brian, who had taken a First in Classics, found Geoffrey impressive.

'He knows such a lot without doing any work. Goodness knows what he could do if he tried.'

'Perhaps that's why he doesn't try? So nobody quite knows,' she suggested mutinously.

She knew Geoffrey found her earnestness a little comic. He made her feel there was something contemptibly pious about her attendance at lectures. It was Brian he liked. And Nell had to accept Geoffrey's style with a kind of mute envy.

At their wedding, he kissed Nell behind the ear and said: 'Such innocents, the pair of you. Touching really. I don't suppose either of you has ever been to bed with anyone else.'

Brian looked smug, but Nell flushed because it was so nearly, so unfashionably, true.

Brian's own family thought of themselves as simple Lancashire working-class; he didn't need their approval of his life as a shabby research student. He didn't talk to them about it either when he followed Geoffrey's advice into something much better paid. Geoffrey had been his mentor all through Nell's marriage; and now here he was, at the door of her neat little house in Plumrose Crescent, telling her Brian was in gaol.

'Come in and have a bite of supper,' she suggested, aware as so often with Geoffrey that her words were totally inadequate to the occasion.

Nell still didn't know exactly what it was Brian was supposed

9

to have done. Something had evidently gone wrong in that mysterious city to which he disappeared every morning on the fast electric service from Royston.

She drank a good deal of wine with a carefully prepared fresh herb omelette, and talked with exaggerated animation as if she had no problems at all, until she could show Geoffrey to the spare room and thankfully collapse into her own bed.

At three o'clock she woke in that bed, drenched with sweat. And two pieces of knowledge thudded into her head one after another.

Brian had known for more than four months he was going to be charged with fraud without mentioning a word to her about it.

And Geoffrey was sorry for her.

She ground coffee beans for breakfast, in an attempt to declare there was still some continuing pleasure in her life. Conversation, however, would not return to normal.

'There's another thing,' said Geoffrey. 'I don't suppose you remember Thynne? From Trinity. On the same staircase as Brian.'

She did remember Thynne; a pale boy, with serious green eyes, who always had an air of elegance without dressing in anything that drew attention to itself.

'One of the partners in Brian's firm, isn't he?'

'Well, I'm afraid he's dead. Rubber tube over the exhaust. Put his head down in the front seat of his Mercedes and closed the garage portals. Such an ugly way to do it.'

For a moment, a vision of Thynne disturbed her: she saw him grey-suited, and still soberly dressed in a neatly striped tie. She tried to imagine him sucking on a piece of school laboratory tubing, but she really only cared about what had happened to Brian, so she replied faintly.

'Do they by any chance say why he did that?'

'He wasn't well, the doctors said. Lupus. Nasty tropical disease. Well, there are lots of rumours.'

'I didn't know he spent any time in Africa,' said Nell dully. 'When did it happen?'

'A couple of months ago. Such a devoted father. Well, you'll remember that, at least.'

'No,' she said.

'Time and chance,' he said, and flashed her his unattractive grin. 'Happen to us all one day. No point in worrying till then, is there? You'll need a pad, of course.'

Startled, she looked round her house, and he explained.

'If you find a job in London. Somewhere to live. Maybe I can help.'

She shook her head.

'It's harder than you think,' he warned her. 'It'll take you a while to sell this place. A friend of mine has a basement flat going in Camden Town. She'll be very reasonable.'

She shook her head again. It was getting quite hard to disguise how frightened she felt.

Nell was so eager to see Brian and share her indignation with him that she woke in the dark on Saturday morning thinking about all she would say to assure him of her loyalty and trust; and as she thought of his innocence, and the unjust world that was so maliciously arraigning him, so much adrenaline coursed through her body that even five milligrams of Valium could not send her back to sleep until just before the alarm went off at seven. As a consequence she was bleary-eyed on the train, though she had chosen a later train precisely so that she would arrive fresh and cheerful. Fortunately, the laminated plastic buffet car, which was all the Eastern Region normally offered its customers, was serving real coffee.

Just outside Baldock, the train stopped in a field for such a long time that the guard came along the train to explain the delay. And the adrenaline began to rage in her blood again as she thought of Brian waiting on the platform for her, needing her help and comfort, and puzzled to know what had happened.

She imagined throwing her arms around his dear, battered shoulders, and holding him to her. She imagined him as he had been in his college days, long-haired, untidy, round-eyed, laughing. She had not felt so tenderly towards him in years, indeed she had not thought of him with any intensity at all. Now she sat and fumed in a field, longing to see him, and imagined his anxiety for her poignantly. Brian, she thought. My one and only love. Don't

11

worry. Nell is coming. Nell will stand by you, and make this horrid dream go away.

The train was forty-five minutes late.

And there he was waiting at the end of platform nine, looking quite dapper and spruce, in a grey woollen suit she did not recognize; a stranger, who gave no sign of wanting to be embraced at all. His charming, disgruntled face looked surly, even reproachful, as if the delay of the train had been her fault.

She searched his eyes for any sign of her own melting tenderness but she could not read their expression; and his mouth was clamped tight.

It came to her that she had not given any thought to what was going on inside him for a long time. She did not even know how he felt about his work, whether it had been what he wanted to be doing, or whether even before this trouble it had seemed to him that life was cheating him, that he had cause to feel his life was being wasted.

'I'm sorry,' she began idiotically.

'These Eastern Region trains,' he shrugged. 'Don't worry. I had a bit to eat at the Railway Hotel and read a paper while I was waiting. Quite a good breakfast. Are you hungry?'

The anger she saw had nothing to do with the delay of the train. Not even anything to do with her, possibly.

'I'll do whatever you like,' she said.

'Well, I thought we might try and catch that French film at the Curzon.'

She was astonished. Not by the choice of film, but by the fact that he had so little sense of crisis that he could afford to do anything so casual. It was reassuring. Wasn't it? Unless, she began to wonder, as he escorted her to the queue for taxis, he was very worried indeed in a way he didn't want to talk about.

He wanted to talk about the film, and did so even as they walked to Geoffrey's flat which was just round the corner from the Curzon. They walked along Shepherd's Market, chattering inconsequentially just as if nothing was seriously wrong, and Nell wrinkled her nose at the Dickensian, knobbly prettiness of the place, remembering Heffers in Petty Cury before Cambridge developers got to it.

Geoffrey's flat had portals of marble and glass, and a hall porter, who sent them along the corridor to a door that looked as though it opened into Fort Knox. In fact it opened on its own to their buzz, since Geoffrey had been alerted to their arrival by the doorman. Inside there was another hallway, lined with paintings. Nell wondered if they could really be the French nineteenth-century oils they appeared to be. Manet? Corot? She speculated. The ceilings were so high; the cornices so elaborate, she longed to squeeze Brian's arm and giggle. But his face was once again as remote as a stranger's.

Geoffrey was talking into a cordless phone, his eyes twinkling with amusement as he waved them towards a little supper.

The table was set with a pretty green embroidered tablecloth which matched the napkins precisely. The plates too were delicately green and gold, with a pattern of entwining leaves. Someone had set out a bowl of thick asparagus, cooked within the last five minutes as far as Nell could judge. Salmon. Freshly cut slices of lemon. Lychees, clementines and fat muscat grapes. Stilton.

'All right,' Geoffrey was saying. 'I understand . . . Of course. I'll explain exactly as you say.'

Later that evening, Nell marvelled again at the bathroom, the extraordinary deep cobalt blue of the sunken bath; the number and thickness of the towels that matched that cobalt precisely; the beauty of wall and floor and rug.

'Of course Geoffrey isn't filthy rich,' said Brian impatiently as they went upstairs to bed. 'He's just a minnow.'

Brian made love to her that night with self-contained desperation and fell asleep at once, while she pondered the various matters that disturbed her until it was nearly morning.

'Don't worry,' she said hopefully as they sat over Geoffrey's scrubbed-wood breakfast table the next morning.

Brian looked up at her without smiling: 'I'm in a mess. I'm sorry. I know you just want to be reassuring, but I can't pretend. You'll find out soon enough. You'll have to forgive me.'

'Geoffrey doesn't think it's serious.'

'Well. It conveniently isn't serious for him. Don't widen your eyes like that.'

13

'Brian, you're talking as though there's a lot you haven't been telling me.'

'It's too late now,' said Brian.

At the trial, which was much sooner than Nell had expected, the case against Brian seemed to turn very precisely on what Brian himself did or didn't know and when he'd known it. He looked so quiet and unhappy as he answered the questions that she wanted to cry for him. The whole thing was over very quickly. Brian was found guilty and sentenced to three years' imprisonment.

'What will I do? What will happen to us? What on earth will Becky say?' she asked Geoffrey, since he seemed to feel himself involved.

Nell's daughter Becky was fourteen. She had grown increasingly hostile to the world in general for having done this thing to her father, and even more hostile to her mother for allowing it to happen.

'The case is all over the local papers. I'd move,' he offered.

'Becky won't like that.'

'You can't be tyrannized by a child,' said Geoffrey.

Nell held on to the words as common sense in a world where all other certainties had exploded.

The estate agent was very enthusiastic about selling the house. Just what people wanted, he said. Nicely kept. Practical. Sell in a fortnight as long as she wasn't determined to get the absolute top of the market price.

'And why shouldn't I want top of the market price?' asked Nell. She had been examining some very surprising bank statements and was acutely conscious of the fact that at the most optimistic figure she could imagine she would be very lucky to have any equity left in the house at all.

'It's a psychological mistake,' he explained. 'Ask too high a price and you get the wrong people altogether coming to look round. They expect more than you've got to offer; bathrooms en suite in all rooms, that kind of thing. Then the house starts to hang about on the market, and people who like it just as it is start to say there must be something wrong.'

'That's a bit complicated,' objected Nell.

'All psychology,' he said brightly. 'It's our job to understand these things. After all, it's in our interest too, isn't it? To get the best price on the house? Just sign this, by the way.'

'What is it?'

'Sole agency.'

'Why should I agree to that?'

'Cheaper for you. Look. Lower percentage. And you lose nothing; everyone comes to us, whoever else they look at as well. You don't lose. Put up a lot of boards, and people start to think you're getting desperate.'

'Psychology?' asked Nell.

'Exactly.'

She nodded.

'Of course it isn't true that you or your firm gain as much as I do if the house makes another few thousand. You do better by selling more houses more quickly.'

A slight change in colour in his cheeks confirmed that her shot had gone home, but she regretted it instantly.

'It's up to you, Missus. Your business who you go to, but there's no need to put on airs with me – everyone knows why you have to sell.'

She stared at him and her own colour came up into her face as she took back the agency forms.

'Don't bother to measure up,' she said frostily. 'I'll deal with this through someone else.'

It was not a clever decision.

In the first week, forty-three possible purchasers from another two agencies tramped round the neatly maintained rooms of Plumrose Crescent. It was an odd experience, seeing her house through the eyes of strangers, apologizing for this and that, cursing her tongue. She took to putting flowers everywhere, opening windows, waxing floors.

And then of course there were the books.

Her mother's voice came into her ears, suggesting unwelcome truths about the odours of her life: 'When people buy a house, they're buying a smell.' Clearly she was being found wanting by the market forces of which those daily visitors were the inspectors.

She would have liked to be out all day long, and leave the job to the estate agents, but her decision had made that impossible. The man in the blue blazer had been confident, however rude. A succession of younger, more diffident figures gave her no such reassurance. Some needed the printed sheet of particulars every bit as much as the potential purchasers; they all behaved as if they were seeing the house for the first time; most needed her help to find where the bathroom was and forgot the interesting features in the breakfast room.

They all apologized for the books.

At the end of a fortnight she began to feel her panic mounting. She began to see that there was a good deal of sense in renting a room in London. It seemed unlikely any building society would continue her present mortgage, let alone let her take out another to buy an expensive house.

Not with Brian in gaol.

Perhaps not ever again.

'I'll go up next week,' she said to her daughter Becky the following morning, over a bowl of Alpen into which she was still careful to sprinkle the requisite amount of bran.

Her fourteen-year-old daughter fixed her with a blue stare of implacable hostility.

'I suppose you expect me to stay with a friend?'

'Well, yes, I suppose so.'

'You don't think of anyone but yourself,' said Becky.

Nell was astonished.

'You can come if you like, ' she said doubtfully. 'It won't be much of a jaunt for you, but I suppose you can look at a museum or something while I'm hunting.'

'I don't expect a jaunt,' said Becky. 'London's dirty, and I hate museums.' She burst into tears.

Nell jumped up in horror and tried to embrace her daughter, but Becky resisted any such attempt.

'Have you asked Daddy what is supposed to happen to me?'

Nell admitted she had not.

'He wouldn't want me to move from my school; he loved me being there.'

Nell agreed that was so, in some perplexity, not wanting to emphasize their dilemma.

Her daughter's face grew thoughtful.

'Why did you lie to those Canadians about the fish pond? You know what happens every winter when there's a lot of rain.'

'I was just trying to make them see how pretty it could look,' said Nell.

'Daddy never told lies,' said Becky.

A mounting sense of injustice had Nell's blood pounding in her temples, but she managed an equable demeanour.

'Daddy wouldn't think I was doing anything wrong,' she said.

Becky's chin lifted in defiant disbelief.

'It's all your idea, moving to London.'

Against her will, Nell began to say a good deal she wished to keep silent about.

'It's so unfair, the way you blame me. Everything isn't my fault, you know. It certainly isn't because of me there isn't any more money in the bank. It isn't my fault Daddy is in gaol either, though you sometimes look at me as if you think it was. It's all right having me to blame, I know that. I only wish I had someone I could hate the way you hate me, but I haven't. I don't hate your daddy, and there's no one else to blame that I can see.'

She stopped.

'Daddy told me he'd done nothing wrong,' said Becky primly. Her eyes were unfocused and she seemed to find that Nell's words confirmed all her secret suspicions.

'You're quite right, he hasn't,' said Nell in an attempt to be conciliatory.

Her daughter saw through this contemptuously.

'You're such a hypocrite. You don't ever say what you mean.'

'I was trying – ' Nell began.

'When you turn up on Parents' Day I can't bear that voice you use; so smarmy.'

'At least I did turn up,' said Nell, lured into self-defence.

It was a mistake.

17

'What else did you need to do? It's not as if you run a shop, or have a career or anything.'

'Your daddy and I decided – ' Nell tried again.

'You never did pull your weight,' said Becky crudely.

The absurd schoolgirl phrase took Nell's breath away.

'Can't you be more just, things are bad enough,' she begged.

But her daughter shook her head, and slid away from the table. Every nerve in Nell's body screamed with the desire to follow and make peace, but she continued to sit at the table. Perhaps I'll go out and buy a packet of cigarettes, she thought. I'll walk to the corner shop. But she didn't move. The quarrel had hurt her. She felt cowed by it. There seemed no point in anything: not even in clearing the table. Not if Becky was going to continue being so unkind to her. Who was she struggling for in that case? No one but herself? The thought brought two tears of self-pity to her eyes, and she had to wink them away angrily. Mustn't get depressed, she thought. No sense in that. But the misery rose in her all the same, and she felt her shoulders heave against her will. Perhaps in her mind she hoped for two soft daughterly hands to come and stroke her head, a little voice saying sorry and even a forgiving kiss, but whatever she imagined, she quite soon heard the front door slam, and could watch her daughter, dressed in beret and scarf, take her bicycle out from the garage.

'Here,' Nell said, opening a window in some agitation, 'don't you remember promising to say whenever you go out on that thing? Where are you going?'

Becky gave her a brilliant smile, as if they had not quarrelled.

'Just posting a letter,' she said. 'I'll be back in a minute.' Nell felt an intensity of relief she could not absolutely explain.

'My legs are wobbly,' Nell explained to her general practitioner. 'And I feel as though my brain's resting on a kind of water cushion. Judders about all the time.'

'Anything else?'

'I wake up in the night with my body pouring with sweat. And sometimes my heart pounds so that I think it's going to jump out of my chest.'

'Stress,' he said instantly.

18

'Of course I'm under stress.'

'I don't want to give you any more Valium.'

'I think I read in *The Times* they've brought out something with a shorter action; only works for a few weeks like any of these things but they say it shouldn't hook you for life.'

'They said that once about the benzodiazepams. You don't want any, do you?'

'Yes,' she said.

He looked surprised.

'I'd like anything that helped me function again. If drink helped, I'd drink, but it just makes me sleepy.'

He was a mild, sandy-haired youngish man with a lineless face, and he could not keep the tone of reproach out of his voice.

'Come now,' he reasoned. 'Drink only stops you facing up to your troubles. Pills too. Now if you would let me arrange for you to see a therapist . . .'

'I haven't time for that,' she said. 'And even if I did, why do I need a therapist? I have perfectly real troubles in the outside world to cope with. Anyone would feel like I do in my situation.'

'Ah,' he said sagely, 'but why are you in the situation? That's where a therapist comes in.'

'I can't afford to pay a therapist,' she said abruptly.

He was really a very concerned young man. In the last election he had flown a banner of the SDP outside his house, and something in the smoothness of his face and roundness of his eyes suggested an eager child. Residents of Plumrose Crescent did not like to admit to being short of money. It was thought of as a moral weakness, and he wasn't used to hearing it so bluntly acknowledged.

'Dear me, dear me.'

'Never mind about that. You can't help me,' said Nell, rising to her feet. 'I know that. I'll have some more Valium, though, if you'll write a script . . .'

'I don't approve, mind,' he said, doing so.

Becky was still adamantly opposed to London. Nell wondered if Geoffrey could be right about moving.

'She'll like it more than staying here. So will you. What about your mother?' he said.

'She died.'

'You've got family, haven't you?'

'Cousins,' Nell said doubtfully.

They were her father's family, however. They had played on waste ground together as children, and she was still fond of Mark, who was the same age as herself, but they had grown apart even before she went to Cambridge.

'We don't get on,' she said flatly.

Geoffrey looked amused.

'Go to London. Do you have friends? I can give you some addresses.'

'I'll be fine.'

'You could go and see Caroline,' suggested Geoffrey.

Nell was stung at once with something very like jealousy. At Cambridge Caroline had been her most admired, most magical friend. When she thought of Caroline, she thought of everything life had once seemed about to offer her. In those days, as Newnham doors closed behind them late at night, no future seemed impossible to either Caroline or herself; and their youth, their good looks, their position as women in a university where men were still so much more numerous, made it natural for Nell to miss the difference in their true expectations. In the late sixties, in their generation, girls like Caroline, from good schools, learned the voices of the disadvantaged, making in the process a new unmistakeable voice of their own which was called classless. Together, the whole generation rejected the values of the 'grown-up' world in favour of their own more joyful lives. Nell and Caroline smoked a little pot, listened to very loud bands with inscrutable and evocative names, and grew their hair long. Caroline experimented with a greater variety of men, some of whom put her off by knowing all about her parents, a titled uncle, and the family acres in North Devon. When Nell took up with Brian, Caroline did not approve, though she was gracious about him when he took a first-class degree.

It was the move to Plumrose Crescent that depleted their friendship and only partly because it took Nell to Royston. Caroline had visited only once, and Nell had found it hard to forgive the way her marvellous eyes had grown round with an amazement she could not conceal.

'It's just like a Sunday magazine,' she said at last, making clear that her disapproval was nothing to do with snobbery and everything to do with Nell's wish to conform. And for a moment Nell had felt a rush of disloyalty, as though it were not her life at all, but something she had only taken on because of Brian.

The split was never articulated, and sometimes Caroline had telephoned with wild, straggly confidences from a life that had never stabilized. The phone calls had fallen off with the arrival of Becky, and the monotonous sobriety of Nell's existence. No one in Plumrose Crescent had ever seemed likely to take Caroline's place in Nell's affections.

'Are you still in touch?' she asked Geoffrey now, with some surprise. Geoffrey had been in love with Caroline, but from a distance as far as she knew. Nell might have been at a distance herself, but for the accident of sharing supervisions with Caroline during her second year.

'I have her new address. She's moved house again, had you heard?'

'We don't even write these days,' said Nell wearily.

'She hasn't married. Doesn't believe in it, she says.'

Like Geoffrey himself, thought Nell.

'Go and see Caroline. You'll need help. She's well connected,' he advised her.

Nell shut her mouth firmly over an inclination to wail.

TWO

Early September was hot and wet, and uncomfortably sweet-smelling, as if a foreign climate lay over Southern England. Nell was determined to find a London base for herself and Becky. For there were no jobs in Royston, and even if there had been she could not face the pity in the faces of those who knew her situation and would now be employing her. And she could see Becky was going through a crisis of her own; the farmers' children from her school class no longer took her off to ride their horses. When girls came to tea, it hurt Nell to see their undisguised curiosity, and read what was being said in their homes in their sharp eyes and the expressions on their fresh faces. When Nell admitted to giving a term's notice at school, there was only token resentment from Becky.

She encouraged Becky with the thought of a new school, but the need to live in an appropriate catchment area made looking for a flat tricky. Nell did her best; combing the small ads and tramping about areas of inner London where schools had some reputation for academic standards. She saw small rooms that were little more than a hole under the stairs. She saw rooms bare and wet at the same time. She smelled old frying bacon, saw crumbs in the sink, and was able to afford none of it.

When she was exhausted she went into a noisy pub full of grey heads and Irish voices. One of her toes hurt with a persistent throbbing pain that suggested she might have done something serious to the bone when she stubbed it.

She would have prayed if she had thought it would help. It didn't seem likely. And headlines glimpsed in the screaming typeface of the popular press confirmed her apprehension. How would Becky cope with this wilderness? 'Eighty-four-year-old pensioner raped and strangled,' she read. 'Young woman caught at tube station and robbed at knife point.' The city seemed to be full of the terrors God daily permitted without interfering. Wouldn't the old pensioner have cried for help? Or the young girl at knife point? If no help had come for them, if the horrors of humiliation and finally death had been permitted only yesterday, in this very city, not more than a mile or so from where she was now sitting, there seemed no sense in hoping for divine assistance in the matter of lodgings.

Stolidly she drank her beer, decided against a meat pie, and tried again.

Waiting for the last train home from Liverpool Street Station that night with the rubbish lying about her feet like the detritus at the end of a market day, Nell found she was crying helplessly. The tears came partly from fatigue, and partly because she had just missed a train by two minutes; but mainly she began to cry because she was losing faith in the possibility of keeping herself afloat. One of the new tramps of eighties London stopped to watch her curiously before shuffling by in an old coat tied with string, in search of a warm place to sit with a comforting bottle of plonk.

A bag lady. Nell looked at her, particularly the way her varicose ankles fitted into shoes that were much too big for her, and felt ashamed at her own self-pity. This is ridiculous, she told herself angrily. This is nothing but self-indulgence, I'm not trapped, I have resources, I'm not alcoholic. I've no business identifying with this poor woman. Supply teachers are still needed. And typists earn seven thousand pounds a year in London. I've seen the shop windows. I must pull myself together. Take off tax, and I can spend about sixty pounds a week on a flat. The trouble was she and Becky would be sharing a single room if she had no more than sixty pounds a week. But I'm Class A in the Registrar General classification, she thought. The highly targeted, most desirable reader of glossy magazines. A house-owner. One of the privileged who had watched their investment rise over the last few years by however many per cent. Except, manifestly, she had no disposable income at all; and probably didn't even have enough money to take a cab home from the station when she arrived back in Royston at 2 a.m.

That was when she had the idea of renting out Plumrose Crescent.

The house was still unsold, as the bank very well knew; they might not be enormously pleased about her wish; but for a short let they might agree to have it produce a little revenue. If the manager felt kind.

Something else she thought of, as she pulled out her ticket to give to the impatient white-faced man at the barrier. She still had the address of Geoffrey's friend Millie, in Camden Town, and it made sense at least to look into what she was offering.

She went to visit Brian at Bleakwood at the weekend. He was understandably sombre, sunk too deeply into contemplation of his own disaster to be much interested in her anecdotes, or listen to her plans.

On Tuesday Nell found her way behind Camden High Street, past a grey hillside of Victorian villas, their windows sealed with rusty corrugated iron. She was in squatters' territory, she concluded gloomily, though Geoffrey had said that Millie had the whole house on a short lease. A little further on, the neighbourhood improved; there were a few estate cars and a teak-framed dormer window or two.

Millie's street was Nell's first pleasant surprise. The house was part of a splendid Georgian crescent, with enormous windows, pretty black frills of railings, and a door painted dark blue. Millie apologized at the unreadiness of the accommodation. The house was not yet completely divided into flats; there was a common entrance, and the basement rooms had access to the bathroom only through an outside staircase. Nell had no hesitation in taking the three rooms she was offered.

Millie had black skin and an Ethiopian profile; she had the kind of beauty that photographs with great purity because of the regular, almost brutal bone structure. Her eyes went up and down Nell's neat suit.

'You sign on yet?' she asked.

'Pardon me?'

'It's Tuesday. Listen, you don't know these crooks. They like you to lose a week. It gives them pleasure. You better get down there before it shuts.'

'I'm planning to get a job.'

'How you going to pay the rent?' demanded Millie directly,

shaking her head. 'Social security pays the rent for me when I don't have work. And just at the moment I don't have work. How old is your kid?'

'Fourteen. I can pay you the first month's rent,' offered Nell.

'Make that two, and we'll forget the deposit. What kind of job are you looking for? Can you use a word processor?'

'I'll take a course.'

'You can play around with mine,' said Millie.

'What do you work at?' inquired Nell cautiously, not wanting to pry but bewildered by Millie's assurance.

'I work in the theatre. When I can. I trained, though – ' she threw out a flashing smile – 'as a biochemist.'

'Are you married?' Even as she asked, Nell felt uncomfortable. The words seemed to come from a different world. She uttered them bravely, as if she half-expected Millie to burst out into laughter at them.

'When I was seventeen,' said Millie shortly. 'A mistake. Then I lived with a couple of guys. And now I'm on my own which suits me fine. Your man is in trouble, Geoffrey said?'

Nell agreed.

'It happens,' said Millie, indicating with a movement of her shoulders that she had no intention of embarrassing Nell with questions.

'Who else lives here?' asked Nell, registering Millie's diplomacy gratefully.

'There's a musician. Don't worry. You can't hear him from the basement. He gets a lot of gigs.'

'Jazz?'

'LSO. A violinist. Comes from New York.'

'I'll move in early next week,' said Nell.

Saying as much made her feel anxious, and her hand went to her pocket where a bottle of Valium nestled soothingly. She wondered how many pills were left. Taking the bottle out, she turned it round to see.

'Hey,' said Millie.

'It's all right,' said Nell reassuringly. 'Only Valium.'

'Haven't you been reading the papers?' demanded Millie. 'There

25

are people suing at this very moment world wide. Those little yellow pills are poison.'

Before Nell could question Millie's unexpected vehemence, they were disturbed by the violinist opening the front door.

Nell saw he was a man of about thirty-seven, who must once have been exceedingly handsome. His face was broad, his eyes large and blue; a thick fuzz of brown hair stuck up around his forehead. A redness in his cheeks and a certain puffiness in the tissues under the eyes suggested that he might have a drinking problem, but he welcomed Nell affably.

'Glad to have you aboard,' he said.

Nell set off triumphantly for Royston, eager to tell Becky that she had found somewhere to live. Her discoveries raced round in her head. There are trees, she would say. And little shops just a minute away, a post office, a grocer's, even a wet fish shop. It's much more convenient than Royston. And the shops stay open late. And there's a launderette, we'll need that because we can't start plumbing in the washing machine. And there's a fine school, everyone agrees it's very good and you can start next week. Becky, we're going to be okay.

She was so eager to explain all this that she couldn't fall asleep on the train. She wasn't thinking about Brian. He had become remote and dreamlike; a querulous, unhappy ghost that sometimes woke her in the night with pain and longing, but whose voice fell silent in the daytime. How else could she function? She kept her pity at bay.

To understand that, there has to be a little history.

Brian had always been the superior member of their family team. To begin with, he was a Mature Student, nearly ten years older than she was, with National Service and a series of odd jobs from butcher's assistant to factory worker behind him. He had a burly physical strength that made him an excellent forward on the college rugby team, and he might have had a Blue if he hadn't been much more interested in Classical Philosophy. He was a working-class grammar-school boy, trailing his Northern origins with pride at a time when they seemed a marvellous indication of intellectual vigour. Then he won First-Class Honours in his first year, and she did not. Both felt this was entirely appropriate.

He developed a paternal, protective and entirely benevolent style towards her. He was the teacher, she the eager apprentice; he knew, and she did not. About everything, really. Sex, learnt extensively and subtly on the south coast during National Service. Politics in the North-West, learnt through his rumbustious Liverpool days on the factory floor. Class, in which he saw himself as spiritually advantaged, in the style of Hoggart's *The Uses of Literacy*, by childhood games, and street wisdom she had never acquired in her pusillanimous childhood in the home counties. He looked exactly as winners those days were supposed to look: fresh skinned, sturdily built and male. She looked up to him, with starry respect. She was suburban; he was Lawrentian. With these masculine virtues he tackled Socrates and Heidegger. All they had in common was poetry, which he loved as Nell did, though he preferred the classical control of the Greeks to her Russians.

Leaving Cambridge, he began to pride himself on his superior worldliness too. House mortgages. Home improvement grants. Dealing with bank managers. He explained; she listened. He knew, and she did not. It was the basis of their relationship.

'Don't worry,' he'd said when they added up the first household bills, which came to more than they could possibly pay. So she hadn't worried. Or not much. Not since. Because she trusted him to make everything come right.

Her mother had always been a bit sniffy about that.

'I suppose *anyone* is more in touch with the world than you, Nell. All the same, Brian is a bit of a dreamer himself.'

It was a description that made her furious, because it was exactly the word her mother had always used to describe Nell's limitations. And Nell felt she knew much better. Brian understood what he was doing. That was why he had decided to leave research in Classics and go into the City.

And he had always been a man of total probity, who would no more have thought of fiddling his income tax returns than stealing from a beggar.

Nell lay back in her seat in the train, then reflected that she felt something rather like happiness. Becky had been unusually solicitous over the last few days. She'd taken to making hot drinks last thing at night, and turning on Nell's electric blanket in good

27

time. And twice she had even got up in the early morning darkness to see Nell off to the station. Nell was enormously strengthened by Becky's new comradeliness, which seemed to acknowledge that Nell was putting up a good fight.

All this pleasure evaporated the moment she saw Becky's face.

'What's happened?' she asked therefore.

'Geoffrey phoned. He's got someone who wants to rent the house.'

'Well, that's good, isn't it?'

Becky's face was dark and expressionless, her round eyes remote. There was usually a ghostly moment when she looked like Brian, something in the relationship of eyes to grin, but she wasn't grinning now. A little frown wrinkled the pure skin between her brows.

'I don't want someone I don't know sleeping under my duvet,' she said.

There was a spot of colour in her cheeks and her underlip was tremulous.

'What rubbish,' expostulated Nell. 'We can't take the bed but we can take the linen.'

Becky was holding something back, she could see. Nell felt suddenly very tired. She's been damaged, of course. What else could be expected? She'd seen that darkness before, in the children of friends. Her heart was squeezed with compassion for the whole generation. How shall we manage to help them? Some families had to cope with absconding parents, readjusted mates, unfamiliar siblings. Who is daddy? This is the man who is living with my mummy. And this is the daughter of the man who lives with my mummy. Let's all be good friends.

My daddy is in goal.

How could she hope to cajole Becky into cheerfulness?

'I'll phone Geoffrey,' she said therefore, hearing the faked jollity in her voice and unable to think of what other style to adopt.

Some of her earlier enthusiasm for the Camden Town house came back as she thanked Geoffrey for his intervention.

'All I need now is a job.'

'Go and see Caroline,' he advised her.

THREE

The seasons were changing. A new school term was beginning. Becky had started at her new school.

On her way to school with Becky, Nell saw chestnuts in the gutter with their rinds split open. She could see the shiny red nuts within. And the country-red, mahogany colour aroused thoughts that weakened her: like certain phrases – 'I love you,' say, or 'we were happy once' – the colour made her faint with longing. And she couldn't afford to feel faint, or entertain longing.

She was free to do as she liked. It was a pleasure succeeded almost at once by the terror of having nothing to do. From the kitchen window she took in a new wetness in the light, a glistening in the stunted pear tree; the pale light caught on the surfaces of leaves. The sunlight was hard-edged. Brilliant. As she wiped up the two breakfast mugs she felt exhilarated and painfully lonely at the same time. She wondered if the two feelings went ineluctably together.

Why not go and see Caroline, she thought. We spoke on the phone easily enough.

I ought to try to find a job. But then, perhaps Caroline could help with that.

Caroline had moved to the wrong side of Islington: 'For space, mainly,' she'd said on the telephone. And as Nell turned north from the Angel she perceived that Caroline was not exaggerating the gap between her new surroundings and the salubrious street facing a canal from which she had moved. The people in the streets looked confused and sad; twelve-year-old boys in padded navy coats, their chalk faces frozen between a jeer and a glare; old West Indian women carrying heavy shopping bags; and white youngsters, fiercer and angrier than any, pushing and nudging.

All this was forgotten as soon as Caroline's door opened, and Caroline flung both arms around her; it was as if fifteen years had not gone by since their college intimacy. Nell was beckoned to an open fire. On a table nearby stood an oxblood table lamp, bottles of vermouth and vodka, a thirties-style cocktail shaker. The walls were lined with books. And Caroline herself looked exactly as she had in the corridors of Newnham.

In contrast to Nell's honey colouring, Caroline had marvellous white skin and black hair, and her eyes seemed to belong to a larger face, perhaps to a larger animal like a lion.

Nell was glad she had taken the risk of coming. The visit had already restored her to a forgotten sense of herself. In Caroline's presence she was no longer just a social security problem; someone displaced from the suburbs, inexplicably connected to the criminal classes. She had a history, which included Cambridge, laughter and all the absurdity of adolescent loves. Now she stared out at the wonderful autumnal sunshine that filled the room from the garden window and smiled.

'At least I've found somewhere to live,' she told Caroline, describing her situation.

'Sounds marvellous,' said her friend, doubtfully. 'I suppose you heard what happened to poor old Nicky Thynne?'

'Geoffrey told me. Do you still see them?' Nell asked, surprised at such continuity.

'I speak to his wife quite often. She has a feminist workshop in West London. In fact, I wondered whether you'd be interested in working for her?'

As she spoke, she got up and Nell could not see her face. Nell looked doubtful.

'It might be fun,' suggested Caroline.

'Doesn't sound fun exactly,' said Nell. 'I mean, I believe in votes for women, of course, and equal pay and things like that . . .'

Caroline shook her head.

'You think the battles are all won.'

Much you know about battles, thought Nell unfairly, knowing from their telephone call that Caroline had problems of her own and would soon be discussing them. Surreptitiously she eased the top off her bottle of tranquillizers, and extracted one with her fingers, hoping it would still her rising panic.

'I mean, think what happened to poor old Thynne. Men have

30

problems too,' she said, with the pill on her tongue, releasing its magical charm to her trembling nerve ends. She was thinking of Brian.

'What do you know about Nick's problems?' asked Caroline sharply.

'Not much, not enough, not in time,' said Nell sadly. She was still thinking of Brian.

'I'll give you the telephone number anyway,' Caroline said at last. 'It was Geoffrey's idea.'

'I'll try and get some teaching first,' said Nell, without a great deal of optimism.

'You should be developing your talents,' said Caroline briskly. 'You've forgotten you had any.'

'Becky and I need to eat,' said Nell.

'You don't expect enough from life,' said Caroline. 'Never did. Waste yourself.'

Nell swallowed unhappily.

'No use lecturing me about self-help now,' she said.

'Silly, I'm not a Thatcherite,' said Caroline briskly.

And she was not, she was a dedicated socialist far to the left of the Labour Party. Before China's paddy fields had been exposed to Western eyes, she had believed in Mao, as Nell had believed in the singing enthusiasm of the North Vietnamese while she was at school. Nell recognized that Caroline had been pulled by all the same strings as she had been herself.

'You should see this change in your life as an opportunity,' said Caroline.

'Well, I'm not ambitious,' said Nell.

It was a lie. But ambition was a luxury when she couldn't even be sure of the next quarter's rent for Millie.

'What are you doing these days?' she asked, genuinely curious.

Caroline looked as though Nell ought to know the answer.

'I'm a poet,' she said simply.

Now this was surprising information. Nell could see that Caroline might well have hoped she would know as much; and was just wondering whether it would be forgivable to ask if she had a book out when Caroline threw a slim volume over to her. It was

31

called *Drowning and Other Incidents*, had a cover in brilliant reds and blues and the logo of a prestigious publishing house.

Some part of the surprise, Nell observed, as she turned the pages for a sense of Caroline's achievement, came from her friend's beauty. It was an absurd prejudice, a Plumrose Crescent cliché, to believe that all women poets were spinsterly, witchy or suicidal; she was ashamed of herself. She read the title poem, and looked up with respect.

'It's like Waller,' said Nell. 'That's the tune of it.'

'Yes,' said Caroline, surprised. 'I'd forgotten what a good ear you have.'

She had been watching a little edgily, but Nell's words relaxed her, and she began to speak spontaneously in quite a new way.

'It's unfashionable, I know, to aim at the lyrical.'

'The last poet I really loved was Larkin,' said Nell, slowly, feeling for words in a way that she had forgotten. 'Someone looking at themselves very quietly, not afraid to say true, rather ugly things. I didn't really like myself for liking him: I felt it was the dinginess of our lives that we had in common. I was unhappy about it, as if the nothing-much that had happened to him was what had happened to me. Of course it was the song of it I was liking. Since then I haven't read much.'

She hadn't said anything of comparable complexity to anyone for a very long time.

'It was the Americans at first for me,' said Caroline eagerly.

Nell remembered Allen Ginsberg's reading at Kings College in the sixties. It was Caroline's boyfriend who had organized the reading. The undergraduates had packed the oak-lined room, most of them supercilious about a poet with a name like a tailor, unwilling to be impressed; all of them finally seduced by the showbiz energy more than the flashes of poetry.

'I liked the lion poem. I liked it because it was funny. Do you remember that evening?' Nell's voice was eager. And suddenly they were both talking happily and freely.

When Caroline got up to take a phone call, Nell found herself looking down at the newspaper on the chair next to her. Johnnie Farrago. The well-cut underlip, and the hint of a suppressed amusement there gave the face some of the good looks of a young

Paul Newman. It was almost too handsome a face for the narrow, stubbly-chinned eighties. He enjoyed a celebrity very much of the eighties, however: his company had bought another company: together the new firm was expanding, there was general financial success. Evidently behind the face of Butch Cassidy lay the brain of a kind that owned banks rather than robbed them.

'Who *is* that?' asked Nell.

A little colour came into Caroline's cheeks: she sat down with studied inconsequence.

'Johnnie Farrago? I met him at the Adelaide Literary Festival. Didn't think I'd ever find Australia exciting, but we all see it differently now it doesn't seem to be so far from Europe, don't you think? And you can stop over in places like Bali.'

Nell said that Bali sounded fun, and waited.

'Well, Adelaide was glamorous too. Parties. Theatre. Operas. Patrick White. The Governor General.'

'And Johnnie Farrago?' asked Nell, amused.

'He was there as a publisher. Looking in on one of his novelists. Adelaide's not all poets, you see, that's why Oz can afford to spend a bit of money. At least I suppose that's why. It was quite a jaunt.'

About this she looked complacent, as though jaunts were her God-given right. Nell thought enviously that it must be wonderful to be so hosted round the world.

'Geoffrey doesn't approve of Johnnie,' said Caroline. A dimple came into her face as she said as much, and Nell observed she was altogether unafraid of anyone else's judgement. It was a confidence that no doubt came from parental assurance, childhood austerity and the knowledge of her own beauty.

'It wasn't exactly instant romance,' Caroline continued. 'We spent the first evening arguing furiously. Poetry. Politics. We didn't agree about anything. Especially not Russia. Anyway, we went off to Melbourne on the same plane. And then there was a week up the coast in a beach hut. But it was really only in Moscow that we became important to each other.'

'What were you doing in *Moscow?*' asked Nell in a small voice.

'Invitation from the Writers' Union. Writers go every year from Great Britain, you know.'

'Are your books known in Russia then?'

'Oh no,' said Caroline. 'They ask committees here for names. You know how these things work.'

Nell didn't.

'Anyway, last year they sent a playwright and a novelist the Russians had heard of quite a lot, so they could afford to send me.'

'And Johnnie was there?'

'He arranged to be there at the same time. Of course he was interested in some other business, something to do with *glasnost*. But you'll know all about that – you read Russian, didn't you? And didn't you live there for a time in your third year?'

'Yes.'

'Well, I was only there a week. Honestly, I never got to grips with the place at all. There was Yevtushenko to meet us at the airport with a green velvet suit, a peak cap and red carnations, and we stayed at the Sovietskaya. All turn-of-century splendour, marble balustrades and chandeliers. Johnnie was at another hotel but we were all invited to the Writers' House – you know, the one that used to belong to the family Tolstoy described in *War and Peace*.'

'Yes,' said Nell. 'The Rostovs' house.'

'Such a feast they gave us there: chicken cooked in walnut sauce. Georgian wine. It was marvellous. And Johnnie knows everyone. Everywhere. He was dining that first night with a popular singer of ballards – I can't remember his name – he had sleepy eyes and a Latin-American moustache. Looked like Brassens.'

'Dunno. Sounds like Okudzhava, but I think he's dead,' said Nell. Her mind was running along other lines. 'When I was there I lived out in the snow hills of Prospekt Vernadskovo, with utility furniture, and most of the time we wore laddered tights and were short of shampoo. What I mainly remember is getting drunk on some harsh pepper and garlic flavoured brew which was somebody's home-made vodka. None of us ever got to see the inside of Dom Literaterov.'

'Well, the thing about Johnnie is he always gets to the centre of things. That's really what I love about him. He's a real adventurer, a buccaneer – you know how some men can be?'

Nell looked down at the photograph again.

34

'Well, congratulations,' she said, a little heavily. 'I suppose you'll be getting married in due course?'

'There is no need to be snide,' Caroline snapped.

'I don't understand,' stammered Nell.

'There's a problem. He's married,' said Caroline.

'And he isn't going to leave his wife?'

'He's sorry for her,' Caroline explained. 'She's older than he is, and fragile. German, you know. Came here as a child. She's very clever at being pitiable.'

'Brilliant,' nodded Nell.

Nell could not pretend to be overwhelmed with surprise. In another life Caroline had confided many troubles with a recognizable pattern. For all her beauty and intelligence, all Caroline's strongest passions had been for unmarryable men. Nell wanted now to be supportive, but she found herself saying as much. Caroline fixed her with those huge brooding eyes.

'You've led a very sheltered life, Nell. Wait till you've tried it alone for a while.

'I'm not criticizing you,' said Nell.

'Yes, you are. You think I'm predatory.'

'No,' said Nell with absolute honesty. 'It just doesn't seem good enough for you.'

Caroline thought about that, and then smiled.

'I remind you that nothing's safe,' she insisted. 'It's because I'm the other woman.'

In Nell's mind the silly, giggling thought formed itself like a cartoon balloon. There's always another woman. Like buses. There's always another bus following on behind. There's always another woman.

And, unbidden, her thoughts went back to some of the more mysterious episodes at Brian's trial.

'What I can't bear to see is how he is so wasted. He's married to the most appalling woman,' Caroline was saying. 'Believe me, Nell. She's totally selfish. Doesn't care about him at all.'

'I see your feminism does not extend to wives,' said Nell, a little more quickly than she intended.

Damn, she thought. She didn't want to quarrel with Caroline.

Why couldn't she say the things that were likely to please? How could she change the subject?

'How do you stay afloat?' she asked, with a conciliatory grin.

'Jobbing,' replied Caroline instantly. 'I do whatever's going. Reviewing. Travel journalism. I went all the way to Taiwan for *Harpers and Queen*. Don't do much political stuff now, except Greenpeace for the *Guardian*. I write a few lines of poetry every morning, whatever happens.'

'What are you working on now?' Nell asked.

Caroline paused.

'It's a play,' she said.

Nell felt her interest quicken.

'Queen of the Night,' said Caroline. 'The black mother figure from Mozart's *Magic Flute*, remember? Did you know she started out as the innocent party in the first version of the libretto? She was a Titania-queen-of-the-fairies figure, nothing to do with darkness and evil. Even in the version we have she's still the one who rescues the prince from the snake. And sends him off to rescue Pamina. It's the Queen of the Night who gives the prince the magic flute.'

'That's why the opera is a mess,' said Nell. 'Or would be without Mozart's music.'

'Exactly. Did you know Goethe wrote about what was supposed to happen afterwards? I thought I might retell the story from the beginning. How the Queen of the Night first asserted herself, what happened to her husband, that sort of thing. Here . . .' Caroline took out a notebook, and handed it across to Nell. 'Look at what there is.'

Nell read as she was instructed, and a new and unfamiliar discomfort rose under her ribs. Not simply envy of what Caroline had done, but a grudging recognition that she was at least trying to realize an adolescent dream, while Nell had been in a Rip Van Winkle sleep.

'Where are you thinking of putting it on?' she asked, as practically as she could.

'Liza Thynne is interested,' said Caroline at once.

'Have I met here?' asked Nell uncertainly.

'Probably. But you won't remember her. She was up at Cambridge a year or two behind us; she read something frightfully unglamorous like Geography. I just remember her slightly because she lived in Old Hall, but she was a dumpy mousey little thing then. No one could ever understand what Nicky Thynne saw in her. Of course she was always very brilliant: she got a First. But we never got on.'

'Doesn't seem the most obvious choice,' said Nell.

'That was *then*,' said Caroline, shaking her head energetically. 'She's not dowdy now. Still short. Still round. But she dresses in Chanel suits. She's one of the whizz-kids of the new London. Geoffrey says her method of marketing women's theatre is going to do as much for plays as Virago did for women's publishing. Well, I'm a bit frightened of her actually.'

Nell looked incredulous.

'Yes. When I was younger I think I made her feel she wasn't beautiful. Now she makes me feel I'm not successful.'

She looked at her watch and, seeing that Nell took the gesture as a dismissal, added: 'Sorry to be brisk. I have a deadline. Eight hundred words to bike round to Fortress Wapping this afternoon. Listen, come and hear me read at the Poetry Society in Earl's Court Square next month. They have a glass of wine first and there'll be a few cheery people there. At least I hope somebody shows up. I'll ask them to send you a card.'

Nell looked at her own watch. She had to be back for Becky.

'If I can,' she agreed.

Becky had arrived home first. She looked smaller and more lost than usual, and Nell would have liked to pick her up as she had done when she was a child and comfort her, but something in Becky's eyes warned her that this approach would not be welcome.

'How was school?'

Becky lifted one shoulder in a shrug.

'They don't try to teach us anything,' she said.

'How can you tell? It's early days,' Nell managed.

'The girls don't want to talk about anything except pop groups and clothes. And the boys all read science fiction and comics,' said Becky.

'Well, that's quite trendy these days,' said Nell hopefully, adding: 'I've made a pot of tea.'

37

She really didn't want tea; bland, inoffensive drink that it was; she would have liked deep rich brown coffee, with thick cream. She wanted something sharp and spicy to eat. She wanted a surprise.

'There's a lot of very interesting science fiction,' Nell attempted. 'Have you read *The Master and Margarita*? It's a kind of science fiction, by a man called Bulgakov.'

'What's it about?'

'Well, said Nell, 'there's a Devil, and a cat that swings around Moscow, and they run a show in the centre of Moscow and give away expensive shoes. It's about how absurd people become when they just think about money. It's all about now really.'

'Have we got a copy?'

'Somewhere,' said Nell uncertainly, remembering her books in their boxes, kindly stored by Millie in the coal hole. Last week they had gone down into it together to recover Shakespeare. She bit her lip. But Becky's face lit up with a recognition of their joint difficulty, and suddenly both began to laugh.

'Is it worth another trip to the coal hole?'

Nell thought it would be worth a journey into the underworld just to have Becky laugh companionably like that more often.

FOUR

Nell did not want to be visiting her cousin Mark. Even before the divorce, her father's family had always made her feel an interloper; like a big scruffy dog, she put it to herself. When she had tried to explain as much to her mother, that pinched little face had become unusually animated with fury.

'What rubbish! Nothing *like* such a good family as mine. Their old man was a pedlar, or near enough. We've always been professional classes.'

'I suppose so.'

'Your education's as good as theirs, anyway.'

'It isn't snobbery. Not exactly, is it?'

'Incestuous, that's what they are,' her mother raged. 'It isn't natural for families to huddle together the way they do. Human beings are meant to spread out and grow apart. They've turned in.'

'They certainly make me feel like an outsider,' Nell admitted.

Her mother was mollified by such outspoken criticism.

'Well, you know what it is, dear – they aren't properly English, are they? I know they were all born here, but it isn't the same. It's what I always said to your father.'

And indeed it was. Nell's mother did not often hear the subtext of her own remarks. 'Blue eyes,' she insisted, when Nell was six and the colour was already sea-green. 'Blonde hair. Takes after me, thank God.' Nell rarely took the risk of suggesting she was antisemitic. 'Married one, didn't I?' her mother would retort furiously. 'What's the sense of using the word if it includes marrying them?'

It was a very long walk along Bishops Avenue and at the far end Nell realized she was already twenty minutes later than she had promised. It wasn't the only source of her discomfiture. The houses were large, grand, set back; not so much detached as

39

displayed, with Georgian fronts and imitation Victorian porticoes and windows secured against burglary with internal iron trellis work. She turned into the street where Mark had his house. Her ideas of space had adjusted themselves to London. In this street, at least, the size of the houses would not have been remarkable in East Anglia. But already Nell felt astonished that a single family could fill both sides of a front door and all the way up to the attic.

Mark's house, when she found it, was a declaration not so much of wealth but of ease. The porch was surrounded charmingly with winter jasmine; two cars were parked in the driveway. Once inside, the comfort was palpable and obscurely worrying. It wasn't just her newly constrained purse. In the grander houses of her East Anglian friends, a kind of crabbiness prevailed alongside the grandeur. Here there was a total lack of puritanical embarrassment. And what is wrong with that, she told herself, mindful of her mother's genteel disparagement, hating herself as priggish. Her father would have liked her to live in just such a house. Dimly, she remembered the big house of her own childhood; the plum trees in the sunken garden, the high ceilings.

It wasn't just the opulence of Mark's house that seemed strange. There was also an air of savage cleanliness, as if whole rooms were scoured with steam daily. The beige-pink carpet looked as if it had been laid no more than a week before. The walls, too, were unmarked. Yet she could hear the voices of children from upstairs. How could they be so well behaved?

Her cousin Mark had the air of the room: his navy jacket was impeccably pressed, and his shirt looked not so much freshly laundered as bought that very day. Happiness shone out of him, Nell observed with a twinge. He looked like the man in the psalm who had lived well and for whom everything good had been prepared by the Lord. His face was attractively furrowed at the cheeks, and the dome of his forehead was preternaturally exaggerated by hair that was just tinged with grey. He had once had a caressing, almost insinuating manner with women, which went along with his beautifully chosen clothes – all lambswool and tawny colours – and the aquiline strangeness of his young face.

How was it done? It wasn't just a question of common sense, prudence, economy. In this house it was possible to believe (as she had done long ago when her father was alive) that money came as naturally into the house as air into the lungs.

Like an asthmatic, she reflected grimly on her own situation.

The news of that disaster was in his face and even more so in that of his wife. They had read the papers. They were sorry for her. She was ashamed to meet the kind eyes that shifted so uneasily away from her own. Kind brown eyes. Asking about Brian.

'How is he?'

She knew she was not expected to give any details. Mark's favourite Eastern European story had always been the one about the frozen bird whose life is saved by being dropped into a cow pat. She could still see his boyish eyes wrinkling with laughter over the turn around as the creature is eaten by a wolf attracted to a rash outburst of singing. 'It isn't always your enemies that drop you in it. It isn't always your friends who get you out of it. And if you are in it. SSHH!'

It was in the spirit of this advice that Nell held her peace. The whole of this room seemed in any case designed like a stage set to assert that there were neither cowpat nor enemies. Not, at any rate, for those who kept the rules.

He's done very well, Mark, she thought mutinously. Why? I was the bright one.

'What are you doing these days, Mark?' she asked. Mark had been a socialist once, with some political ambitions; a historian with a passionate commitment to reform, an energetic organizer of famine lunches. 'I heard you went into the City.'

'I'm not a merchant banker,' he laughed. 'I manage companies.'

She couldn't imagine what that could mean.

'On a day to day basis?' she asked slowly. 'Do you look into a screen, or what?'

He laughed again at her naiveté.

'No, I look at papers. Talk to people. Make decisions. That sort of thing.'

'You must be getting the decisions right,' she said.

'Well, making any kind of decision is most of it,' he agreed.

Unavoidably her thoughts strayed in a puzzled kind of way to Brian.

'Mark wouldn't put up with you,' Brian had always chaffed her.

'He's bright but he isn't bookish. He doesn't respect people who sit around with their heads in a book.'

Well, I'm not bookish now, she thought. I'm out in the world. Nell had never thought the possession of money had much to do with virtue. Somehow, not having it now felt like a moral inadequacy. Then and there she decided to take the job at Feminist Arts.

Mark's wife had breasts like a French hooker, absolutely clear skin and bold black eyes; she was very confident in her own body. She wore black boots tight round her calves and a short wool skirt that could have shown a flash of stocking top with a little urging. The clothes were not high fashion, but hers was not a fashionable shape. She had the solidity idealized by men in cold countries. Mark, she saw with a pang of envy, was happily in love with her.

Their children looked in briefly: two daughters; the sturdy, streetwise children of the professional classes, with pert features and spiky hair; the harsh stones of small earrings glittering in their ears, the shortness of their new wool skirts. The eldest girl looked like Becky; there was the same flower-like vulnerability, the same smile that suggested they were unprepared to be ambitious. Poor Becky, Nell thought. Mark would always admire and worry for these lucky children; he would know how to protect them. She felt a little ashamed at her own sense of injustice. A line from a forgotten childhood song came into her memory: 'Someone to watch over me'. There'll be no one to do that for Becky, she thought.

'Let's have a bite to eat,' said Charlotte.

From the table rose a spicy odour that took Nell back to that same childhood; the scent of pickles, smoked fish, cream cheese and rye bread. Such a different smell from the scents of onion bhajis and poppadums, and all the other delicacies of the Asian subcontinent from the shops in Camden Town. This was the smell of Eastern Europe. The smell of those houses of her childhood, carried on into contemporary London. And the tablecloth itself was familiar; stitched and patterned like those of her childhood aunts. And in another elusive resemblance, like the tablecloth in the flat of a Russian woman she had visited in Moscow in her final year. In Moscow she felt the same stirring of something warm and welcoming, something unEnglish, something altogether alien to Plumrose Crescent, something she liked and admired and had missed. Something she and Brian had never had together, something she could not yet quite articulate.

'Bea looks like your father, doesn't she?' said Charlotte, speaking of the elder, darker girl.

Nell had not thought of her father in a long time, and said as much. She could see the resemblance, and in doing so remembered a grin, black hair and laughing eyes.

'He was all right, your father,' said Mark tolerantly. 'My dad used to get very angry with him, but I thought he was a good guy.'

Nell was surprised.

'What did they quarrel about?'

'Business mostly. He was never one of the world's great organizers, but he had a lot of energy.' He shrugged. 'Uncle Jack enjoyed life.'

Nell supposed he had. It had not seemed a virtue to her mother.

'He loved himself,' she said harshly.

She saw Mark remembering the divorce, the abandoned responsibilities. She wondered whether the shrug included his desertion, his womanizing and indifference. Then she looked down at her plate. She had eaten the whole of it without thinking, wolfishly; it was the first good meal she had been able to eat for weeks, perhaps since the disaster.

'Some cake?' offered Charlotte, sensing as much.

Nell looked again at the table; it was something from a Viennese café, tarts piled with fruits, strudels.

'From Louis' shop,' said Charlotte. 'Help yourself.'

Nell took a cake and put it on the plate.

'I don't think either Brian or I were ever natural entrepreneurs,' she said boldly. 'I think I believed in the mousetrap story. You remember, making the best possible mousetrap? Excellence? It's not a despicable ethic.'

'I never thought Brian ever had much interest in making money in any way,' said Mark, completely ignoring the story about the mousetrap.

43

'I suppose he's never been what you'd call a yuppie,' said Nell, flushing. 'If you don't mind me using the word.'

It wasn't altogether what she meant to be saying. It broke the comfortable mood. Mark had brought them a glass of white wine. It was a good wine and the pressure of Nell's need, and her cousin's embarrassment in the face of it, had begun to disappear.

'Brian was a dreamer. Talented, very talented,' said Mark, looking dreamy himself as he savoured the quality of the wine.

'To be like that you need a patron,' said Charlotte.

'That's what's wrong with it,' Mark agreed.

'There was a time when Uncle Salomon supported Heine, however reluctantly,' said Nell, still brave, and referring back to the world they had once had in common; the literature of their university days.

Mark looked at her blankly and she had to explain.

'Uncle Salomon. He was a wealthy Hamburg banker. Heine made fun of him.'

'Heine?' he said uncertainly.

'The poet,' said Nell unhappily.

'I have heard of him,' said Mark, grandly, as though some distinction were thereby conferred on Heine.

'Well, he has been celebrated,' said Nell.

'I thought he was rather successful?'

'Yes.'

'Did he have to be a *schnorrer*?'

The fall into a vernacular which might belong to Woody Allen surprised her. She supposed New York had made it acceptable. Mark looked more Jewish than he had when they were both younger, Nell thought. She remembered his sober, public-school cadences which were deliberately anglicized more than her own.

A flash of alarm ran through her as she realized what she was thinking.

She smiled to disguise her thoughts, and accepted more wine. More cake. Affection. Familial togetherness. Let the conversation patter on around her. She perceived the decency, the kindness in them. The warmth. The friendship that would embrace her if she would only trust it. And she knew that she was unable to be part of the world they inhabited, and didn't understand why. It was

44

so much more generous, so much warmer than Plumrose Crescent. What did it mean to say it was Philistine? Did it *have* any meaning?

'What's so really wrong with yuppies?' asked Mark, who was sharp enough, she remembered. 'Everybody has it in for them.'

'Well . . .' Nell floundered in her desire not to be rude.

'I'll tell you one thing,' said Mark, 'they aren't hated because they are rich. They aren't the richest in the land. Don't you think it. That's not why they're hated. It's because England doesn't trust traders. Never has. The English don't like people who buy and sell. They think it's cheating to buy cheaply and sell at a profit. And another thing. It's nothing to do with cheating. The English *expect* to be screwed by the gentry. Don't even mind. But let someone of their own class get above himself, and they want blood.'

'I don't want to have a political argument.'

'You and Brian were always sentimental about politics. Shall I tell you what I think? About yuppies. I really admire them. Their independence. Anyone who can keep going. Listen. I believe the whole of the Midlands could be transformed if people could be encouraged to float their own enterprises.'

'The Midlands?'

'Yes.'

'Look, Mark, Brian and I lived for five years in the Midlands. Who exactly are going to help themselves in this way? The coal-miners? The people laid off from the hosiery factories?'

Mark laughed at the return of her animation but he wasn't pleased, and she was annoyed with him.

'I think I'd better be going,' she said. 'I have to be home when Becky gets back from school.'

'Don't fuss.'

'I don't mean to be quarrelsome. I'm upset.'

'I know, Nella – I want to help you.'

The childhood nickname nearly broke her down. She thought about Becky, and how much help she needed, but her pride rose inside her. Mark was wrong about so many things. She knew he was. She'd have liked to make him see that. There was something absurd about thinking he had everything morally correct just

45

because he had prospered and she had fallen accidentally into a particularly foul cowpat.

'You've certainly moved to the Right,' she said angrily. 'Weren't you once hoping to lead the Labour Party?'

He laughed without taking offence.

'I can't quite believe in it all any more,' he said. 'They don't even believe in state ownership in Russia. Why should I believe in it here?'

'All the decent people I know hate the idea of profit and greed,' said Nell primly.

'Please,' he said.

'You're a Thatcherite,' she accused him.

'Not really. But I'm not a socialist any more either. Sorry.'

She thought of the long arguments she'd had years ago with her mother who had always hated socialism; some of her old exasperation mixed with new unhappiness as she listened.

'At least I'm not a snob either,' he continued, clearly more riled than he wished to admit. 'I like people to get on by their own efforts. Now your mother really was an eccentric old loony. I don't mean to offend you – '

'Don't call my mother loony!' she shouted.

She'd often thought as much herself.

'You know what I mean. I've known a lot of very decent, middle-class Tories. She wasn't one of them.'

'You've no manners, Mark,' said Charlotte.

The light was just beginning to go. Nell phoned Liza Thynne at her Studio of Feminist Arts from a payphone on her way home.

On Thursday it was Caroline's reading at the Poetry Society. Nell decided it would do her good to go.

Earl's Court Square had a decayed grandeur. The portals of the Poetry Society opened on to a bookshop and at six o'clock Nell, who was early, stood around for a time there, studying the books, and observing that Caroline had three to her name on the shelf. Much had happened in English poetry, she decided, since she had looked into it with enthusiasm at Cambridge. In some ways it was much easier to read. In those forgotten days undergraduates who cared about poetry had volumes of Olson and Ed Dorn on their shelves, and knew the meaning of the Maximus Poems. Things were neater now, and better printed. Nell recalled mimeographed poetry sprawling over pages of A4. She remembered the passionate theorists of Projective Verse, the demand for 'composition in field' as the phrase was then. She could still hear the drugged, reverent tones in which the poems were read aloud. Where was Maximus to Gloucester now? Where was Gunslinger? Now the poems had reassuringly returned to stanzaic shape. There were rhymes. And most of them were about fathers, mothers, old age and childhood. Recognizable themes. Recognizable pleasures.

The reading was upstairs and after a while Nell made her way up the grand curving staircase, examining as she did the faces of poets staring down at her; Ted Hughes and Philip Larkin, both in their own ways sombre; an impish Donald Davie, a solemn Geoffrey Hill. Would any of these grand figures be upstairs and waiting to hear Caroline read? Nell had no idea what to expect. This was the centre. The National Poetry Centre. Plumrose Crescent was at the peripheries, and she had come in from those lonely parts to find her natural home.

The drinks, it turned out, were downstairs; an elegant spiral staircase led into a small room full of people drinking white wine. They seemed, perhaps because of the scale of the photographs up the stairs, strangely smaller people than she was expecting; indeed all the men were an inch or two shorter than she was. None of the figures from the staircase were standing in the room. Caroline herself was dressed in a pale grey silky dress. She was standing with a stubbly-haired man with a beard, with whom, it seemed, Caroline shared the evening's programme. Nell wondered if everyone apart from herself was either a poet or an aspirant poet, and whether everyone taking a drink was also going to the poetry reading. Caroline introduced her to three people very rapidly, and then moved on to another group. Nell perceived she was nervous.

Nell wished she knew more about contemporary poetry, and listened to what was being said around her.

'I'm in Northumberland next week.'

'Isn't that William's patch? I did a very good gig with him last month.'

'Another book-signing?'
'I don't know why we bother.'
'I won't read for nothing outside London.'
'I like to see the rare unsigned copy.'
'Glad about your award.'
'I'm going to sit in my garden shed for the next three months.'
'I'm skint as a rat, of course.'
'Send me some poems for next month.'
'Haven't got any. Haven't written any this year.'
'Have you been to Struga yet?'
'Went three years ago.'
'What do you think of Peter's new book?'
'Haven't read it yet. Haven't had time.'
'I'm judging again this year. Knocks me out for months. Anaesthetizes the nerves that respond to language.'
'Did you see the *Observer*?'
'Did you hear what that bloody woman said on *The Critics*?'
They were summoned at this point to the serious business of the evening. A number of the party were invited to dinner, however, and were unable to stay.

As Nell joined the people who were making their way into their seats, she became aware of some tension between Caroline and the man who was billed to share the evening with her.

'No, I shan't read first,' he was saying. 'Never do. Won't start now. Why should I?'

His supporters, who had all held themselves a little aloof from the general dance of wine-sippers at the party, grouped around Caroline aggressively.

'I'm nervous too,' she said with a charming smile. 'But it really doesn't matter if you feel so strongly about it.'

'Nervous?' roared her fellow poet, his Geordie accent now vehemently obvious. 'I'm not nervous of these Southern gits. Why should I be nervous?'

He flourished a small silver pocket flask.

'It's a question of dignity and what's appropriate. I'm the senior poet. You'll agree with that?'

'Absolutely,' said Caroline, drawing away slightly from the hot fierce face that he thrust against hers.

'Very well,' he said, mollified. 'If you'll agree to that, you can read when you like.'

Saying as much, he sat down heavily in a chair in the front row nevertheless and waited for her to mount the platform, which she did rather helplessly.

Caroline's nervousness did not prevent her from beaming round at the audience. She was going to read a group of poems from her last book, she said, and she didn't know if they were sad or funny. The audience purred at the offer. And really her reading was as easy to enjoy as a television sketch, thought Nell, admiring the ironic pauses, and the way Caroline effortlessly brought laughter from an audience relieved to enjoy themselves. Even the chat between the poems enchanted her listeners. She would read some updated Elizabethan sonnets next, she suggested; and gave an introduction to their themes, with a certain self-deprecating slyness as she spoke of men's disloyalty and women's pain that brought an answering hum of approval from the audience. They like her, thought Nell.

Two seats away from Nell the Geordie poet had fallen asleep. His mouth was open. His breath went gently in and out between his lips, with an occasional bubbling noise rather like a baby's sucking in sleep. Nell wondered if he would wake up in time to perform himself.

About this, however, she need not have concerned herself.

Mounting the platform when his turn came he glared round at the innocently expectant faces, and without any preamble began to read from a typescript secured in a battered black file.

Nell, who had expected a growl or a roar, heard instead a quiet voice enunciating every word with tender precision. He spoke of the ancient mystery of leaves, birdsong and the light of early morning. He spoke of puddles, and rain and city streets. And as he read she felt rather like a dead tree suddenly coming into leaf herself. Of course, she remembered. *That* was poetry. That was why she had loved it.

Glancing around, she saw the audience loved it too. They were looking up at the poet with startled faces as if they hadn't expected to feel anything much and were not altogether sure what to make of the experience.

And Caroline? Nell saw that Caroline was frowning very slightly, as if her triumph had been dampened by the surprising excellence of this performance. Nell was saddened to see as much, and to admit that there could be a rivalry and competition even in the purveyance of poetry.

FIVE

Liza's Feminist Arts workshop was small, heated by a Calor stove, and piled high with papers as well as books. There were posters on the wall announcing opposition to cruise missiles, Apartheid and changes in the abortion laws. There were announcements of events promoted by gay activists of both sexes. The far end of the main room was dark and smelled of Nescafé and sour milk. None of the windows opened.

In all this ambience of concern, Liza was at first sight anomalous. She was brisk and spruce, and her expression suggested that people who knew the score had more sense than to expect to be treated well. Her stance was somewhere between a boxer and a blues singer. She was dressed in elegant beige; her considerable weight poised on disconcertingly good legs, her small feet in light tan court shoes. As Nell came in, she was standing at a desk with the telephone receiver in her right hand and reading something held out at the length of her left. As she read, and listened, and gestured to indicate her awareness of Nell's arrival, she chuckled with good humour. Her eyes were a glittering blue.

'Groucho's will be very nice,' she said into the phone. 'Better make it dinner for eight, I should think.' She motioned Nell to sit down and continued: 'I'm glad to hear you say so. Very kind.'

The telephone rang again the moment it reached the cradle.

'That will be the Beckenham wife,' said Liza comfortably. 'Ursula, you take it.'

Ursula, in cardigan and dungarees, did so.

'Do relax,' Liza said to Nell. 'I'll be with you in just a moment.' Without batting her eyes, she reached across to click on a portable tape recorder and spoke into the middle distance very rapidly. 'I'll send her a little note. Dear Mrs P. You really must not imagine you will get anywhere by sobbing to yourself in the mornings. Tears never helped anyone, and certainly never softened the heart

51

of a man such as you describe. So, now, orange juice, vitamin pills.'

The telephone went again, and Ursula picked it up at Liza's nod.

'Your son,' she told Liza.

'Ask him if it's urgent. I'll be home about four; there's cold ham, and pots of salad in the fridge. Now then, Nell,' she concluded kindly, 'I've been hearing about you from Geoffrey.'

When Nell began, tentatively, to express polite condolence for her husband's death, Liza cut her short with a brusque wave of her hand and commented: 'Well, he was never a hero.'

She studied Nell's face as she spoke and Nell, who had been wondering if they might talk about loneliness and the strangeness of living without a man after fifteen years of marriage, could see that something quite else was on her mind.

'We pretty much went our own way, as you must have guessed. But the children adored him.'

Nell had guessed nothing.

Ursula, who helped Liza as and when required, had none of the features of that Lawrentian figure for whom she might well have been named twenty-odd years ago, by a mother much under the influence of *Women in Love*. Ursula looked tough. A vegetarian, she was winkling out the anchovies from the pizza brought in from the local cafe when Liza delivered Nell into her hands.

She led Nell into the office in a businesslike fashion.

'I'm afraid this is an old-fashioned Apricot,' she said. 'Can you cope with the user's manual?'

'Yes,' said Nell dishonestly, and after about two and a half hours her hopeful assertion became true.

A whiff of pleasure filled her. I can do anything, she thought.

Liza looked in on her at teatime.

'It's about time Caroline called in again. You'll have heard about her play?'

Nell said she had.

'A wonderful idea. The trouble is,' said Liza, 'the play hasn't really developed. Lacks bite. No political edge.'

Nell said she knew Caroline had some very political ideas. 'Of course, she's a poet,' she concluded uneasily.

52

'We particularly *wanted* a poetic play. Everyone is bored with realism. We wanted something bold, and stylized, and new. Something with a bit of colour. We shall have to get a cast together with a lot of experience in devising, that's all,' said Liza. 'And workshop it ourselves.'

'Will Caroline like that?' asked Nell dubiously.

'Of course,' said Liza. 'She's trying to do too much, that's what it is. Her mind's on other things.'

Nell thought one of them might be Johnnie.

Later that week, Caroline looked in to see how she was getting on.

'I've been having the most wonderful time,' said Caroline.

Nell looked up from the promotional material she was copying.

'Doing what?'

'Guess.'

'Something to do with Johnnie?'

'Everything to do with him. We've been to Paris. I can't tell you what heaven it was. I'd never realized his family were French. Of course, they've lived here since 1940 and Johnnie was born in the Cotswolds. Still, a Parisian background counts for something, don't you think?'

'I suppose so.'

'He showed me where they used to live. Wonderful old square. Not far from Rue des Rosiers – do you know that part of Paris?'

'No,' said Nell.

'Place des Vosges. Archways, and secret flowery courtyards. Streets full of vegetable shops and pedlars. I love it.'

'Yes,' said Nell. She pressed the key which made her typeface italic.

'Johnnie had a marvellous flat lent him by some kind of minor diplomat. And it was so romantic. We talked about poetry and death, and his family and everything. I'd no idea the French behaved so badly after the war. So bigoted. It's not as if they had anything to do with what happened in Vichy.'

'You mean his family were collaborators?'

'Goodness, I don't know about that. They come from Algiers originally.'

'I see,' said Nell.

'And Johnnie is wonderful. It isn't even mainly sex,' said Caroline.

'No,' said Nell.

'If *only* I could trust him.'

Nell made none of the comments that came to her mind.

'How are things going here?' asked Caroline.

'Much the same,' said Nell.

'The play must go on,' said Caroline. 'Well, that's not your worry. Just tap away: we'll have a drink at lunchtime.'

As Nell returned to her copy typing she felt a querulous sense of injustice, because she had thought the theatre would be her world all those years ago. She had done nothing about it, of course, she told herself, as she copied the letters Ursula brought in to her, so she couldn't begrudge Caroline the opportunity.

The following week Liza held auditions to find the four or five girls needed to play the characters in Caroline's play. Nell had already noted with surprise how many actresses with names known to her from television had replied to the original advertisement in *Stage*; now she had to write rejecting unsuccessful applicants. She couldn't help querying one such rejection.

'We want people with skill in devising,' said Ursula flatly. 'People with experience of working as a group. That one's a star, she'll unbalance the whole thing.'

Nell wondered how Caroline would feel about that, but clearly Caroline's feelings were not especially important.

As the girls appeared and went downstairs into a cellar which had been designated the rehearsal area, and disappeared until lunchtime with Liza, Nell wondered idly how the characters were to be redistributed among an all-female cast.

'How on earth can that work?' she asked Ursula.

Ursula exploded with righteous fury.

'If you knew anything about London's fringe theatre,' she said, 'you'd know. There are absolutely brilliant all-women companies. The Women's Theatre Group, for instance. Absolutely great. Tours all over England. That's the whole point, that's why we have a grant, to give women actresses an opportunity they wouldn't get in the male-dominated theatre. I mean, think about it, no one finds it odd if you have just six male parts, do they? Or one token woman to excite a bit of sex interest. Why should it be different?'

'Perhaps both are a bad idea,' Nell suggested dubiously.

Ursula fixed her with a contemptuous look and gave her a list of Arts Club venues to type envelopes for.

Nell made the mistake of expressing some unseemly envy to Becky over an Indian takeaway that evening.

'It's a choice,' said Becky unsympathetically.

'Is it?'

'You could go on supply, and don't tell me Liza Thynne pays better. I don't believe it.'

Nell perceived the choice which Becky was prepared to consider was not encouraging.

'I don't think I want to teach,' confessed Nell. 'And they send you all over the place. You don't know what schools are like in South London.'

Becky's blue eyes opened even more roundly.

'Are you serious? *I* don't know what schools are like?'

The inversion was new, like the sadness in her face.

'I thought you liked your new school.'

'You wanted to think so, you mean. You just believe whatever makes you feel comfortable.'

'I thought the girls who came home with you the other day were lively,' Nell continued on her own line of thought.

Becky snorted with amusement.

'You're such a snob, Mummy, do you know that?'

Nell was startled, not so much by the accusation as the way in which Becky had chosen to address her. Becky hadn't called her 'Mummy' for ages. Perhaps there was something seriously wrong. Nell approached the subject warily.

'There's nothing very grand about doing Liza Thynne's promotional leaflets on an Apricot.'

'She's smart, though, isn't she?'

'Wait a minute,' said Nell. 'Becky, tell me what's troubling you.'

But Becky simply shook her head.

'Don't bother your head about me.'

Nell felt the rejection as she was meant to feel it.

That night she lay on her back and stared up at the ceiling for a long while, unable to sleep. There is no area of my life, she thought, which is not a disaster. I haven't been very intelligent about anything. Even the things I have tried most patiently and lovingly to do right have gone badly. She thought about Brian, which she tried not to do very often, and fell asleep remembering how touching and absurd their early married days had been.

The weather changed in early December into a savage cold. The wind came along the waste land behind Millie's house, and blasted Nell as she turned into the main road towards Camden Town tube station. She shivered even in her old cashmere coat. The sun was bright but the air was harsh and Nell was too happy to see Geoffrey draw up at her bus stop to wonder what he was doing there.

'You're looking a bit peaky,' he said kindly enough.

'It's the cold.'

'You're still thinking of poor old Brian.'

'Of course I am,' said Nell indignantly.

'Nothing's obvious. Fidelity is very touching, but there's not a lot of it about,' offered Geoffrey.

Nell couldn't think of a reply that didn't sound unbearably prissy.

He drove along Adelaide Road and then turned smartly down Primrose Hill to avoid the slowing traffic.

'I'm worried about Caroline,' he said.

Nell was surprised.

'I thought she was doing rather well.'

'In a sense, yes. Very nicely.'

Nell decided she knew very little about what Caroline was actually doing. She had been away for the British Council in Yugoslavia, and on her return had been teaching a creative writing course at Arvon in North Devon. She said very little about either experience; but her voice on the telephone had begun to be brusque and forbidding; whether through exhaustion or whether because of troubles with Johnnie, Nell was uncertain.

'She has to work too hard,' she said at length. 'She runs around the country on trains the whole time.'

'She should have married me,' said Geoffrey, lugubriously, shaking his head and then flashing a smile that had more self-mockery than Nell usually observed.

Nell found herself wondering how familiar he was with Caroline's present relations to Johnnie; and suddenly found herself asking as much.

'Johnnie Farrago,' said Geoffrey cautiously. 'Everyone knows Johnnie. Caroline ought to know better.'

'Caroline is in love with him.'

He turned to her in surprise, and then laughed before he could say whatever it was he had been thinking.

'Well. I suppose it's the kind of love you're missing,' he said. 'It will be better for Brian if you make sure to get some. Becky doesn't need you watching her do her homework every evening.'

'She doesn't seem to get much homework,' said Nell wearily. 'I'm hopelessly monogamous, Geoffrey.'

'It takes two,' said Geoffrey. 'Haven't you ever wondered whether Brian is quite as you imagine him?'

Nell had begun to wonder precisely that, especially since her last visit to Bleakwood, and she felt her heart clench shut alarmingly as though Geoffrey might suddenly be going to tell her something she didn't want to hear. She still didn't trust him; she suspected him of malice; and she blinked her eyes rather than ask him for more information. They slowed into W11.

It was unfortunately true that her need, if not for love then for sex, had begun to embarrass her nightly. That very morning she had woken from a dream of her fellow lodger, the violinist Kit Martin. In her fantasy she had opened the bathroom door to find him dressed only in a shirt. Without a word, he had lifted her bodily off the floor, so that he could thrust himself into her while she hung above him, impaled as if on a friendly tree. Guilty, even in her dream, she nevertheless stayed where she was until an orgasm of extraordinary sweetness overpowered her as she woke up.

In the cold light of morning she met Millie in the hall, cheerfully opening post, and could hardly force herself to return a smile.

'There's more to life than learning to use an Apricot,' said Millie, studying her face. 'Even people on social security get to see a film now and then. Why don't you go out some evening?'

Nell thought about her reluctance to do so. She found it hard to shake off the schoolgirlish feeling that there was something faintly pitiable in a women going out alone. At the same time she didn't want to do any of the things that she could do at home. Didn't want to read. Didn't want to watch television. And her body was sated with sleep.

'I haven't been to a concert in ages,' she said doubtfully.

Her own post included a letter in a square mauve envelope, which at once recalled Plumrose Crescent. The sight of the Royston postmark made her fingers tremble so furiously that she tore the letter in opening the envelope. It was from her neighbour Melanie, the doctor's wife, she saw; and was penned in large, rounded handwriting like a schoolgirl's.

Dear Nell,

Dick and I often talk of you, and what good neighbours you were. It's not so long ago since we were popping in and out of one another's kitchens, is it? I really can't tell you how things have changed since you left. London must be so very different from Royston; I do hope you are settling in as well as you can, and that poor Becky is enjoying her new school.

Please don't think I'm complaining, but I felt you should know that several new people, all men, in fact all American Air Force men, have moved into your lovely house. I don't know whether the nice young couple you introduced us to have found themselves in some kind of trouble, but we certainly haven't seen them recently. Probably you know all about this, and I'm just worrying over nothing. But every night a lot of young girls come to the house, and they do have parties until very late at night. In fact Dick was unable to get to sleep until nearly dawn Tuesday last week, and you know how important it is for a doctor to get a good night's sleep. Of course, everyone has a right to do what they like in their own house, but I think a lot of people in the Crescent are a bit worried about what is happening in the dustbin area. The dogs are to blame, of course, but sometimes the front garden is completely covered with rubbish and – well, you know how Dick feels about hygiene.

There was a postscript of good wishes from one or two other neighbours in the Crescent and the point was made. Nell stood holding the letter in her hand. Whether something was wrong or not (and it certainly seemed as if something unusual was going on) clearly her neighbours in the Crescent vehemently disapproved of her renting the house.

She wasn't surprised. I'll have to go back and sort things out, she told herself without conviction. Something cold and constricting settled round her heart.

She didn't ever want to go back to Plumrose Crescent.

Then she tried to remember the bank statement. Had any rent arrived after November? The last instalment had been late; the rent ought to have gone across by bankers' order on the third of each month, and it hadn't turned up until the tenth. But this month? She didn't know. She would have to telephone the bank to check.

On an impulse she knocked on the door that led to Millie's sitting room.

She found Millie looking morosely beautiful. In purple sweater and tight trousers, she had the air of wearing a mini-skirt that only just covered her buttocks. She was sitting with her legs across the end of a couch watching television. On screen, a man was lying back in a trance of delight while the sound track mused about the joys of investing money with the right building society.

'All these people with savings,' said Millie. 'Who are they? The whole of telly advertising is competing for their funds, and I don't know anyone who isn't living on an overdraft. You want a can of beer?' she asked.

'Thanks.' Nell hesitated.

Millie didn't sound cheerful.

'Is something wrong? I don't want to pry . . .'

Millie shrugged.

'A job I didn't get. Shakespeare. The guy said I must be crazy to audition for Miranda with my looks. He wasn't being racist, just didn't feel I could possibly do it. And I've been sitting here thinking: Shit, maybe he's right. Only *The Tempest* was part of my childhood too, and if he's right I'm kind of culturally disenfranchised one way or another. I didn't get the part at your Feminist Arts either, by the way . . .'

'I know,' said Nell awkwardly. She had typed the envelope for the letter of rejection herself. 'I don't know what they're looking for, but they turned a lot of very good people down without seeing them. I'm sorry if it's made you feel unhappy.'

'When troubles come they come not single spies.' Millie flashed a grin as she warmed to her list of complaints. 'There's a gas leak in the kitchen. The hot water isn't hot. The management want some repairs to the roof. And I haven't any money.'

Nell was embarrassed even though she had paid the rent till the end of the month.

'Liza Thynne doesn't pay me for ten days,' she began.

'Please,' Millie said. 'I know.'

Nell wondered whether she should explain about Plumrose Crescent.

'If that feckless louse Kit Martin paid up there wouldn't be a problem. Three months he owes. And he isn't really short, he just finds he's spent all his money before he gets round to paying me. Well, he told me he was unreliable when I took him in, but he's so damn charming I thought I'd give him a chance. You'd think a woman of my age would have more sense.'

There was a genial tolerance in her face as she spoke about Kit which raised Nell's eyebrows: it was almost as if Millie expected to be treated badly by attractive men. As if she didn't mind. And yet, in her own way, she was as solidly beautiful as Caroline. Her face had the impassive splendour of an African carving; it was the kind of lineless face that cameras worship; broad across the cheeks, heavily moulded on the lips. A female face, sensuous and yet too tough to be called feminine. It was the face of the next generation, thought Nell: perhaps all women will soon expect to support their men. The willingness to indulge and protect was the other side of Millie's independence.

'I know so little about you, Millie,' she said.

'Baby girl, you don't know much about anything,' laughed Millie.

And then their conversation was interrupted by Kit Martin, triumphantly at the door.

'Rent,' he announced. 'All of it. Here you are.'

'What did you do? Rob a bank?' asked Millie, taking the notes in any case and folding them as she spoke.

'Sessions work. It just turned up out of the blue and I thought virtuously, that's for my Millie. Count it if you don't trust me. Moreover, I'll take you out to celebrate if you like.'

'I'm busy,' said Millie, but Nell knew she just wanted to be coaxed.

For the first time she let herself look at the man who had entered her dreams so intimately. She saw a man in his thirties, heavier than he ought to be and perhaps a little drunk, whose face was alight with joyful, uncomplicated egotism.

Look out, she told herself. This man is always going to be trouble for somebody.

She looked at Millie's face; transformed, she saw, by more than financial relief. The line of her mouth had softened. She's in love with him, thought Nell.

She cooked Chinese vegetables when she came back from Feminist Arts the following night, because Becky loved hot sour tastes these days; it was a dish that took more preparation than she had expected. Becky ate it while reading a book and Nell managed sturdily not to ask for her approval.

Instead she watched the child's face, the fair skin, the tender lips, and wondered what she was thinking. Her own mother had always exploded in fury if Nell brought a book to the table. It wasn't good manners, Nell knew, but what made it hurtful was the gesture of deliberate exclusion. Nell remembered she had never been allowed to seal herself away like that. Was such privacy healthy? Nell wasn't sure. She wondered if there was anybody now that Becky allowed to enter her thoughts. She doubted whether the noisy schoolfriends she had seen even wanted to know what Becky was thinking. What was she reading? Surreptitiously Nell bent her head to make out the cover of the paperback that absorbed her daughter. It was Borges.

When Millie brought *Time Out* in to them and reminded Nell about concerts, Nell looked the paper over like a stranger to the city she had been perching in since the autumn.

'Book now, pay later,' advised Millie, seeing her hesitation and mistaking the source of her low spirits.

Nell said she would think about it.

SIX

'Come downstairs, we're having a design session,' suggested Liza the following day.

That's more like it, thought Nell. I remember those from college days. She agreed enthusiastically.

Downstairs in the long, bare-boarded room sat a group of young women who might have been sixth formers. They looked up with the same half-suspicious challenge in their faces that she saw sometimes in Becky's, but with them she felt unfazed and unhurt. Seeing as much, their expressions softened and they began to chatter.

They settled themselves in a circle around buckets of children's poster paints on newspaper. On the floor. Caroline, too, sat on the floor, though Nell observed she was looking less spry than usual, as if her first session with the girls earlier that morning had taken it out of her a little. She barely responded to Nell's cheery wave.

Nell began to enjoy the game.

'I want you all to imagine your character, and think of your favourite colour.'

'I don't have a character,' said Nell gleefully.

'Then be yourself,' said Kate, the designer. 'Now. Write your name, everybody . . . That's right.'

Caroline looked mutinous, like a lovely trapped animal forced to keep her claws turned inwards.

'Everyone finished? Lovely, Nell. Now, I'll put them all up while you are doing the next one.'

Nell felt gratified by the unexpected praise, as if she were back in kindergarten. Briskly, the sheets were collected and attached to the walls.

'Next I want you to paint what you see from the window of Sarastro's castle,' said Kate.

The sheets in their bold primary colours were pinned up on the walls. In yellow, the scrawl of her own name N E L L sat on the wall alongside Caroline's primmer lime green. Could this really help Kate to design a set? She felt sceptical and saw from Caroline's humped shoulders that she saw no point in the exercise.

Nell drew a garden with several sheep. Did Masons keep sheep? Mutton didn't seem a very holy dish. Perhaps for wool, Nell conjectured, by now thoroughly enjoying herself, and prepared to stay for the rest of the morning at this new and entertaining game.

Only Caroline looked restive; she kept adjusting the pale gold scarf at her neck, and fiddling with the heavy beads that hung down between her lapels. Disloyally Nell thought the well-cut trouser suit looked out of place as she sat on the dusty floor. It was very cold; the Calor stove could not cope with the icy draughts that blew under the door and shook the window frames. Nell was glad she was dressed like the others in an old skirt and a heavy sweater.

'You've all been reading the books I gave you, haven't you?' asked Ursula.

They had, and their faces lit with the eagerness of those who meet print mainly as pleasure. It was more than a clash of generations, thought Nell, as her eyes found in Caroline's face something unusually close to bewilderment.

Ursula was directing the play, and she sat crosslegged on the floor while the girls all turned towards her like sunflowers towards the sun. There was a pale, long-legged girl who looked rather shy, and a tough-faced girl with gold sleeper earrings. The sharpest of them, a girl called Mandy, had a formidable, cat-like confidence. She was slant-eyed, with a hint of Tartar blood in the high pointed cheekbones, but her voice had a Derbyshire quality.

'I think we should start in the castle. This Sarastro is holding Pamina against her will, right? And trying to make her see her mother as a villain?'

'Wait a minute,' said Caroline. 'I think the bit before is rather important. Has to be in, I think. We have to show how the Queen was behaving in a way that isn't usually allowed to mothers. Because mothers aren't supposed to be creative, are they? They are supposed to be teaching their children how to create.'

64

'Well, I think we should get rid of the Queen,' said Mandy. She was munching a cheese and pickle sandwich, and her tongue came out and cleaned her lips reflectively.

Exactly like a cat, thought Nell.

There were murmurs of group approval.

'But the Queen,' said Caroline, speaking carefully although visibly rocked by the suggestion. 'She is the whole point of the play, don't you think? She represents the female creative spirit which men are afraid of.'

'All that is so boring,' said Mandy flatly.

There were murmurs of agreement around the room.

'Boring.'

'The Queen is a silly old bin bag,' one of the girls whispered.

There was a repressed giggle. It was rather like being back at school, when some naughtiness had been punished by demotion to the C stream, thought Nell.

'We're not interested in the Queen's problems. It's Pamina we care about,' declared Manda. 'And sexual harassment.'

Once again she carried the group with her.

'I don't know. Mothers are important,' conceded Ursula. 'I think this is the moment to have a bit of group thinking. Pencils? Paper?'

Everyone settled cosily.

'Now then,' said Ursula. 'Off you go! Try and remember your mothers.'

There was silence as everyone wrote all they could. Nell watched their neat, childish handwriting cover the lined paper. They were remembering as they were bidden; unbidden into Nell's thoughts came Becky with her sad hostile little face. She doodled, writing nothing. You can't win, she thought. If Caroline is right and mothers' creativity is bad for children, how unfair that I should have a daughter who so resents me.

Rather to Nell's surprise, Caroline seemed excited by Ursula's game, and was scribbling intently. At Ursula's invitation, she began to read her jottings first:

'My poor mother kept me going all through my childhood. My father was always explaining to me how stupid she was, and how she couldn't think, couldn't see, couldn't be clear. But when I was ill and called out in the night she was the one who used to pad along to my room with drinks of water. It was never my father. Shouldn't think he even heard. Certainly never came along to put calamine lotion on my spots.'

Nell saw Ursula's eyes meet Mandy's as Caroline continued to read, and a great silence filled the room after she finished.

'Next,' said Ursula in the pause.

'My mother was a stupid cow,' said Mandy.

There was uproarious agreement.

'When my father buggered off there was just me and my sister, and my mother didn't know what to do for the best. She just shacked up with one man after another, each one worse than the last, until my sister ran off. I don't see my sister much now, and I don't live at home, so I don't have to worry. People ought not to get trapped into families.'

Mandy's piece brought approval, and the eager exchange of personal reminiscence about crowded accommodation and early sexual witness. An atmosphere of clammy intensity began to fill the room as one girl after another read out their pieces, and Nell wondered how any of their material could fit into Caroline's play. Ursula's approach seemed to be militantly democratic.

'Let's begin again,' she suggested.

'Where?' asked Caroline suspiciously.

'Well, in the castle. Let's pretend. It's all far too naturalistic at the moment. We need some games, a nursery rhyme or two, something to bring a bit of poetry into it.'

'I've got a limerick,' said the pale girl. 'Would you like to hear?'

'Look, I don't understand,' said Caroline wildly. 'What are you planning?'

'We're going to strip the play back to the bones,' said Ursula.

She smiled. She had particularly sharply triangulated eye teeth, Nell observed, which gave her the expression of a complacent wolf.

'Let's look at the exercises I gave the girls to do yesterday.'

'I've got a piece. Shall I read it?' said the girl with sleeper earrings.

'No, let's do the abortion scene first,' Mandy insisted.

66

'Abortion?' said Caroline, still carefully. 'Do you think that's quite right? I mean, it doesn't *feel* right to me.'

'It's one of the problems women have,' said Mandy. 'And this is a play about women's problems.'

'How would Pamina *get* pregnant?' asked Caroline, intending to defuse the situation.

The group burst out laughing.

'Don't be silly!' said Caroline wildly. 'Try and have a bit of sense. We are talking about something quite subtle. Someone like Pamina can't just sleep with the gardener. Is it Monostatos or not? You can't just let the audience *guess*.'

Ursula said, very seriously: 'I'm all for letting the audience do as much work as possible, actually.'

'I don't see that it matters in the least which man made her pregnant,' said the girl with the sleeper earrings. 'It's still Pamina's decision what to do, isn't it?'

'I remember,' said the pale girl with the face like a madonna, 'when I found I was pregnant, it could have been one of three men. I didn't see it was their decision what I did.'

'Did you ask any of them?' demanded Mandy eagerly. 'I wouldn't.'

Murmurs of agreement buzzed round the group.

'The play,' said Caroline. 'Can we get back to the play?'

'Let's hear from Mandy,' ruled Ursula.

'I need someone to read the other part,' said Mandy.

The pale girl stood up a willing volunteer, and Mandy jumped up beside her, as bouncy and nimble as a sixth-form netball player, to stand in the bare-boarded centre of the circle.

It was really a remarkable performance.

Mandy was Pamina discovering her pregnancy, soliciting help from an attendant. Her body moved from eagerness to fear of the drug she was offered; the potion once taken, she began to mime acute physical pain. She bent forward groaning. She grunted abominably. Her lithe young body took on the grotesque postures of childbirth and sexual congress in turn, as if agony and physical pleasure were of similar intensity. When she had finished, she brought a little round of applause from the group, in which Nell joined with a sense of disloyalty.

67

'Brilliant,' said Ursula. 'That'll give them a little knock.'

'They may just be sick,' said Caroline with unwonted rudeness.

'Oh, we don't want it to be too bland,' said Ursula. 'Do we, girls?'

'Maybe not,' said Caroline, 'but where does this particular gobbet fit into the story?'

'We don't know yet,' said Ursula serenely.

And she smiled her big-toothed wolf smile again, undisturbed by the dismay in Caroline's face.

That normally assured face, Nell saw, was ravaged now by anxiety; unfamiliar hormones had drained the blood from her marvellous aristocratic cheeks. Her skin looked sallow. Tiny lines Nell had never observed before had appeared at the side of her nose.

The group was against her, and Caroline felt helpless in opposition to them. They had joined together and as a collective force they were far stronger than she was. She stood, tapping her teeth with a pencil, turned inward in thought, gathering her forces to resist the pressure. Nell saw her loneliness. She felt the girls' hostility as a kind of betrayal. The sisterhood was supposed to be a support network, and instead it had its own antagonisms and its own collective rejection.

The girls, taking a lunch break now, were laughing comfortably. Mandy was eating an apple; the pale girl had brought out her knitting. Caroline frowned in perplexity, and seemed to come to a decision. She beckoned to Mandy.

'Can I talk to you?' she asked with a brilliant smile.

Mandy looked up but went on eating.

'Yeah. Do you mean now?'

'Just for a moment. About your scene. I liked it very much,' said Caroline hastily. 'Would you mind?'

And she led Mandy off to the other side of the room.

Nell saw the other girls watch as Caroline and Mandy gestured and talked just out of earshot. Their own faces were implacable.

It was a good idea, Nell reflected, to try and pick them off one by one, but the girls silently watching had already formed a biological organism of which Mandy was a living part. They were silent in her absence, waiting securely for her to take her place among them on her return.

Caroline didn't have a chance.

Nell returned that evening intending to sort out the situation with the tenants of Plumrose Crescent. Geoffrey would know about them; the pleasant academic couple had been friends of his; there must be some way he could prevent a group of American servicemen turning her once-loved house into an off-station brothel.

On her way into the house Kit Martin waylaid her.

'Your kid said not to worry, she's gone round to stay at Rhoda Dee's. At least I think that's the name: she said you'd know.'

'Yes, I know. Marvellous,' said Nell.

It was the first sign of any kind of normality, she decided, thinking of the big cheerful girl who had come round on another occasion to borrow Becky's history notes.

It also left her with nothing she needed to do for the evening, and she was just wondering what she felt about that when Kit said: 'Listen, I've got a couple of free tickets. Can I tempt you out?'

She hesitated. And then he smiled.

Absolutely against her will, Nell felt herself responding to that smile, even as she wondered about the sense of it. It was such a thoughtless, primitive response, to find charm in even white teeth. What are they to me, she warned herself, these excrescences of bone? It was part of animal evolution, she supposed. When dentistry was dangerous, teeth must have been hopeful signs of likely survival. Hence the sexual response. She was rather ashamed of it.

'Where were you going?' asked Nell.

'Ronnie Scott's,' said Kit.

She wasn't sure she was interested in a night club.

'Of course you are,' he said impatiently. 'It's Betty Carter.'

Nell had never heard of Betty Carter, and Kit began to describe how he had first seen her five years ago at the Blue Note in New York. It all seemed an alarmingly long way from Plumrose Crescent, but his enthusiasm was infectious.

And then there was his smile.

Walking up Old Compton Street she was reminded, by a pungent odour of garlic butter from a pretty French restaurant, of an almost forgotten hunger for good food. It was not the only appetite that she felt restored to her. She had a sense that she was seeing the city at night for the first time since she had come to live in it. This was Kit's piece of the city and he was going to give it to her, and it was his time of night, and she knew she wanted to share it. He was feckless and charming as Millie said. And she enjoyed being protected by his arm and welcomed in, because of him, by the enormous black doorman. There was a long and impatient queue of people waiting for tickets, and Nell experienced an ignoble satisfaction at the thought of being let in as a privileged guest.

Kit took her down into a big red cave of a room, with illuminated photographs around the walls, a bar at the side and tables everywhere. It was dark and noisy. He took her arm and steered her down to the sunken central square where a table in front of the piano and a melancholy saxophone had evidently been reserved.

'You have to sit close,' he explained. 'Food is quite cheap here, drinks aren't. Eat if you want, and we'll have a beer.'

I deserve a bit of fun, Nell told herself. I'm not doing any harm. Brian wouldn't mind. Anyway, it's all Brian's fault I'm in this mess, isn't it? If a little part of her quivered guiltily with a thought that Millie might mind very much, she put it to one side. I'm hardening up, she told herself. Rather like Caroline said: That's what life is like now. It wasn't the life she'd wanted, but it was the only one on offer.

She ordered a steak and tucked in without even feeling for the bottle of Valium.

Betty Carter wore a turban hat of shimmering blue and diamanté; her dress was black, cut down to the small of the back, and showing her unsupported breasts at the front. She has a fine body, thought Nell, wondering how old she was. Sex. That's what it was. She's never had to deny herself sex. Probably she couldn't imagine denying herself anything. She had that assertive American ethic of joy, the pursuit of happiness which Nell's own dour upbringing had made somehow unclean.

On the table she saw Kit's large muscular hand; it came over and took hers, and she squeezed it back gratefully. It felt quite innocent, she thought, like two schoolchildren. It was the music that made her blood race.

Betty Carter's face had a bold, simian vitality; the mouth was long and slightly pushed out by her strong jaw; her eyes snapped with vitality. It was her stance that was remarkable; a kind of sexual crouch, head jutting forward, spread hips, bent knees. At one point she turned her back on the audience to announce the names of her excellent trio of musicians behind her: the boy on the piano was only eighteen and when she looked at him there was a protective maternal mockery in her long-lipped smile. There seemed to be love and respect between them. Was it only showbiz fake? Nell shook her head. Everything didn't have to be nasty, surely?

'She's nearly sixty. What spirit, never mind the technique,' said Kit.

He put his hand absentmindedly on her knee. She didn't object, but she hoped he would think it was because she was listening to the music.

Whenever Betty Carter turned to face her trio, she turned her buttocks to the audience, holding the microphone as she did so, not ceasing her peculiar crooning counterpoint against the familiar melodies.

'Spring can really hang you up the most,' she sang, looking straight into Nell's eyes.

Nell knew exactly what she meant. This was spring, here in this underground red-lit room; she could feel it, looking at this sixty-year-old woman. Her enormous sexual presence was justified by her music; and Nell responded to the song of love, with Kit's hand on her knee, and his smile ready to leap out at her whenever she turned to him for confirmation. It was impossible to talk. It made her throat hurt even to try. But the audience loved Betty Carter. They were willing to be silent, and Nell was happy to be there with them.

In a quite different way, Nell saw, Betty Carter was happy to be there too, and said so. 'I'm a late developer,' she murmured, 'even if I did sing with Ray Charles.' She had just broken some international surface, and Nell could taste her joy, even when she offered traditional bitter advice about men and made a wry joke about a song she had recorded ahead of Tony Bennett. 'And guess who made the money?' she chuckled.

It was all very extravagant and wicked, and Nell was touched with a kind of greed; a greed for making something happen in a short life, of which Kit's hand on her knee was a small part.

About Carter's joy she thought: I'll never have that! And in the same moment she wondered what is it *worth* when she goes backstage afterwards and crashes with fatigue? Who's there then to *know* how good she is? This is her reality, here on the stage; *this* is when she is most alive, what keeps her so juicy. And she is still remarkably juicy, there's no masculinity in her face, or her body. Does she take hormone therapy or what? Do the band take drugs? Did she screw the band, the way she suggested with her body pushed forward so you could see the mound of Venus under her shiny dress?

'She's great,' she said simply, as the set ended. Kit's approval shone back to her.

Afterwards she saw Betty go to the bar on her own and get a drink. A quiet woman, not gesturing with particular verve. Looking her age and much smaller.

Kit approved of Nell. She could feel that. He liked the way she had responded to the singing.

'Tell me about yourself,' he said.

My *self*, she thought, startled. She hadn't thought about such a thing in a long time. Did she have a self? She wasn't absolutely certain she knew what it meant. There was a financial self certainly at the head of her bank statements; someone else who sat at her Apricot WPC and typed out other people's words. Someone who met Becky's accusing eyes over Alpen in the mornings. But someone within, constant, unchanging? She wasn't sure. And while she thought about it Kit was talking to a friend at another table and a bottle of whisky and two glasses appeared before them.

'Present,' said Kit.

In the quieter piano music that followed Betty Carter's performance, she found herself saying:

'I'm not sure who I am. I'd love to do that. I mean do what Betty Carter can do for a whole room full of people. Is that what it's like to play the violin?'

'Not the way I do it,' he grinned.

But he was surprised by what she said, she could see that, and not altogether pleased. Ambition is not attractive, she conceded ruefully. Though it was not a simple greed for celebrity she had in mind: or even a lust for money – that eighties equivalent of fame's spur. What she wanted was a way of being alive. She knew she hadn't explained it properly.

'I've stopped believing in that kind of salvation,' he said.

Surprised by his choice of words, she knew it meant he had understood what she was feeling. At the same time, she guessed he was rejecting something that had been destructive for himself. He had wanted to be another kind of violinist, she understood suddenly.

'What went wrong for you?' she asked therefore, with a directness which had something to do with the large slug of whisky she had taken. And he put his hand back on her knee while her mind went on working, irritably, reaching after the truth of what she felt, like a small animal.

'I was supposed to be a prodigy,' he said, and his seriousness caught at her. 'When I was five, my teacher thought I was Menuhin. I guess I peaked too soon. After six years in the orchestral line-up, I know what I am and what I'm not, and I live with it. And, let me tell you, I've seen an awful lot of unhappy people take their bows in the Queen Elizabeth Hall. I don't gripe about applause. It's not what life is about.'

'It's not the applause I want,' said Nell slowly. 'Just something I could have been I haven't become.' She shook her head, knowing she still hadn't quite said it right.

'Fame corrupts all that,' he said, shaking his head.

'You know what Akhmatova said about fame?' said Nell queerly, betrayed by the heavy-lidded darkness of his eyes into talking from her innermost core.

He didn't know who she was talking about, but he wanted to be told.

'If I can't have love, or peace, or justice, let me have a bitter glory.'

'All that art stuff,' said Kit. 'It's just another self-deception.'

Nell thought about that. It was so Anglo-Saxon. In his words she could hear his assumption that safety was a norm anyone could fall into, instead of a great privilege as it was for someone living in Stalin's madhouse. And when she spoke of glory Akhmatova wasn't thinking of *success*, but *love*; the love of many people for her work; for poetry which meant something to millions in Russia and meant nothing at all in England. She tried to explain as much.

'I think that's so wrong,' he said eagerly. 'What a daunting error! To encourage us to give up the only happiness there is, our relation to other human beings, for an idol, for our own self image. People justify themselves,' he said. 'They make their rules to include themselves. I know writers, they work maybe eight hours a day, and then drink and cruise the streets a bit. And that's their life. Ordinary people try harder to make sense out of things. They have to. They only have one life; they haven't got this crazy strategy for bearing the pain of human loneliness, so they have to find others.'

'Are there *any* working strategies?' she wondered.

'It's all about love,' he said crookedly. His hand was gentle and warm above her knee.

'Oh no, not that,' she said. 'Please. The whole romantic love myth. No, I don't believe in that, not any of it. There has to be something else.'

'Would you like a friend?' he asked her.

'I need a friend,' she said slowly.

'Let's go back,' he said, offering her his hand as he stood up.

They left half the bottle of whisky on the table, and in the taxi on the way back they kissed. Kit had a hot, sweet mouth and a narrow tongue, and Nell enjoyed it. Her hands went up willingly around his neck; she wanted him to keep on kissing her fiercely.

But I won't go to bed with him, she thought. That would be treacherous, I should feel guilty, I'm not that kind of woman.

His hand inched her skirt higher, though, and the first

unmistakeable streams of excitement began to run through her body.

Careful, she told herself.

'Don't do that,' she whispered, taking her mouth away from his and speaking into his ear.

He turned her head back again quite firmly, without replying, and her lips were soon eagerly returning the pressure of his.

Nothing much can happen in a taxi, she told herself. I'll pull myself together when we get back. And meanwhile she let herself enjoy the feel of his fingers on the skin above her stocking tops.

''Ere we are, Gov,' said the tolerant voice of the taxi driver, and she disentangled herself from Kit's grasp outside Millie's house.

Kit opened the door for both of them and brought her inside.

Even as she reproached herself with the necessity of behaving decisively, she made out the face and form of her daughter in the hall.

'Becky, what are you doing here?' she managed, her hands instinctively straightening her mussed hair. She put on the light. Becky looked very pale, and her eyes were dark and strange.

'I was waiting for you. Geoffrey phoned.'

'At this hour?'

'He phoned several times. He said it was urgent.'

'I thought you were staying with Rhoda? Never mind,' said Nell.

Her eyes could focus clearly now, and Becky's manner disturbed her.

'Thanks for taking me to the club,' she said quite formally to Kit, extending her hand.

He took her hand, not entirely comprehending that he was being dismissed.

'It's a bit late to return a phone call now,' he objected holding on to her hand.

Nell took it away with an undignified little jerk, which she was afraid Becky witnessed. There was no question of pleasurable sensuality now; the expression in Becky's eyes filled Nell with panic.

Going downstairs to the flat, she said, with as much fake jollity as she could muster: 'I hope you had a nice evening.'

Becky said nothing to this.

'Something to do with a signature,' said Becky, her voice icy with contempt.

'He can't want that tonight,' objected Nell.

She could not deny what her daughter was thinking without making everything worse. As her head cleared, she was perversely angered that she was being pilloried for so little.

SEVEN

Nell sat on her own bed, looking down at her feet. She was not pleased to discover the evidence of such unromantic lechery in herself. What on earth had she been playing at? Would she really have gone up the corridor into Kit's part of the house if Becky had not been there to waylay her? She feared she might well have done so. And she could hardly justify her behaviour by any overpowering affection. In her memory, Kit had become little more than a shadowy figure turning away in the passageway, a hand ruefully pressing her shoulder. And a likeable grin. She knew nothing about him; and aside from the brief conversation about her own only half-acknowledged ambitions, he had shown little interest in her. An evening of drunken lust, she thought remorsefully, no longer excited by any such emotion and uncomfortably remembering Becky's black, strange gaze. When I see Brian at the weekend, she thought, I'll tell him about the whole episode.

At least if he is ordinarily friendly I will.

And if he will really listen.

She went to sleep with Brian's familiar face in her thoughts, and woke up feeling mainly relief that nothing sillier had happened.

That morning it was very cold, and in the kitchen Becky looked quite ill herself.

'Did you have a good evening? I thought you were staying the night with Rhoda,' Nell risked.

Becky looked up inattentively.

'It was okay,' she said. 'Have you phoned Geoffrey?'

'Coffee first,' said Nell, who had successfully put that particular question out of her mind.

'Mum, what are we going to do for Christmas?'

Nell was opening her post.

'If the tenants pay up,' she said, 'we'll manage something. What would you like? Clothes? Records?'

Nell and Brian had always preferred the New Year; a new year was important, an image of opening out and hope in a secular age. But Becky had other needs.

'Mark phoned,' said Becky. 'He asked if we were staying in London for the holidays.'

'Of course we'll be in London. Can't see where else we'd go,' said Nell. She was surprised and pleased at the sign of Mark's continuing friendship. She had behaved badly, she now thought.

'Are they very religious?' asked Becky.

'Shouldn't think so.'

'Because they're Jews, aren't they? There are a lot in my class and they take it very seriously.'

Surprised, Nell realized she had no idea about Mark's convictions; but just assumed all people in her generation thought more or less the same way.

'I don't know,' she confessed.

'Nice of you to say that,' said Becky, rewarding her with a half smile. 'You don't often admit you don't know things.'

Nell repressed the burst of resentment those words induced, and returned the smile fully and warmly.

She telephoned Geoffrey before setting out for Feminist Arts.

'It's a question of transferring funds,' he said.

'What funds?'

'To help Brian,' he explained.

'I don't think Brian has any funds to transfer.'

'Yes. Well, in one sense that's very clearly true. But he's owed money. I hoped he might tell you himself. You needn't sound so suspicious – I'm not tricking Brian.'

'Who are you tricking then?' Nell knew she sounded suspicious. That was how she felt, though she couldn't have said why. It was something to do with the mixture of patience and urgency in his voice.

'It's a way of safeguarding both of you,' said Geoffrey. 'I wish you weren't so difficult, Nell. We'd like to put some money into your name. To keep it safe for a while. I want you to open a building society account.'

'I see. So nobody knows you're giving it to Brian?'

'We won't be giving it to Brian. We are giving it to you.'

'Who are *we*, exactly?'

'The firm.'

'I don't like the sound if it,' said Nell.

She didn't mean to be perverse. She needed money very badly. The post had contained a number of demands: rates, water, fees still owing for Becky's last term at her smart school. And then there was indeed Christmas. She thought of Becky's pale face. What sense was there in behaving as though Geoffrey were putting some kind of parchment under her hand to sign in return for her soul?

'I'm not very happy about those lodgers you found me,' she said distractedly.

'I know,' said Geoffrey. 'They had to go back to the States. I hope their subtenants are paying up.'

'I want you to get rid of them,' she said.

'They're not working out?'

'They are not,' said Nell, as firmly as she could manage without bringing up the dustbins.

'Very well, leave it to me,' said Geoffrey. 'No problem there. I'll see to it when I go up next week. Have you got my invitation? I'm having a grand New Year party.'

'I don't like parties,' Nell said, hearing herself sound like a sulky child. 'Especially when I don't know anybody.'

'Well, Caroline is coming,' said Geoffrey. 'A lot of old friends will be there.'

Nell had no more Valium and at first she didn't mind. It didn't seem worth asking for a repeat prescription. On the way to work there wasn't time, for one thing. But what a lot of nonsense is talked about it, she thought with a certain smugness. I'm not addicted to the stuff at any rate, she reflected as she walked towards Liza's workshop.

Caroline had telephoned in to say she had a temperature and wouldn't be coming in until the afternoon and Nell, who took the call, found herself sitting in on a conversation between Liza and Ursula with a mounting sense of disloyalty. She was dismayed to find they were far from displeased that Caroline was to be absent, though Ursula was sceptical about her degree of illness. She seemed to have given up on Caroline altogether, while Liza seemed preoccupied with other worries.

'Have you heard from Geoffrey recently?' she asked Nell.

Nell said she had been invited up to his New Year party, but decided against mentioning the morning's urgent phone call.

Liza studied her face in a brooding uncommunicative way.

'Poor Nicky,' she said finally.

Nell had never heard Liza mention her dead husband unless in response to a direct inquiry. Today she looked pale and anxious, Nell saw, almost as if she had been crying. But perhaps it was the pressure of other anxieties. She was a woman whose abilities were altogether administrative rather than intuitive; someone who controlled the world by filing and sorting, for whom it was difficult to imagine a passionate life. She had two children of Becky's age, though, Nell remembered. For a moment she had a vision of Liza, asleep and defenceless, with a child in her arms, as sharp an image as if she were hallucinating. Now what's this? Nell thought, surprised, and felt the room judder strangely to one side.

'Is Brian coping?' Liza asked.

Nell felt an enormous rush of relief, because people so rarely broached the topic of Brian with concern.

'He doesn't talk much about how he feels, but I *know* he isn't happy,' she said. 'He doesn't seem to see any sense in trying to make the best of things.'

Liza made a rude noise.

'Dear me, we do ask rather a lot, Nell,' she said.

Nell guessed she was thinking of her husband again.

For the first time she put together in her mind the connection between Brian's being in gaol and Nicky's suicide.

And somewhere in the same box, she perceived, was Geoffrey.

But even as she felt the knowledge flood her with anxiety the room took another swing to the right, and her hands began to sweat, awkwardly.

Embarrassed, Nell felt in her pocket for the familiar consoling bottle. Of course she had no more tablets, she remembered now.

'Does anyone have any Valium?' she asked abruptly, more con-

80

scious of pressing physical need than any impression she was likely to make.

Ursula and Liza exchanged glances.

'You want to get off that stuff,' said Ursula.

'I *am* off. That's the whole trouble,' said Nell impatiently.

Liza sighed and fiddled in a drawer of her desk.

'There used to be some here,' she said.

Nell recognized the sudden resurgence of hope with new desperation. Good heavens, she thought miserably, I *am* hooked.

But when Liza produced the bottle with yellow tablets left in it she did not refuse them.

Ursula and Liza went back to a consideration of the latest draft of Caroline's text. Presently Liza said: 'She'll just have to let us get on with it in our own way. Personally, I'm happy to give her the whole week off. All she knows how to do is criticize language.'

Nell decided to say no more, and Liza began to talk with some intensity about the local council's indifference to AIDS.

'Men do run the world,' Liza sighed.

Nell thought that, in her own experience, the truth was much more clearly that some men did and others did not.

'Which bit of the world?' she asked, smiling, hating her own ingratiating spirit, conscious that she wished to please and not contend; that she needed the job. That she didn't feel entirely sympathetic with Liza Thynne's aims.

'The public world. And the home, of course. Most homes anyway.'

That Saturday visiting Bleakwood she found Brian more than usually taciturn. He hadn't read any of the books she had brought last time. When she began to explain eagerly what he should do if he wanted to start an Open University course towards a PhD he said, 'Dear sweet Nell!' with a bark of laughter that brought the lines of bitterness round his mouth into greater sharpness.

She tried a little general conversation: 'Did you watch Ben Elton this week? I didn't like him at all at first, all that *pressure* in his voice used to make my throat feel tight. But he's witty, isn't he? And what he says about this government's behaviour is true.'

'I don't bother with television much,' he said acidly. The snub made tears start in her eyes. The hostility in his voice seemed so unfair.

'Look, I'm not having such a great time myself,' she began, 'tapping away at a word processor isn't much fun. And I haven't worried you with half the stuff I have to decide about.'

This amused him, though she couldn't see why. He seemed to feel he knew far more about the world she was confronting that she did. So she asked him icily what to do about the money Geoffrey was proposing to put into a building society. In response he looked at her as if she might, perhaps, have suddenly taken leave of her senses.

'Take it, of course.'

'Where's it coming from?' she asked abruptly.

Her question produced the first animation she had seen in many visits:

'Now tell me why all of a sudden you worry about that? You never worried before, why should you worry now?'

She didn't know how to reply to him.

'Poor Nell, saint and martyr,' he sighed. 'Hands clean always, because you don't see what's happening. If you don't *look* it can't be your fault, can it? How innocent you always felt, I know that. But you *were* implicated, my little Nell, people *are*, you know, if they take the fruits of other people's behaviour. But you wouldn't like to admit that. You'll never admit that.'

Nell was more shocked by his own implied admission of guilt. How could she be implicated in anything bad, unless he himself were guilty of it?

She felt her eyes open into an extraordinary wideness as the astonishment of her rethinking overwhelmed every other reaction.

'But Brian, you said you've never done anything wrong,' she said, ashamed of the pathos in her voice.

'The worst thing I ever did was not to know what I was doing,' said Brian. 'But you didn't just not *know*, Nell. You actually didn't bloody well care.'

She rose from her seat with great dignity. She knew what was being said now and she had not been working for nearly a month in Feminist Arts for nothing.

'You blame me for being a wife. Is that it? Well, I wish I *had* gone on and struggled and done all the things I wanted to do! I certainly *never* wanted to live in Royston and look after your neat little house. I had ambitions too.'

He was standing alongside her now and shaking with rage himself.

'You think you are so virtuous, coping with this and that. If you tell me one more time about that bloody Apricot word processor I'll hit you.'

Nell held on to her dignity precariously. Her every instinct was to throw both arms around him and hug him to her. Far from feeling virtuous, a residual guilt about her behaviour with Kit Martin meant she had absolutely no desire to strike a moral line.

'Darling, I'm sorry, I'm sorry,' she said, tears streaming down her face.

'Are you?' said Brian. 'Well, you don't know what you're saying, unfortunately.'

She was angry with Brian for the whole train journey back to London.

Looking down at herself in the bath on Sunday evening, it occurred to Nell with a pang of alarm that she had lost weight. Her breasts, which were normally rounded and perky, hardly broke the surface of the water. She could not remember whether the bones of her ribs were normally so easily detected. Standing on the scales, naked and still wet, she made out that she had indeed lost half a stone. It seemed a great deal to lose in a month, Nell thought, though she supposed there was no need to invent a horrendous disease to explain it. Gloomily, she thought back. She never had breakfast and, since Becky had been out with friends, had eaten nothing for lunch. She ought to eat, but her stomach closed against the idea. Perhaps with another pill? Were there any more pills? She checked her bag desperately. The top had come off the pill bottle Liza had given her and the contents were scattered among the lipsticks, small change and pencils at the bottom of her handbag. In a panic she scrabbled for them, aware all the time of yellow dust, which meant those that were left had already disintegrated. She was tempted to lick at the dust. Christ, I'm an addict, she acknowledged to herself miserably. I crave the stuff with every cell in my body. This is a nightmare. Unfair, unfair, she wanted to shriek. Damn it, haven't I enough troubles? She knew she would never get to sleep without some kind of chemical help.

Millie saw her face as she came out into the hall.

'You got some kind of problem?' she asked.

'I'm a junkie,' Nell said tonelessly.

Millie looked incredulous.

'A Valium junkie. I've lost half my pills, and I don't think the doctor will give me any more, and without them I can't sleep and can't eat. I'll die.'

Millie clicked her teeth and shook her head.

'Why didn't you just stick to dope?' she suggested.

'Have you any?' asked Nell eagerly. 'The trouble is, when I tried it at college, I could never take the smoke in properly. Maybe if I could eat it?' She laughed, a little breathlessly: the situation was so absurd. Was she really trying to solicit solid marijuana? She was beginning to break down altogether.

'I don't care,' she said miserably, in part in answer to her own thoughts. 'I have to carry on, get in to work tomorrow. I have to sleep tonight. I must have something.'

Millie shook her head.

'I've got some Scotch,' she offered.

Nell thought back to those first terrified days after Geoffrey had appeared, thought of the time she drank a whole bottle of ginger wine and the release of falling into a deep dreamless sleep, and the headache in the morning.

'It'll make me feel sick,' she said doubtfully.

Over the Scotch Millie spoke with authority.

'You are not approaching your GP right. Now this is what to say. Are you listening?'

Nell nodded slowly, the alcohol dimming her sense of the problem, but not reaching it, not curing it.

'You tell him you can't come off cold turkey. You need to give up maybe two milligrams a day, not more. Understand? Then he'll give you some of the two-milligram white pills. And you can get yourself through till Christmas. Then you better take some kind of notice of this because Valium – well, that's as hard as heroin to give up. I'm not exaggerating. It takes thirty-seven days.'

'You mean housewives all over the country are going through thirty-seven days of this kind of hell?'

'Well, women are brave,' Millie shrugged. 'It's mostly women. Why are you so surprised? They have to give birth, don't they – if they can stand all that, they can stand anything.'

Nell wasn't sure she had any intention of giving up Valium but she took Millie's advice about how to get the two-milligram pills out of her doctor.

On Monday afternoon Caroline arrived looking haggard and shivering, and Nell saw she had influenza. It was unlike her to go out into the world when she was ill, and Nell decided to speak out against her unwise bravery.

'Why go on if you're sick?'

'Have to. It's in the contract.'

'You can't make yourself ill because of a contract.'

'Yes, I'm freelance, I have to,' said Caroline wearily.

'Even people on social security can stay in bed if they have flu,' said Nell.

'No, they can't. They have to be up and going to the Job Centre or retraining or something,' said Caroline.

She gave Nell a wan ghost of a smile.

Nell knew exactly why Caroline, who was not one of the meek of this world, was experiencing such a pressure to keep her word. It was part of the war with the group, a war which Caroline could scarcely be said to be winning. The play had taken a very different shape as the weeks progressed. It opened now with Monostatos, made over into a hermaphrodite, who acted as a rather jokey link man. The Queen had dwindled into a charmingly designed black and white wooden puppet who was brought on stage from time to time to be ridiculed by Sarastro's minions. Very little of Caroline's original dialogue had been left. All this Nell knew because she had typed the changes.

So she understood the defeat and disappointment that underlay the white febrile look on Caroline's face. There was another quality, however; an uneasy triumph, a guilt, which she could not quite explain.

'Funny thing,' said Caroline after a while. 'Shall I tell you what is making this so peculiarly difficult?'

'Do.'

'Liza's brilliant PR.'

'How so?'

'Well, I'm having all these interviews. Television. Colour supplement. Liza knows how to raise people's profiles. And she's raised mine. I'm getting more attention for this play, which isn't very much my piece of work any more, than anything I've ever done in the past. I don't see quite what to do about it.'

She paused.

'No, it's worse than that. I can't make myself refuse what Liza is setting up. Is it greedy of me? Is it even sense? You know how little control I have over what Ursula and the group are doing. What do you think, Nell?'

Nell floundered.

'Exactly,' said Caroline.

'Why can't you speak up for what you want?' asked Nell.

But she knew. The girls had no respect for what Caroline wanted. They didn't even see her beauty, poor Caroline, only her being ten years older and increasingly desperate.

'I *wanted* to do this,' said Caroline. 'I wanted to work with a group. It's such a noble idea. East German, really. I'm tired of Western narcissism. The collective is so much more worthwhile.'

But she looked very unhappy.

'Sorry to moan on like this. It's the headache. Honestly, my temperature was over a hundred this morning. I can't read my stuff out to them, Nell. Their hostility stops me. I'm frightened of them somehow. And then,' she admitted, 'so much of my energy is elsewhere. Thinking about Johnnie and what he's doing.'

Nell decided not to take up that problem for the moment.

'It's hard to get through to a hostile audience,' she said. 'It takes a lot of spirit. I could do it for you . . .'

She stopped. Nell had once been a great reader. Not as Caroline was, someone who could charm an intimate audience into acquiescent pleasure, but a figure on a stage who could take an audience whose knees were aching, and whose interest had dwindled to a box of chocolates, and fight them into following a complex piece of Shakespeare.

'I suppose it might help,' said Caroline, doubtfully.

Nell picked some of Caroline's best lines to read out. At least she hoped they were Caroline's. There was an odd echo of Chekhov. As she reached the second sentence, she heard that odd stilling of the room she remembered. She knew it meant everyone had begun to listen intently. Eyes were fixed on her. A little ripple of excitement ran along the nerves of her back. This was something she could do. She could do it well. She read on, and as she did so, sent her voice lower and quieter; and old trick which only worked if the audience allowed it to do so.

They all leaned forward.

'I would like to wake up on a clear calm morning and feel that every good thing I have ever done could be blown away. But I can't. It is terrible to be a plain woman, isn't it? To be kind and generous counts for nothing with men. Only beauty matters. They don't care about the soul, only the flesh. What does any man know of the problem? Do they have to look into their mirrors for an answer? No. They have only their souls to manage and the world is theirs.'

It was easy.

She had done it.

'Wonderful,' said the pale girl with the face like a madonna.

Nell was intoxicated with a sense of power and hope. But she had only read to help Caroline, and she wasn't sure whether she had convinced them about the lines in the play, only won a little admiration for herself. Greedily, however, she enjoyed their applause.

EIGHT

Mark rang to ask Nell round for a Sunday brunch in the days before Christmas and the New Year.

'I've invited some interesting people,' he promised her.

'I'm sure you have,' she said, wanting to convey gratitude but somehow hitting the wrong note.

'University people. I think there's a publisher too. Maybe one of them will suggest a better job for you?' he said.

Nell was still flushed by recent applause and did not respond to the possibility.

'I'm very happy with Feminist Arts,' she said. She wasn't sure what he heard in her voice but his own grew sharper.

'It's your crazy ideas that damage you,' he said. 'Don't you know that? You are so stubborn. Think of your daughter. She probably doesn't give a damn about alternative theatre. Why should she have to do without just because you want to be involved with a lot of pretentious dykes? I can't see why the taxpayer funds them.'

'Your government . . .' she began.

'I'm not a Tory,' he pointed out.

'You believed in literature once,' she cried out. 'I know you did. Conrad and Lawrence. You talked about them.'

'Do you think what these women do has much to do with literature? Now let me finish. Don't argue. I know what you're going to say. Not the point, because I'm not sure I do believe in literature, not any more; it's got nothing to do with my life now whatever I once thought. I was conned into thinking it mattered to me at university, but I know better now,' he said. 'Writers are for writers. They don't interest me as people. I've never heard one of them on a book programme who had anything useful to say. Names. That's all they know about. One another's names. A name made great is a name destroyed.'

'Very biblical.'

'I don't admire them. Who needs all their cleverness? Give me a good airport blockbuster, at least that must be damned hard work to produce. Don't interrupt. And don't give me any rot about self-expression. What kind of self do writers have to express anyway? They're sour and they're bitter. And life is very simple when you come down to it. Everyone knows what a good life means.'

'The thing is, Mark – ' she interjected.

'All that fancy talk,' he raged. 'We were taught lies. We were taught that literature changed society and it doesn't.'

'Well, Auden knew that,' she said. 'Poetry changes nothing. Makes nothing happen.'

'Can't you think of anything that isn't a quotation?'

But maybe he is right, she thought. Maybe it *was* literature that had damaged her, and especially the Russians; Dostoevsky with his vision of shining goodness and Tolstoy with his hope for shared human love. Maybe that's why she wasn't safely in Mark's solid world of material wellbeing.

'I don't care what people do as long as they make contact with the world,' Mark was saying.

She had missed the connection with what went before.

'I suppose you are right. I *am* out of touch with Thatcher's Britain,' she admitted.

'Yes? Well, don't think you would have got on so well in the Gulag,' said Mark sharply.

'The point is, I *prefer* to work as part of a group,' she retorted, an oblique dig at Mark who had once been a socialist.

Approval of the group, however, was not to be Nell's for long. And the quarrel, when it came, surprised her the more since she had begun to feel some truth in what Liza and Ursula were saying about women's lives.

Several of the girls, including Liza, had joined Nell and Caroline in the now familiar Victorian pub, all brown wood and mirrors, for a glass of beer. The girls didn't usually like to drink beer at lunch: it got in the way of work, they said. But this time they were excited by a play the workshop was considering for its next production. Nell listened idly at first. Ursula's commitment to the welfare of the planet no longer sounded strident to her. It was only when Liza began to declare that there was never any need to work on the bomb in the first place that she felt inclined to enter the discussion.

'They worked on the bomb because Hitler worked on the bomb,' she said.

They were unimpressed by her assertion.

'They should have refused all the same,' said Ursula, gesturing with her fork, and suspiciously removing the curve of a shrimp. 'American warmongers.'

'Aren't you by and large glad America came into the war?' asked Nell.

'I don't feel war was the only way to answer Hitler,' said Liza. 'There were other things that weren't tried. Weren't done. Roosevelt could have been made to open the gates. That would have been more use than the war, if you're thinking about atrocities.'

'But American Jews didn't care,' said Ursula equably. 'They were too busy getting in to the right clubs.'

'Not getting in, you mean,' said Nell. 'Why think of the Jews as powerful? They damn well weren't powerful then.'

Blank eyes met hers, and she realized that they weren't interested in the dead, why should they be, why indeed should she?

'The United States went into the war for its own disgusting reasons,' said Liza finally.

'I don't care,' said Nell wildly. 'I don't suppose the English came in primarily to help the Poles.'

'We have to stop wars altogether now,' said Ursula. 'Or the planet will blow up.'

'Yes,' said Nell. 'I agree. But we have to fight against torture and murder too.'

'Of course,' they all said patiently.

Liza's eyebrows were raised in polite astonishment at her vehemence and Nell felt the absurdity of her lonely anger. Nothing anyone had said was in the least antisemitic, she could see that, and yet she sensed their indifference. In a moment they will sweetly point out, she realized, that the bomb was used against the Japanese anyway. But the focus in the argument had changed.

There was a gap separating her from the eyes that confronted her own. They knew about the camps, of course, but distantly. It was not a story that touched them, not a threat they felt sharply. Her voice came from too far away to make any sense. And for her, perhaps because of her father, perhaps because she had always known what would happen to her as a half-Jew in Hitler's Europe, she could only see that last war as a simple struggle against absolute evil.

Caroline, too, she saw, was bewildered by her intensity.

As they returned to the workshop, she tried to defuse it herself, but instead began the whole discussion again.

'Did you watch *Shoah* on Channel Four?' she found herself asking. 'On Sunday.'

'I don't *need* to do that. I know all about that,' said Liza. 'I don't have to go through all that again.'

'You don't know,' said Nell furiously. 'Not the details. It had to be organized so cleverly. *What do you know about what ordinary decent people let happen?*'

'Not all that again,' sighed Liza.

Conscious that the discussion had gone against her, Nell continued to fume through the first part of the afternoon; and when Ursula came to ask her to read a part, her emotions were still uncomfortably volatile.

Caroline was embroiled in a fight of her own.

'There's no feeling left in the play,' she was saying. 'It's just agitprop. All right. Now, I've lost over that damned rape scene. Maybe that works. I don't know. But can't we compromise over this one? It's not the politics I object to, it's the language. You don't seem to have the slightest sensitivity to cliché. Don't you understand? I have a small, not very grand, reputation as a poet. These are words I would never write.'

'I write poems too,' said Mandy rather huffily.

'Yes,' said Caroline.

'We all thought that speech of Sarastro was rather fine,' said Ursula.

There was a pause.

'Look,' said Caroline. 'I've been pretty easy to push around up to now. Can't you try to see things my way? Just over this bit?

You've changed the whole structure. As I wrote it, the Queen of Night was disabled by love. That made some kind of sense to me. What is this new tribe of Amazons doing here? What has that to do with anything?'

'We're trying to make a political point,' said Ursula.

Nell's attention wandered.

Her last visit to Brian had gone badly. He had yelled at her not to come back for a fortnight, because it made him ill to quarrel. She found that altogether unjust, because all the quarrelling had come from him. She had done nothing more than chatter to him about her daily life. She had asked so little of him, reproached him so rarely. Blamed him not at all for the situation they all found themselves in. When she found tears trickling hotly down the edge of her nose, he mocked her:

'Goodness, anyone would think it was *you* being punished. You are really amazing, Nell. I'm the one locked up here, you know.'

Did she have the right to be happy when he clearly wasn't? It didn't feel right, certainly. I do care for him, she thought with remorse. The pain of it came through to her for a moment; but it was so paralysing she protected herself from the knowledge.

She woke from her reverie to find Ursula and Caroline glaring at one another in white fury.

'This is a democratic organization,' said Ursula. 'You must abide by the decision of the group.'

'Oh no, I mustn't,' said Caroline, and walked out of the room. Nell gasped in amazement.

And then Liza said: 'Well, that's no great loss,' and Nell found herself standing on her feet.

'You've no sense. And absolutely no compassion, for all your do-gooding talk,' she said, and strode out after her friend, catching her up in the office. Caroline was astonished to see her. Nell threw her key down on the desk next to the Apricot, and picked up her own coat to leave.

'Are you sure you can afford this?' asked Caroline, impressed but doubtful.

'I'm sure I can't,' said Nell.

She wasn't really sure what had so angered her: the self-satisfied piety of the girls or her telephone call with Mark. Both were very bad reasons to throw her next month's rent out of the window.

Caroline seemed to feel the same.

'Let me take you for a proper lunch,' she said. 'Celebrate our freedom.'

Nell agreed, her voice a little hollow, and then they were in the street. Caroline held up her hand. A taxi, nosing behind the traffic, made its way obediently across to the kerb. In a moment they were flying across London and Nell felt her spirits revive. Caroline waved aside Nell's offer of half the fare.

'I had good news this morning,' she said. 'The Arts Council have made me an award, so I can see a few months ahead. First time in a long while.'

In less than twenty minutes they were sitting in Caroline's favourite restaurant: a wine bar with shiny, cherry-painted tables and simple white hotel plates. A beautiful boy with a light jacket, straw hat and a plastic bag marked ROUGH TRADE walked in ahead of them, and then turned and greeted Caroline effusively.

'What are you doing these days?'

Nell and Caroline sat at a table opposite a girl who was smoking and talking feverishly. She had large transparent plastic earrings and a very short skirt. Nell observed that underneath it her stockings had a visible tear from which a ladder had already begun.

Everyone knew Caroline and smiled and tried to catch her eye. Caroline's own gloom had evaporated and she whispered to Nell across the table.

'You were wonderful. I'll never forget the way you spoke up.'

Nell tried to enjoy the feeling of having behaved well, but with a little knot of panic in her stomach she remembered she now had no job and that there might be no income from the house in Plumrose Crescent until after Christmas.

'Listen,' said Caroline. 'I've thought of something. There may be a job going in Television Centre.'

'On an Apricot?' Nell inquired.

'Well, I suppose there'll be some typing, bound to be, but some of it will be reading scripts.'

'I don't suppose they'd want me to start till January though, would they?' asked Nell.

Caroline took in the significance of the terror behind Nell's smile.

'Wait a minute. I thought Geoffrey said you were getting some money?'

'How do you know that?' asked Nell, with a funny shock. 'I thought I was supposed to keep it such a damn secret.'

'I see a lot of Geoffrey these days,' said Caroline.

'So you screwed it up,' said Becky when Nell explained to her why she wasn't going into work on Monday morning.

'Don't worry. Caroline said she knew somebody,' said Nell.

'I'm sure she knows everybody,' said Becky. 'Will that necessarily help?'

'She said she'd phone when she got back from Struga,' said Nell with diminishing confidence.

'By then she'll be having lunch happily with Liza Thynne,' said Becky, shaking her head vigorously.

Nell had considered that likelihood herself, but had put the thought aside. Now she looked at her daughter with a mixture of anxiety and admiration.

'Don't be so smart,' she said, and waited for Caroline to phone.

After five days she decided her reluctance to take the initiative was silly.

'How have you been?' asked Caroline. Before Nell could reply, she plunged on: 'I can't tell you how awful it's been over here. I never *reached* Struga. My mother's been at death's door, knocked down by a car, rushed to hospital, just awful.'

Nell thought Caroline's distress sounded evenly divided between missing her jaunt to Struga and her mother's accident.

'And Struga was my last chance to see Johnnie before he goes off to South Africa. I was out when he phoned and I haven't heard again all week.'

'Awful,' agreed Nell. 'I wonder, did you have a chance to talk to that friend of yours in Television Centre?'

There was a pause.

'You remember,' said Nell, trying not to sound agitated. 'About some kind of job for January.'

94

'I don't want to preach,' said Caroline stiffly, 'but your really mustn't be so trapped inside your own problems, Nell.'

'I suppose not.'

'Of course if I'd had any news like that you'd have had it at once,' said Caroline.

'I suppose I would.'

'I'd like to help you. Let me think. If you're absolutely stuck,' Caroline suggested, 'I could phone Liza Thynne for you.'

There was another pause as Nell considered that, remembering what Becky had said.

'No thanks. I'll find something,' she said eventually. 'One word processor is very much like another.'

'I'm going away for Christmas,' said Caroline. 'See you at Geoffrey's New Year party.'

'Expect so,' said Nell.

NINE

Before that, however, there was Mark's party.

Becky hadn't wanted to go to Mark's brunch; so she made it impossible, by arriving back home at four in the morning, looking black-eyed and tottery, and refusing to be woken when Nell needed to set out. Looking at Mark's brilliantly set table Nell though of the half quiche in the fridge with a mixture of guilt and irritation. Was it altogether her fault that Becky lived so bleakly?

There were quite a few youngsters of Becky's age at Mark's party. 'Suitable friends,' as Becky would have put it, picking up Nell's wish for her happiness as some kind of criticism.

Nell looked around the room. There were neighbours too, some of them with a strong physical resemblance to Mark, in well-cut suits and sparkling shirts. Nell knew, without being told, that they were Jewish. It wasn't easy to identify the clues to that knowledge. They weren't particularly dark or heavy featured. Then there were several people who had been at London University with Mark, whom she half recognized. She knew Mark had in part structured the gathering for her benefit, and wished she could feel more relaxed.

She was recognized herself with enthusiasm by a pale girl with a narrow face and pursed lips, who seemed to think Nell knew all the details of her life. She had separated five years ago from her husband and now worked in the social services.

'Of course, in principle, I'd like to marry again if I found the right man, but it doesn't seem to happen. Anyway, I like living alone,' she said.

Nell said she couldn't imagine feeling like that.

'It's the freedom. The space. I'm not sure I would want to give it up.'

'It must be very hard work, your job.'

'Exhausting. I'm up at six most days, and driving around. I don't get back till eight.'

'Scary too?' inquired Nell.

'Sometimes you get people who shout at you,' she admitted.

Nell was astonished by her brave goodness.

'Where do you live?' she asked. And the girl coloured with embarrassment.

'Well, I've got a pretty little house. In Dulwich. Very charming.'

Nell understood. The girl was guilty because her family equipped her with the money to live in a decent house. She wanted to say: Good heavens, you deserve some luck; you work hard, you're ill paid, and the community is lucky to have you serving it. But she said nothing.

I don't belong here, thought Nell unhappily, not among these cheerful, sensible people. And the thought made her feel lonely. Their lives were open in their faces. She could tell they got up early, just as they got into bed at the right time the night before, with the right partners. Not one of them would even lie awake finishing off a last chapter. Even if they did, they would not get up late for work. They keep the rules, she told herself. And prosper. That's the point of the rules. I don't, and that's why I don't fit.

In some ways it was her own fault. She felt uneasy as she looked around the women, and couldn't imagine any of them responding eagerly to Kit's open lips in a taxi. But that was only part of it. There were routines, she thought, rituals. Nothing elaborate, nothing pretentious.

Everything in its place. Everything in proportion. Balanced. Nothing eccentric. Had she ever risen to their standards, even when she was living in Plumrose Crescent? Probably not. And they would not understand how she could live gratefully in Millie's basement, though that wasn't exactly bottom of the pile. Rebelliously, she wondered why not. Their parents might well have climbed up from even meaner housing, she supposed. Like her own father. She felt their disapproval as a moral judgement.

They were both joined by a baldheaded gnome of a man, with a lined face and tired eyes. It was as if he had been stricken with premature ageing. And yet there was something likeably direct in

97

his gaze. Nell observed that his plate contained neither fish nor meat.

'Are you a vegetarian?' she asked him.

'I'm certainly not kosher,' he said at once.

'I hadn't thought of that, and in any case, I expect Mark is,' she laughed.

'In the house,' he agreed. 'Won't stop him eating giant prawns in the Chinese restaurant, however. Such self-tolerance is part of his generation and getting rarer and rarer.'

Nell's spirits had begun to lift a little, as Mark came over to take her by the arm. He led her towards a good-looking man of about forty with blue eyes, black hair and an outdoor tan.

'This is Johnnie Farrago,' said Mark importantly. 'And his wife. She's a close friend of my own wife. Almost a relation, really.'

Nell could see in Mark's face that he did not approve of Johnnie Farrago, and wondered how much he knew about Johnnie's life. She decided that he knew a good deal, and that was why he was so solicitous towards the tired woman at Johnnie's side.

'I remember you,' said Nell, confused to have her London circles overlap. She could not meet his eyes for thinking of Caroline.

His wife, Jana, looked unutterably exhausted. She had a shattered face, the kind loved by Lucien Freud, with huge black eyes, deep lines and very straight hair. Her voice was a low and very charming purr, still accented from her displaced childhood.

'Johnnie, find me another drink,' she asked. And, turning to Nell with a smile which lit her face so that for a moment she looked almost beautiful, she said: 'I'm not myself. I was up all last night with a sick child.'

'Can I find you a glass of wine at the same time?' Johnnie asked Nell courteously.

If he knew of her connection to Caroline there was no sign of it.

Even in her fatigue, Johnnie Farrago's wife was dressed with extraordinary chic; her black dress had a simple gold band at the hips which must have cost the earth, thought Nell. Jana had the kind of gaunt, rangy body on which clothes hung like French models and she wore her black hair like a twenties ballerina.

'You must come and have lunch one day, if you aren't too busy,' Jana said as they waited for their wine.

Her grin had all the peaky charm of a child in a French film.

Nell said that she would like to, and recognized that in this room Jana was as out of place as she was. More so, because she seemed to represent that great Central European displacement that had brought so many Jews to this country before the Second World War. Yet she could hardly be part of that; she was too young, Nell reasoned. And her name suggested Czechoslovakia.

'My family went back,' said Jana promptly, when asked. 'Silly, wasn't it? They believed in Communism. Until Slansky. That's how I came to marry Johnnie. He rescued me.'

Johnnie did indeed have the air of a hero, a face and body style which would have been at home in the Western states of America. Nell found something alarming in Jana's fragility alongside Johnnie's gunslinger good looks, and remembered Caroline's part in the situation guiltily.

That morning she had woken to an odd dream, of a childhood where she still put out her hand to a father. She was dressed in a white coat, about six years old, with white gloves which itched and chafed her wrists. And there she was, in some gallery of strange women, pretending to look down into her prayer book, and peeking instead through the rails at Mark in the seats below. Her dream was suffused with golden light; she could see a green ceiling and painted stars. There was darkness in the windows, so it must have been a winter evening. When she woke up, she knew she had dreamt what she did because she was setting off to enter Mark's world as someone displaced.

'About publishing,' said Johnnie Farrago, returning to her side with glasses of red wine. 'Mark tells me you are interested.'

'Well . . .' said Nell, embarrassed.

Jana took a glass of wine, gave another brilliant smile, and moved away.

'I'm not sure I can help you with anything very interesting,' said Johnnie. 'I can't tell you how beleaguered we are with the fall-out from the last takeover.'

Something in Johnnie's clean-cut good looks definitely alarmed Nell. Aryan, she decided, surprising herself by the thought: it was like being in the presence of an SS officer. Yet here he was, accepted on Mark's hearth, and married to a sweetly Jewish wife. He was too large; there was a sort of granite quality to his face which would smash anything in his way. She absolutely could not imagine wanting to make love to him. He was too invulnerable, too untouchable; it would be like making love to a piece of cliff, she thought to herself, a little appalled to find herself thinking so of Caroline's lover, a little embarrassed to be thinking of him as a 'lover' at all in this world where home and family values were so warmly and securely enveloping.

'I was thinking of something secretarial,' she said baldly.

His slight surprise at so humble an ambition was instantly readable.

'I suppose that's different.'

She didn't want to work for him, she decided. She would have liked to say something that would startle his air of complacent control.

'I'd like to help Brian's wife, of course,' he nodded.

'I didn't know you knew my husband.' Nell was startled.

'Oh, but I do. I know everyone. And in any case Geoffrey is very fond of him.'

Without knowing why, Nell felt very frightened suddenly, as if she were about to learn something that would permanently damage her.

'You're an innocent,' said Johnnie, sighing. 'Did Brian ever speak of a girl called Babar?'

'No,' said Nell. 'Funny name. Is she enormous?'

The polite deadness of her voice concealed the anxiety she now focussed clearly.

'Tiny,' said Johnnie. 'A bit silly, really, but Brian liked her. She worked in City Trust with him.'

'What are you telling me?' asked Nell.

Johnnie said: 'I grant you Brian was a very moral young man. But even the most moral young men make mistakes.'

'I don't care,' Nell said. 'It doesn't matter now, when he's in such trouble. Even if he did fall for a silly girl called Babar.'

Johnnie looked amused.

'I don't believe Brian did anything wrong,' Nell insisted.

'Don't you?'

Suddenly she wasn't sure.

'How much do you know about it anyway?'

'Babar's been working for me,' he said.

She believed that much at least was true. Did she believe the rest of it?

'About a secretarial job . . .' he began.

It was out of the question. She could not bear to owe him anything. She said as much in a blurred, hopeless voice, and he nodded.

'Get in touch if you change your mind.'

'I won't,' she said.

Inwardly she added: I'd rather go on the streets.

Johnnie shrugged. 'It's no skin off my nose. Ask Brian about Babar.'

Carefully, Nell put down her glass of wine and walked away, her heart now beating so noisily that she could hardly hear anything else. For all the malice she had seen glinting in Farrago's eyes, she believed him. Her heart clenched as she went to sit on one of Mark's white leather sofas. There were so many clues she had ignored, it now seemed, she thought as she sat on the creaking leather. She had been asleep.

Brian had shown her only perfunctory interest for months before the disaster. Hadn't he always been tired? Why hadn't she taken him up on that? Didn't she mind? The truth was she had expected the tiredness. Melanie, the doctor's wife, had spoken of the same problem. Plumrose Crescent wives *expected* their husbands to be tired. Did they also expect them to be unfaithful? She thought of Melanie's conscientious little husband, and could not believe as much. But then she had not expected it of Brian either.

Were they right then, Caroline and Geoffrey, and all of them who took for granted the shifting pattern of sexual relationships, and were so undistressed by changing partners? Was it normal, expectable, *forgiveable*? She wasn't sure.

Meanwhile people were being invited to another room: evidently the bits and pieces she had taken for a buffet lunch were no more than appetizers, and a full meal lay waiting next door.

'Aren't you going to eat?'

The voice at her side made itself heard through her distress.

'You don't look like you need to diet,' the voice continued. It was an American voice, she decided, turning sideways to shake her head politely.

The man who had joined her was a rather surprising guest to find in Mark's house, because his clothes looked curiously rumpled, as if pulled on in a moment of urgency. He was about fifty, Nell guessed, though his face could have been taken for someone much younger: his smile was so innocent, almost irresponsible. As he sat on the couch, his trousers rode upwards and she made out a pair of short green socks. Neither shoe had the laces done up. An academic, she decided. And indeed he introduced himself as Professor Irving Stoneman.

Struck by the unexpectedness of his appearance, she made herself smile with perfunctory civility, even though she went on thinking about Brian and his relationship with the mysterious Babar.

'How do you come to be here?' she asked.

'I'm a relative of Charlotte. You know, Mark's wife.'

It was no good. Nell found it impossible to listen. She was thinking of Brian and Bleakwood. Her weekly journey, the unhappy meetings, the letters she had written with her pathetic bits of news, which he had never acknowledged as soothing.

'You look a bit out of things,' said Irving Stoneman kindly.

'Yes,' said Nell.

'It's not like New York.'

'I don't suppose it is.'

He shook his head over the difference.

'The interesting Jews over here don't seem to belong to communities. Why is that?'

'I suppose it depends on what you mean by interesting,' she said.

'No, it doesn't.' He shook his head. 'Everyone knows what they mean by interesting. I mean the ones who do things which give a city character. You know, thinkers or writers, or painters or even scholars. I'm a psychiatrist, by the way,' he said.

She thought about what he'd said.

'It's a deeply conservative community,' she said. 'Solid. Decent. I was thinking earlier on how much I'd like to be part of it myself.'

'Would you?' He looked surprised. 'You're the brilliant cousin Nell, aren't you?'

'Mad Nell,' she corrected him.

It was something of a surprise to imagine Mark or Charlotte describing her in such terms as 'brilliant'. Or even having such terms. Perhaps they offered the brilliance as a kind of excuse? On another occasion she might have been amused; even today she felt her spirits rise a little, though the thought of the new abyss that had so recently opened under her feet made her sceptical. Now she was not only Nell-the-Unfortunate-without-enough-money; now she was Nell the betrayed.

'Tell me about yourself. What are you working on?' he asked her. 'Something in the theatre, isn't it?'

She lifted her chin defiantly.

'I'd like to work in television,' she said.

She saw a different kind of interest cross his face.

'Really? I was on the box myself a few weeks ago. You have a good face for television. Relaxed. Which is very important. Good bones.'

Nell decided she liked him, and was just beginning to enjoy herself when a girl who looked like an undergraduate appeared, with fresh peach skin, and hair shaved like a prisoner, so closely that it was possible to make out every bump on her perfectly formed skull. Her nape and neck, however, were tenderly shaped and she still looked enchanting. She was carrying a plate of food, and she said: 'You're being very good, Irving. I've brought you some low-calorie tasters.'

With the girl's appearance, Stoneman's expression changed; the shrewdness in his eyes became as drowsy as a stroked cat. Nell recognized the unmistakeable transformation of sexual interest. Indeed, his voice dropped to a purr as he introduced them. Indignantly, Nell realized she had been enjoying the flirtation. Perhaps unfairly she disliked the girl on sight, not only for her youth but for something opportunistic and self-absorbed. Her bright eyes darted too eagerly around the room, looking for advantage.

'Is that Sir Ralph Halpern?' she asked, staring over Nell's shoulder.

'Who is that?' asked Nell, who rarely read the business section of *The Times*.

Stoneman shook his head, and put his hand on the girl's neck in gentle reproof.

'Excuse me,' said Nell, smiling briefly. She left Stoneman standing where he was, with his hand on the girl's neck, so as not to have to show her jealousy. Because she was jealous. Not of Brian now, and not altogether of Stoneman. She was jealous of youth and beauty and confidence, and an easy sexual rapport. And it made no sense. Damn it all, she told herself, I'm no older than Caroline. I'm not finished yet.

Coming in at suppertime, Nell found Becky already asleep. It was rather surprising. She put her hand on the girl's head, which felt moist but nevertheless cool, and wondered if she was getting flu. She should have been more severe about her behaviour the night before, Nell thought, conscience stricken. And, compounding her sin as an over-indulgent mother, decided to let the girl sleep on, unmolested.

Nell felt anger, like a single flame in her gut; it fanned out dangerously to make her heart bang and her head pound with blood. No one likes to be cheated, nobody likes to be deceived. And for people like Nell, who have seen themselves as uncomplaining and stalwart, the blow is always worse.

At least while that central flame burned, it was possible not to weep.

She wandered upstairs to knock on Millie's door. Millie surveyed her from head to foot and listened to her tale of Johnnie's disclosure, and Stoneman's rapid transference of his sexual favours.

'You aren't using your natural assets,' said Millie flatly.

'And what the hell are they?' asked Nell, accepting a Scotch and swallowing it without much attention.

'You're a damn pretty girl, Nell. But it looks like you're turned off in some kind of central place. Were you happy with that Brian of yours?'

'I always thought so,' said Nell.

She wondered if that was honest. She had told herself Brian was home for so long it was hard to admit that she might have been lying to herself.

'Maybe I was just coasting along,' she said thoughtfully. 'He felt safe.'

'Safe?' queried Millie. 'Who is this other chick, anyway?'

'Does it matter? Someone young and sexy and charming and not turned off, I expect,' said Nell despairingly. She was thinking of the furry-headed girl at Mark's brunch.

'You're anxious,' said Millie. 'Congenitally anxious. That's *why* those little yellow pills don't send you to sleep. They just bring you back to the ordinary human state.'

'I feel anxious with reason,' said Nell, stung. 'I'm worried for Becky and I can't help caring about Brian. I'm lonely.'

'Come here,' Millie said, and led Nell across to a long mirror. 'Let's talk about signals.'

Nell looked at her own image suspiciously. Her hair was bushy and difficult and stood out all round her face if she allowed it; tonight she had swept it back behind her ears and on top of her head, and she knew the style gave her the look of a queen. She explained as much to Millie.

'Exactly,' said Millie. 'That's the signal. Not accessible.'

'Hmm,' said Nell.

'There's a letter for you, by the way,' said Millie.

It was another letter from Melanie, and Nell looked at it for a moment wondering whether she could stand any more bad news.

'A Christmas card?' Millie suggested encouragingly.

With misgiving, Nell opened it. The card was there, a cosy fireside card, nothing elaborate, just a token, with a note scribbled on the back. Nell squinted at the note timorously:

Dear Nell, Dear Becky,
Happy Christmas to you! The American Air Force has gone, and not before time. Last week there was a police raid on your

105

house. It was very exciting – lights going on in the middle of the night. I've never *heard* such a noise, just like the television. The next day they'd all disappeared. Do write some time and tell me how you are getting on. We often talk about the old days, and how quiet things were then.

There was a postscript on the other side of the page.

Did you know, by the way, that they have drawn cartoons on some of your pictures? I do think it was a mistake to leave them behind, but I suppose you had to let the place furnished with something. Anyway, your friend Geoffrey recovered that strange print of yours with a Chinese horse.

Nell folded the letter away silently. She didn't care.

'Have you put in any other tenants, or shall I advertise myself?' she asked Geoffrey briskly when he telephoned a day or two later.

'I hope you're coming along to the New Year party,' said Geoffrey. 'You've nothing to worry about in Plumrose Crescent, Nell. The rent will be coming just as usual. I've got some very nice quiet industrial chemists.'

'How many?' asked Nell suspiciously.

'One industrial chemist and his live-in industrial chemist sweetheart. Dress up, won't you,' said Geoffrey, 'for the party. There are a lot of people want to meet you.'

Nell knew that in fairness she should ask Brian whether there was any truth in what Johnnie Farrago had told her. But she couldn't face it. She couldn't face the journey to Bleakwood at all. She knew it was cowardly, but there it was. And she felt mutinous. Why did she always have to do what was fair? She had tried so long to do her duty, and much good it had done her. So she decided to take the easy way out and write a letter.

'Dearest Brian,' she wrote, 'Please don't mind if I don't show up this Saturday. I'm feeling very tired. Sorry.' She didn't send love and she didn't put in any bits of news about Becky, or Mark's party.

In spite of Millie's advice, Nell dressed with deliberate chastity for Geoffrey's party. Her feelings over the Irving Stoneman incident had upset her: she wanted to feel she had reached an age when sexuality was no longer the main pivot of human action. No doubt there was a mournful quality in believing that the sexual game was over and it threw an uncomfortably sharp light on all the other games that could be played. If people were not primarily male and female, then the glamour of occupation became the only legitimate excitement. It was all very fine to be considered interesting for what you did out of bed, but in that case it was very important to do something much more interesting that Nell had yet learnt how to do.

Geoffrey was not having his New Year's party in his own flat. 'Not big enough, dear,' he explained. He'd borrowed a pretty house in a cottagey cobbled mews in Chelsea. The noise of the party could be heard along the lane as Nell approached. Then the door opened and her coat was taken from her in one movement, and suddenly she was afloat in a sea of people. There were so many faces Nell did not know that she was filled with an over-whelming desire to turn on her heels, reclaim her coat and head back to Camden Town. Only the thought of the nothingness that waited for her there and the emptiness in her own heart persuaded her to stay. And the wine, perhaps.

There were men in butlers' gear walking round filling glasses: without any volition on her part, there was soon a glass in her hand. There was a great deal to drink and platters of cut vegetables accompanied by an array of exotic dips. She let the movement of people swirl her about, out of the first room and into the next, where the density was slightly less. There was no sign of Geoffrey himself.

In the second room, sitting on a chaise longue, a tall and extremely thin man with one of his legs looped over the other was sitting between two young girls, both plump in the breasts, and wearing very short skirts. He had his hands on the knees of one of them and fondled them informally and without particular attention as he spoke. The girl's face was inscrutable. If she found it exciting she made no sign. On the other hand she made no objection and appeared to be listening to his words.

Nell stood for a moment to listen herself. The man addressed a series of questions to a young, Irish-faced man sitting opposite. 'So you like books. For pleasure. You teach them? Do you claim you are teaching pleasure?'

'I love books,' the man said, unfazed and good-natured.

'But you surely can't claim to take your guidance from books, can you? I mean, is that what you're saying?'

'I *don't* take my guidance from books,' said the younger man equably. 'Because I'm a Catholic.'

'How embarrassing.'

'I can't help that,' said the Irishman, shaking his head without anger.

'I mean I've never heard anything so embarrassing,' repeated the man on the couch. 'This man reads all his books as a Catholic.'

'But that isn't what he said,' ventured Nell, startled.

Perhaps fortunately the man was too drunk to notice the intervention, and pressed on with his own personal aggressive catechism.

Nell moved away.

In the next room there was a buffet: scotch eggs, smoky sausages and a huge ham. Nell took a plate of food in sombre mood. By her side, a man she did not know was staring at her. She looked away. His face filled her with instant dislike. Why doesn't he shave, she thought angrily: though indeed he probably had; it was simply that his beard grew very strongly: she thought she could see the blue points of it at his chin and upper lip. She disliked the redness of his lips; she never liked red lips. But it was the eyes she disliked most. They were so bold and dangerous. And at the same time, they were dark brown; the colour of a dog's eyes, she told herself angrily; eyes that were dark like that ought to look down and be loyal and quiet and not stare so rudely. She wondered where he came from. He was dressed in a brilliant white shirt and a formal suit, unlike almost everyone else. She stiffened her features formidably because she had no wish to arouse any kind of speculation.

A quick glance a few moments later showed him still looking at her, with a kind of amusement she did not relish, as if he knew exactly what she intended to convey by her frozen profile, and was making his own decision about whether to honour it.

Nell decided to move to the other side of the room and help herself to salad. To her discomfiture she found the man at her side even as she collected her plate.

'Don't I know you?' he asked.

'No. Absolutely not,' she replied coldly.

'The desires of the heart are as crooked as a corkscrew,' he said, smiling and shaking his head. She was startled. He didn't look like the kind of man who would quote Auden. But he was moving away still amused, though whether at himself, his failure to engage her interest, or Nell's alarm she could not be sure.

It was only going back with a plateful of gleaming salad that she wondered whether he had not perhaps been in the courtroom at Brian's trial. She had seen so little then she could remember nothing with certainty. But one thing she was sure of: whoever he was, he was part of some terrible, shady London underworld of which she wanted no part.

She sat down. She had a sense that her life was about to change momentously, but she could not have said why.

Geoffrey had said there would be a lot of people she knew. So far there were none that Nell could see. She moved around the rooms looking for familiar faces, overhearing scraps of conversation between people who did not seem to see her. For a time, she stood in a group around a large man with a beard who seemed to be either dead or asleep.

'Poor Haffenden.'

'So sad.'

'So talented.'

And then she saw Liza Thynne.

It was such a relief to recognize anyone that Nell moved towards her eagerly. Liza Thynne was resplendent in a turquoise dress that floated silkily about her figure so that she seemed to rise like a spangley cloud before the admiring group of young men and women who were grouped around her. To each of these she spoke in turn, without any of them uttering a word, as if she divined their innermost thoughts.

109

Fascinated, though nervous, Nell was drawn to overhear: 'Upper State, New York, in October? Lovely, Simon. All those marvellous coppery trees. I'll have Ursula check the calendar first thing tomorrow . . . But do you think we're quite ready for another play about battered wives, Julian? Yes, I did catch your programme about nuclear waste, as a matter of fact . . . These mushrooms are delicious, Mark. I hope they aren't wormy . . .'

'Hello,' said Nell.

The flashing blue eyes froze for a moment.

'Ah yes,' said Liza with great sweetness. 'Geoffrey said you might come. Well, you'll be glad to hear we have a very fine new temp. This is Mark Topley, and this is Julian; I can't remember the name of this very pretty young man. Never mind. This is one of Caroline's friends.'

'Nell Bolton,' said Nell, rather curtly.

'Bolton?' said Liza. 'That's right. I'd forgotten that. Brian's wife. He used to be a friend of poor Nicky. Are you having a good time?'

'Lovely,' said Nell.

'I didn't know Brian had a wife,' said Mark Topley.

'There it is: surely the fate of wives,' said Liza. 'The play is going on tour next week. We've got rid of all that boring old opera stuff. You'd hardly recognize it, Nell.'

'I don't suppose I would.'

'Even Caroline is pleased. And Mark is going to write about it, aren't you, darling? Now, I wonder where that man with the tray of crudities has wandered off to?'

'There's a table with food next door,' said Mark Topley.

'The whole secret of these parties is to keep a firm sense of one's own centrality,' said Liza comfortably. 'Why don't you boys run along and find me something pleasant to eat.' She spoke as though sending a group of toddling children about their business, then turned away and smiled at Nell. It was a forgiving smile, profoundly free of rancour.

'Have you found a job yet?' she inquired.

'No,' said Nell hollowly.

'Speak up a little, dear.'

'No,' said Nell. 'I haven't.'

110

She didn't want to go back to Feminist Arts, either, but felt it would be uncivil to say so. It was not evidently what Liza Thynne had in mind.

'Do you know, I think I can see someone here who may be able to help. I mean a friend of mine. He works for the BBC and always has wonderful production ideas.' She gesticulated. 'Over there. Look!'

'I think I *can* see someone I know,' said Nell helplessly.

And indeed there was a bearded Cambridge contemporary who had once edited a literary magazine while playing rugby for his college.

'Ripper Jarvis,' Nell exclaimed with dubious enthusiasm. He approached, put his arms round Nell's waist and gave her a smacking kiss.

'Little Nell,' he said. 'How are you enjoying the big city?'

'No, *no*,' said Liza Thynne, who obviously doubted Nell's ability to concentrate on more than one thing at a time, 'Over *there*.'

And Nell's eyes met those of the dark-faced man from the buffet table. He raised his own glass in ironic recognition, and began to move towards her. She was just too late to keep Ripper at her side for protection.

At first sight, she had imagined a dark stubble at his jaw; it was not so; but there was a kind of darkness there, as if he would have to shave very often to keep the stubble at bay. He was just the kind of man she distrusted. There was something assessing in his eyes which she did not like: less as if he were judging her than pricing her, she thought with indignation. Although he was dressed in an expensive suit, he did not look neat or even particularly groomed. It came to her that his flesh beneath the well-cut shirt would have a pungent odour. For some reason, the thought did not repel her.

'His name is Theo Walloon,' said Liza. 'You'll have seen it in *Private Eye*, but you don't have to believe all you read. Be nice to him.'

Nell felt considerable reluctance to be steered in Walloon's direction, but she allowed herself to be dragged after Liza's sailing figure like one of the creatures following after a brass band in

George Barker's poem for his mother. Walloon's voice, as she had already heard, had the edge of a London cockney. She guessed he was Jewish, but was somewhat offended when his alert gaze covered her face, and his first words suggested the same conclusion about her.

'Have you noticed this is a totally *goyishe* room?'

Nell found herself angrily wanting to repudiate the relationship.

'Don't be too sure of me.'

'We can use Hitler's definition for my purposes. Your mother wasn't Jewish, is that what you mean?'

'Partly. I wasn't acculturated either,' she said stiffly.

'That's not significant,' he said, grinning broadly.

'Then what is important? Blood?' she demanded.

'You don't have to look defensive. I'm a great joiner,' he explained. 'I'm a man who liked to feel part of things. I don't fit anywhere either.'

'Why should that be?' asked Nell. 'And is it true?'

He seemed not to hear, as if he were mainly meditating for his own benefit.

'I remember once in some *judenrein* bit of the Midlands, I thought I'd look in on the local *schule*. Poor *schmuck*. I was looking for the Jewish community. I found about nine men, glad to see me because I made up a *minyan*, but still hostile. Very hostile. And I'm not being paranoid, I know exactly why. I didn't look like a Jew to them. And I have to say they had so thoroughly taken on the colouring of the Midlands that they didn't look like Jews to me either.'

She missed what he said next in the noise, and had to bend towards him.

'Are provincial Jews so different from London Jews then?' Nell asked, intrigued.

His eyes narrowed speculatively, and she felt a little colour coming into her cheeks as he registered the difference in her attention.

'Nell Bolton,' he mused. 'I've heard that name.'

'Liza just introduced us,' she said.

She did not see how she could possibly mention a job.

'In some other connection?' he suggested hopefully.

112

'I'm afraid not,' she said.

Not yet, she wanted to say. Damn you, I've done nothing yet. It wasn't fair. She wanted to scream at his amused, handsome face: I've spent the last fifteen years in Plumrose Crescent bringing up a daughter who doesn't approve of me. And looking after a husband who had been up to a great deal I don't know about. I've been missing lots of opportunities. Even to herself it sounded like an excuse.

And suddenly there was Caroline.

'Darling! I'm so glad you came. Come and meet people.'

'I *am* meeting people,' said Nell crossly, not wanting to be towed over to start again somewhere else. But she need not have worried, because almost at once Caroline herself had been seized by an elegantly dressed young man who looked like a schoolboy and they were chattering with animation.

'Oh yes, the yuppies had it coming to them. Let them pawn their Porsches, drown in their champagne, rot in their second homes,' she heard Caroline saying.

'Wealth always goes to people who know how to get the highest profit for the lowest risk,' sad the young man. 'They can't be decent.'

'All that asset-stripping,' Caroline agreed. 'Spivs, my father used to call them.'

Walloon's eyes met Nell's once again with a knowing amusement that invited her own glance of complicity, but she loyally rejected the implied criticism of Caroline. Caroline might say anything in a moment of party euphoria, but she was incapable of petty prejudice.

Liza Thynne was once again at her elbow.

'Well?' she cooed, 'have you arranged it all?'

Nell blinked, and Theo looked bewildered.

'You said you were looking for somebody bright for the front desk, Theo.'

'So that's what you're up to,' he laughed. 'I wondered.'

Nell tried to pull away.

'Fine, fine,' said Theo. 'What exactly are you looking for, Miss Bolton?'

Nell told him stolidly what she could do. Even as she did so, and guessed that the job would this time be hers, an unfocused feeling of disappointment mitigated her relief. With reluctance she recognized that she would have preferred to be on very different terms with Theo Walloon.

When twelve o'clock came it was Ripper Jarvis who put his lips to hers with bruising enthusiasm and, though Nell did not object, she felt it was not much of an augury for the New Year.

TEN

'Kit Martin is back,' said Millie one morning about a fortnight later.

'I didn't notice he'd been away,' said Nell.

This was a lie.

'On tour in Europe with a modern music group,' said Millie. 'Six weeks he's been on the road.'

'That must be very tiring.'

'Perky bugger, he is,' said Millie, apropos of nothing.

Nell thought she understood the new and pleased complacency on Millie's face.

'I've found another job, Millie,' she said, without grudge. She didn't say anything about Theo Walloon.

It was very pleasant at Television Centre. No one asked Nell to type. She made appointments, and drank coffee made in a real-coffee machine. She also made phone calls and wrote things systematically into a diary. And she looked pretty.

She looked prettier than she had since her first week in Newnham. Her face began to glow, her skin looked translucent, paler, smoother; her hair shone with new energy.

Compared to dealing with Liza, or Becky, it was, thought Nell, a doddle. The great and famous turned out to be not only harassed and anxious, but touchingly grateful for her help. Drinking in the BBC bar, they told her their troubles, and Nell began to feel not only a pretty girl but a wise and wonderful one. Inevitably, those men who saw her as wonderful wanted to take her to bed, which is the nature of the tribute men pay to intelligence and prettiness. Of Theo Walloon, however, she saw little.

In her spare time, of which she found guiltily she had a great deal, she began to compose outrageous lyrics and this is what she was doing one Friday morning when she saw Walloon making his way purposively towards her.

Nell hastily changed disks, so that her own could be put safely back into her handbag, and brought up the file of current production schedules before Theo Walloon reached her. He seemed preoccupied.

'Mellonhead? Is he in?' he asked brusquely.

'Not back from lunch yet,' she said, covertly admiring the hair at his neck which was visible under the open-necked shirt.

He was wearing a blue pendant with lettering she could not quite make out. He sat down and tapped his teeth with a pencil.

'What sort of mood was he in? I need him friendly,' he said.

'He's never exactly cheerful,' she said dubiously. 'But he wasn't sending me out for Rennies and clutching his belly as he was yesterday.'

'Good. That's something. I want his help.'

Nell looked surprised. It was news to her that anyone at Walloon's level of power needed anything.

'A programme,' he explained. 'I want his support next week when it's talked through in committee. You know we're doing a *Great Man* series?'

She nodded.

'Well, I want him to back my Great Man idea.'

'What kind of Great Man do you have in mind?' asked Nell gaily.

He looked at her moodily.

'England,' he said, shaking his head. 'What is Greatness in England today? It's hard to know, isn't it? There's Class, that's still real enough. And then there's Money. That's always meaningful. And then I suppose there's Success, which is more difficult. But Greatness . . . ?'

'What does he do, your Great Man?' asked Nell.

'See what I mean – you have to have some way of categorizing him. Well, he's not rich, he taught in Cambridge for twenty years and then quarrelled with the Department. The point is, a lot of people who matter value his mind. He's a thinker. An art historian. He's retired now. Gone off to live in a small farmhouse in Tuscany.'

116

'Then I know who you must mean,' said Nell, startled because Brian had once made her go and hear some of his lectures while he was still teaching in Cambridge. 'You must mean Bronstein.'

'You've heard of him?'

'I read a chapter of his about the character of Florence, oh, ages ago, when I was at university. And my husband used to talk about him a great deal.'

He looked at her rather oddly.

'You must be the only person in this building then. I tried for an hour to explain how extraordinary his contribution to civilization was, bringing together art and science and history as he does, and that idiot who calls himself Head of Programming said: "If he's so famous, why isn't he on television more often?" So instead of Bronstein, the first programme in the *Great Man* series will be about an action painter who started out in the North of England and has made a million out of silk-screen. Remind me what your name is.'

Nell told him again, a little sadly.

'Well, I'll explain to Mellonhead that there's someone out here in reception who has heard of Bronstein even if he hasn't. Might make him think. I can't guarantee that, of course: it's too unusual for him. But if he lets me do the programme I'll take you to Tuscany with me to help. Would you like to come?'

Nell felt her breathing constrict for a moment.

'Yes,' she said.

'That's a promise,' he said, nodding and pointing his finger. 'Remind me.'

Her infatuation was such at that moment that she was almost tempted to send up a prayer to the mysterious Lord of Chance, who presumably regulated the affairs of Central Programming along with other inconsequential behaviour on the planet.

Nell did not hear the outcome of Walloon's discussion with Mellonhead because she was summoned to Becky's school in response to a letter she had written two months earlier.

The headmistress peered at Nell out of simian eyes and said thoughtfully: 'So, you've been worried about Becky. I can't say I'm surprised.'

'Not *about* her,' Nell explained. '*For* her. I don't think she is being sufficiently stretched. Well, interested. I mean by her school work.'

'She's a difficult child,' said the headmistress.

Nell knew that was so and felt a quiver of disloyal agreement even as she protested.

'Why exactly did you ask to see me now?' asked Nell.

'Her truancy, primarily. But we always like to understand the problems of the family.'

'Are you telling me Becky fails to turn up for school?'

'Obviously. Last week she only appeared on Wednesday, and that is because there was a Crisis Day and the teachers were making their own protest.'

'I see.'

'She has a number of very undesirable friends, who think themselves far too streetwise. Altogether, I think it's very important to take the matter in hand, otherwise we shall have to consider calling in social workers, and that's always so unpleasant.'

'We are not a problem family,' said Nell indignantly. 'I don't say we don't have problems, but that isn't the same thing, is it?' She stopped. 'I'll have a word with Becky this evening.'

ELEVEN

Nell set out the table for supper at seven fifteen. Becky had not yet returned and Nell turned over in her mind how best to approach the question of where she had been all week. Then the telephone rang. It was Caroline.

'How are you?' she asked, for once pausing to hear what Nell might say.

'I have a delinquent daughter,' said Nell. 'I don't know where she is now but she wasn't at school all week.'

She felt like bursting into tears.

'Come on,' said Caroline. 'Relax. Don't you remember what we were like? How is work going?'

'*Work's* okay, but what's the point of bothering if Becky's ruining her life?'

'Don't panic till you've talked to her,' advised Caroline. 'Have you got a minute?'

'Of course,' said Nell.

'Things are very wrong here,' said Caroline, in an odd, shaky voice.'

'What, particularly?'

'Well, the cover of my latest book, for one thing. It's absolutely foul, and they say it's too late to change it if we're going to make the spring list.'

Nell waited.

'And Liza's sending my play on tour, and there isn't a line left of mine in it. They've even changed the title. Imagine, they're calling it *Queen of the Amazons*. It's become a kind of romp about a tribe of women and a girl who's fallen into the hands of a city gent.'

'Is it intolerably bad?'

'No, very funny, actually. Liza wrote a lot of it. Still, it's galling.'

None of this quite accounted for the tremulous voice, and Nell waited for more.

'The worst thing is, Johnnie's packed me in.'

Nell couldn't think what to say. Her own situation had made it difficult for her to listen to Caroline's anxieties in the last few weeks. She couldn't help it. Maybe she had simply been insufficiently tempted. But she couldn't feel Caroline was justified in believing Johnnie belonged to her.

'Don't lecture me,' said Caroline. 'Don't tell me I should have seen it coming. I did see it coming. In a way. But we didn't quarrel, or anything.'

'I suppose it was always on the cards,' said Nell.

It was the wrong thing to say. There was a pause.

'I'm sorry you feel low,' said Nell.

'Well, there it is,' said Caroline. 'How is your Theo Walloon, by the way?'

Nell had rashly confided her adolescent fancying during lunch earlier in the week.

'Unreachably sexy,' said Nell, aware that such minor misfortune made her companionable, and hoping the admission would make up for not knowing the right way of expressing sympathy. She didn't tell Caroline what Walloon had said about Tuscany.

'This is going to be boring,' said Becky, as Nell made clear that she intended a serious talk.

'I just want to know,' said Nell, 'where you've been and why and who with.'

'Is that *all*?' asked Becky, with a mocking lift to her voice which recalled Brian at his most scathing. 'Don't worry. I've been with nice people, children of friends. *Cambridge* friends.'

'Doing what?'

'Listening to music. Lying around.'

'Screwing?'

'Your generation!' said Becky. 'That's all you think about.'

'Just listening to pop records! Are you insane? You could wait till the holidays to do that, couldn't you?' said Nell hotly. 'Don't you want to do anything with your life?'

'I can't imagine *what* to do with my life,' said Becky. 'If I knew something I wanted to do, I would try and do it.'

Her tone had changed and she looked tired and vulnerable, like a rather scraggy doll. Nell wanted desperately to put her arms round her and hold her close.

'I know,' she said instead, to Becky's surprise. 'All the same, try and get a few good grades. It's such a bore without them later on. Cheer up – I've got a steak for supper.'

Nell had not forgotten about Brian in Bleakwood, but she thought about him remotely, unhappily; almost as if he were a figure in a dream, someone she had mislaid, whose face and voice she could still recall, but whose significance she could not altogether decide. She had gone back to visiting him; it seemed only fair; they didn't quarrel now; didn't say much about anything, really, though when she explained her new job at TV Centre with a modest triumph, his mouth had curved in a kind of mirthless smile, which for a time took away all the pleasure she had been taking in the experience. Admittedly, it was not exactly a glamorous job in itself. Perhaps only a woman who had spent fifteen years asleep in Plumrose Crescent would find it exciting. With Brian stuck inside his own prison gates irrecoverably it didn't seem appropriate to complain about his lack of encouragement. So Nell went on writing letters dutifully, to allay the guilt of being happily out in the world while he was not. And she didn't ask about a petite little secretary from City Trust called Babar.

One day in March the postman brought her a letter from a sister in the prison hospital. Nell read it with incredulity. Brian had been savagely attacked by another prisoner and was suffering from a broken jaw.

The news set Nell's heart banging with sympathetic fury. What a monstrous world! How could the prison authorities be so out of control? The thought of Brian at the mercy of such thugs entered her dreams and she woke the next morning in tears, and begged the day off from work to travel up to Bleakwood.

In spite of the letter's warning she was quite unprepared for the state in which she found Brian. He was attached to an intravenous drip and the necessary clamps and bandaging made it hard to recognize him. In addition, he was, as far as she could tell, unconscious. He made no response whatsoever to her whispers, and showed no sign of registering the kisses she pressed to his forehead.

A nurse with a face rather like the underside of a plaice, watched her the while without any evident emotion.

'Five minutes more,' she said phlegmatically as she caught Nell's tear-filled eye.

'What happened?' Nell asked. 'How?'

'Set upon,' replied that lady. 'That's what.'

As Nell's face continued mutely to inquire for details, the nurse proceeded stolidly: 'They will do it, you see. Provoke one another. They need something to do, I reckon.'

Nell was furious.

'I can't believe Brian *needed* to be beaten into this state,' she said. The nurse showed no sign of hearing the edge in Nell's voice. Nell addressed the problem of making contact with Brian again and then gave it up.

'Will he be all right?' she asked nervously.

'Well, that I don't know, Mrs Bolton. It was Ripper Bruce, you see.'

'What has Brian to do with Ripper Bruce?'

'Maybe he made a joke about Scotland,' said the nurse, shaking her head. 'Or maybe they knew one another before Bruce came in. He only came back inside this week. I don't know.'

Not my business, her shaken head implied.

'When will he come back to consciousness?'

'Tomorrow, most likely.'

'I'll be at work tomorrow.'

'Can't help that. You'll have to leave a little note.'

Nell scribbled: 'Keep your pecker up, darling. Don't worry, we'll get to the bottom of it. I'll write to the governor if necessary. Back next weekend. Love, Nell.'

A letter in handwriting recognizably Brian's arrived on Wednesday. Evidently whatever was wrong with his jaw had not affected his hand or brain. Her first reaction was one of enormous relief to see the familiar scrawl. It was not, however, an affectionate letter:

'For God's sake, don't be an idiot! Don't do *anything*. Aren't I in enough trouble? Brian.'

That evening Geoffrey telephoned. She hadn't heard from him for a long time.

'I'm worried about Caroline,' he said.

Nell told him what had happened to Brian.

'Yes. Do tell him to be sensible, won't you? Caroline has been quite ill, by the way.'

'I heard she was unhappy.'

'You might go and see her.'

'I don't think I should be of any help. About Brian, though?'

'Now don't be a baby, Nell. If he'll just keep his mouth shut nothing worse will happen.'

'His mouth is wired up at the moment,' she said with some acerbity. 'So there's no need to worry about that.'

'Exactly,' said Geoffrey.

Nell felt a prickle of alarm under her ribs.

Geoffrey's concern for Caroline struck Nell as excessive when she ran into her two days later at TV Centre. Nell had been having lunch with two of the younger producers, Bob and Jolly. Bob, Nell judged, was about twenty-three. He had come to Television Centre straight from Bristol, with an undergraduate track record in experimental drama. Spruce and short-haired, with a downy-skinned, highly-bathed look, he was very different from the theatre groups of the seventies she remembered. Jolly looked a decade older, and more familiar. She was a harassed girl, with deep lines etched at each side of her nose. Her eyes were pale blue and there were deep anxiety pouches under them. Both Bob and Jolly drank nothing but Perrier with their lunch, and ate nothing but salads. They watched Nell's cheerfully heaped plate with scorn and resentment.

'I feel the cold,' Nell pointed out, 'and I never get fat.'

'Animal fat,' said Jolly, 'lays down all kinds of bad cholesterol in your blood anyway.'

Nell shrugged and sipped her glass of wine. Bob and Jolly had their heads together over a new idea for adapting a few sketches of Dorothy Parker; rather to Nell's embarrassment they were soon discussing the possibility of using Caroline.

'I don't know about a *poet*,' said Jolly, shaking her head.

'Parker was a poet,' said Bob, 'and Caroline's not just a poet. Not a bit. I saw her *Queen of the Amazons* a couple of months ago when I was in Bradford, and it was the best thing I'd seen in the North-East. Real theatrical attack. Good political stuff. Modern. Really the voice of this generation.'

'What I'm after,' said Jolly, 'is something like Penny Simons used to turn out.'

Bob had never heard of Penny Simons and contented himself with looking wise and sceptical.

'I've been replaying some of her old programmes,' said Jolly. 'From the sixties. They have a kind of period quality, of course. Even so, I don't know how she did it.'

Nell thought she knew exactly how Penny did it. She was sharp and she was kind, and the combination was rare. Just before coming down to lunch, indeed, Nell had been waved into the room where Penny was sitting reading a novel by Jean Rhys.

'Join me,' she'd invited.

'Aren't you going down for lunch?' Nell asked, taking in the opened bottle of Scotch on Penny's desk, and the half-filled tumbler.

'Hate that canteen food,' said Penny in her most gravelly voice, the tones most deeply those of the stage between the wars. 'And I'm busy.'

'A lovely book,' said Nell, nodding at the Penguin Jean Rhys approvingly.

'They might do it,' sighed Penny, 'but not in my time. I'm on my way out, you know. End of the road. Have you heard?'

Nell had heard rumours.

'They say I'm lucky. I'm not exactly retiring young,' said Penny. 'What will you do?'

'Live on my pension,' said Penny with a little barking laugh. 'Sit down and tell me how things are with you.'

Penny was a large, heavy-boned woman, with a finely cut, masculine face. She was related in some undisclosed and illegitimate way to one of the stage's leading theatrical knights. As she had aged, the resemblance had become startling. Perhaps she enjoyed the resemblance; certainly the way she wore her hair bore a decided similarity to his, even to the way the quiff fell forward over her heavy eyebrows. As she patted the chair by her side, Nell saw her left eye was badly bruised.

Nell frowned over this recollection while Bob and Jolly went on comparing notes about Dorothy Parker.

'Mellonhead has never read her.'

'Oh, surely!'

'Can't get the flavour at all. He's too English.'

'I never liked all that Algonquin charmed-circle stuff myself,' said Bob. 'Look, I've got Caroline coming in this afternoon. Maybe we should think of something else. I'm getting a few pilot schemes together.'

'There's Theo Walloon,' said Jolly. 'Over there.'

'Where?' asked Nell with sudden alertness.

'I think he's looking for you,' said Jolly. 'Well he was, earlier this morning.'

'Was he?'

'You were powdering your nose or whatever.'

'Did he leave a message?'

Nell watched Theo striding out of the restaurant as eagerly and precipitately as he had come in.

'No. I think he's abroad for the rest of the week.'

'Goodness, there you are,' said Caroline, as she came out of Bob's and Jolly's office. 'How nice you look. How's Becky?'

Caroline looked wonderfully well herself. Her hair was clean and shining, and her face was alive. She was wearing a very short, tight skirt and high heels. She perched easily on the edge of Nell's desk top, and swung her legs like a schoolgirl.

Nell said: 'Becky's okay, thanks. How are *you*? Geoffrey was worried.'

'Quite right,' said Caroline airily. 'I was absolutely at death's door, done in, finished. But last night the telephone rang and it was an old friend from New York. Remember Norman Hanks?

Broke my heart in the seventies. The novelist? Well, anyway, his second wife left him this year and he wanted a bit of sustaining.'

'I see.'

'He's lost a lot of hair,' said Caroline. 'Still, it was like old times.'

'You've been seeing Bob and Jolly,' said Nell. 'Have you been given the Parker commission?'

'Well, Bob did offer it to me,' said Caroline. 'Nice boy. I probably won't do it. I'm horribly busy at the moment, and I'm off to Sweden at the end of the week.'

'Did Geoffrey tell you what's happened to Brian?' asked Nell.

At this, Caroline shifted on the desk and dropped her eyes.

'Yes. I'm sorry, Nell.'

'Do you think Geoffrey knows something he isn't telling me?'

Caroline eased herself down from the desk top and for a moment stood quite still, as if assessing Nell.

'Surely the best thing to do is just leave all that alone?'

'That's really what Geoffrey was telling me,' said Nell. 'You know something about it too, don't you?'

'That's *all* I know. That some things are better left alone.'

'*What* things?' asked Nell. 'What *kind* of things, Caroline?'

'Things that get you bashed about.'

'Does Geoffrey know about those? *Does* he?'

'I must go,' said Caroline. 'I'm supposed to be in West London.'

'Is Geoffrey connected with Brian being in gaol?' asked Nell. 'He must be. You *know* he is, don't you? I always suspected it.'

'I'm sure Geoffrey's always done the best he can for Brian.'

'Yes? What *has* he done, exactly? What has *Brian* done, if it comes to that?'

'I don't understand these things,' said Caroline.

She yawned; a pretty dismissive yawn.

'Johnnie Farrago knows about it. Or says he does,' remembered Nell. 'I'll talk to *him*, if you won't tell me anything.'

'Please, Nell,' said Caroline. 'Please don't. Don't get in touch with Johnnie. It's too embarrassing.'

'I should have asked him more questions when I met him. He's a friend of Mark's. I don't have to say I'm anything to do with you. Perhaps he's actually involved as well?'

126

'What's *happened* to you, Nell? You never used to be so aggressive.'

'No, I know.' Nell gave a short bark of a laugh. 'That's true.'

'I don't like to hear you sounding so bitter.'

For the first time since Nell had arrived in London it came to her that perhaps she really didn't care what Caroline did or did not like to hear.

On the way out that evening Nell helped to carry Penny's case to her car.

'You're a good girl,' said Penny. 'I'll be in on Monday. By the way, that Theo Walloon was looking for you.'

'I wish he'd look hard enough to find me,' said Nell.

Becky was out when she arrived home. Nell wished she didn't care, but she did. She felt empty. Her own loneliness swept through her like a bleak March wind across a patch of waste ground. She watched the six o'clock news indifferently; politicians, policemen, mothers cut off by the Gas Board in Cheshire, victims of famine in Africa, they all walked across the screen with their parts to play. When Mrs Thatcher, in the royallest of blues and triumphantly well groomed, began to explain how concerned she was to look after those who could not help themselves, Nell switched the television off.

On an impulse, she telephoned Mark.

'I'm worried about Becky,' she confided.

'Yes, well, is there some way I can help?'

'I need Johnnie Farrago's telephone number,' she said in a rush. 'I met him at your party and I think he can give me some good advice.'

There was a pause, as Mark calculated what she might in fact be up to. Nell wasn't sure herself.

'How could he do that?' Mark inquired mildly.

'Vacation job,' she improvised craftily.

'I think Johnnie's in New York this week,' said Mark. 'Still, I'll find his number for you.'

He was puzzled, but not altogether incredulous, she judged. With the number in her hand she drank down a whole tumbler

127

of Scotch, to give her the courage to use it. Farrago, however, was indeed in New York; Jana explained as much; and though Nell wrote down the telephone number of his hotel, she knew she would not ring him that evening. Jana's voice sounded even deeper than she remembered, but there was something else in it; a blur, a fuzziness that suggested she had just been woken from sleep.

Just then, Becky arrived with a school bag bulging with books, which she banged down on the table, observing the bottle of Scotch and the tumbler with a portentous sniff as she did so.

'There's a pie in the oven,' said Nell. 'I see you have a lot of homework.'

Becky looked in the oven, and groaned.

'It's a home-made pie,' said Nell defensively. 'I don't mean I made it at home, but the woman at the shop did and it tastes good. Even if you don't feel like heating it up.'

'I'm not very hungry,' said Becky.

She flung her bag on the floor and took out a stack of exercise books. Nell would have liked to ask where she had been, but stifled the impulse in the relief of seeing her bent over the table with an apparent purpose.

'I'll go up and have a coffee with Millie,' she said instead.

In the hallway she met Kit Martin and to her own annoyance found herself blushing.

'I've not seen you about,' he said.

'I heard you were back,' she managed.

'Come and have a drink upstairs,' he suggested. 'Renew acquaintance.'

'I don't know about that,' she said.

'Why not?' he asked innocently.

'I was just going to call on Millie,' Nell temporized.

His smile widened.

'So was I. She's out, though. We'll just have to console one another.'

Nell thought about it, since she was herself most vehemently in need of consolation. While she hesitated however, Becky's voice called up the staircase.

'Nell? Nell? A man called Walloon phoned. He says it's very important. Something about going to Tuscany on Monday.'

TWELVE

Theo and Nell flew to Pisa, and there hired a low-slung sports car, so that within minutes of their arrival they were sailing out into the fresh sunlight of a Renaissance painting.

Nell felt magically happy, and hoped it was not too callous of her to do so. Millie was looking after Becky: Brian was recovering in hospital: everything else that was wrong could surely wait until she returned.

It had been raining just before they landed and there were still glints of wetness in the air as they drove through a landscape of tufty trees, shimmering olives and neatly arranged vines.

'Those trees,' she said. 'I always thought the Florentines made them up. Will we have a chance to look at any paintings?'

'I don't suppose so,' Theo grunted.

Whatever his intentions were in taking Nell on this jaunt, he had so far been mainly preoccupied. Now he pulled up at the side of the road, took off his jacket and untied his neckerchief.

'Tuck these out of the way, could you?' he asked, opening his shirt so Nell could see the black and wiry hair and the blue flash of his pendant again. 'This is not going to be a doddle. Bronstein is a very difficult man. And his wife is even worse. Or so they say. They say a great many unkind things, of course, I don't suppose they are all true. They say she looks twenty years older than he is, and protects him very craftily.'

'She's Russian, isn't she? Didn't she get her exit visa about the time of the Sinyavsky trial?'

'Something like that.'

'I remember. She was homesick. She went *back*,' said Nell. 'To Moscow. A very stubborn lady.'

He looked at her and said: 'I didn't know that.'

The he smiled and patted her hand gratefully. It is a great snare, thought Nell, to be prized for one's usefulness.

They stopped in Gaioli-in-Chianti for a strega and Theo showed the man in the bar the map of the paths that led to Bronstein's farmhouse. The man grinned widely.

'Bernardo,' he said delightedly. 'I saw him this morning. You go up to the Madonnino and turn down the hill. Look!'

'Perhaps we should eat first?' wondered Theo.

There was no restaurant in Gaioli, however. They would have to go back twenty kilometres along the road to Raddom. On balance, they settled for a ham roll with salad, and Theo bought some grapes from the next-door shop.

'He seems popular, locally,' observed Nell.

'Yes. I wonder how common that is these days? The hills here are crawling with ex-pats. Maybe the English are just more popular than the Germans? I agree it's a good sign.'

The afternoon light was going as the car bumped along the dusty, unmade-up path to Bronstein's farmhouse. It was completely dark when they parked in front of the main house. Light streamed from the open door, but there seemed no other sign of life.

'Don't worry,' said Theo, 'They don't lock up in Tuscany.'

He took Nell's arm to guide her reassuringly into the house. It was the first time he had touched her since they set out from Heathrow at eleven that morning, and the easy, unimportant gesture sent an electrical shock through her whole system. Damn, she thought to herself.

The kitchen was roofed with fine red tiles, and beamed with the local chestnut. Bronstein and his wife were sitting on either side of a scrubbed kitchen table, sharing a bottle of local wine. Bronstein had the same flat face and preternaturally black hair, Nell saw, that had been so dramatic at the lectern in Cambridge, when his prodding finger made decisive points. He had been radiant then, twenty years younger, with a marvellous, spiky rhetoric; and his face was still pale and oddly luminous, as if his spirit burnt like a lantern beneath the white skin. It had always been a bitter spirit, and his withdrawal to Tuscany had not made him calmer.

'Theo Walloon. From the Beeb. My assistant Nell,' said Theo.

Bronstein grunted. He poured himself and his wife another glass of Chianti.

'We need two more glasses,' he remarked.

Bronstein's wife carried her head at a challenging angle, with a kind of defiance in her expression that princesses usually avoid. She must have been an extremely beautiful woman before the anger in her eyes and lips made itself felt in little downward lines.

'Where are the film crew?' she demanded without preamble.

'Ah yes,' said Theo. 'They will be coming across from Milan in a day or two, when we've more or less sorted things out. Don't want them under your feet any longer than necessary,' he explained.

'Don't want them at all,' said Bronstein. 'Hate the whole plan.'

'Painless,' Theo assured him.

'Her idea,' said Bronstein. 'She's convinced herself it will make us a great deal of money. I've explained, but there it is.'

'I suppose you expect me to produce some supper?' asked his wife.

'Quite unnecessary,' said Theo hastily. 'We'll just retrace our steps. Now that we know where you are.'

'Hopeless. You'd have to go about thirty kilometres and then the jokers would be shut,' snapped Bronstein. 'I suppose we can give them some dried sausage and a bit of cold pasta, can't we?'

He got up and walked to the sink and pressed a button, so that a huge, grinding noise filled the room.

'Well water,' he explained.

He rinsed two glasses and returned to the table.

'What are you working on just now?' inquired Theo. 'We're very sorry to disturb you.'

'He's been working on a science fiction novel,' said his wife, opening the fridge, which seemed to contain very little food. They were obviously getting on extremely badly.

'No one with any sense would do anything so absurd,' said Bronstein irritably.

'I agree,' she said, with a kind of triumph in her face.

'You'd deny the moon was reflecting light if it suited your argument,' he said.

131

His wife laid the table with cutlery and a few thick white plates, in silence, and Bronstein poured wine for Theo and Nell.

'I don't believe in the novel,' he said. 'Any novel. I have reached an age when I can only believe in efforts directed towards increasing human happiness. And what novel can be said to do that? Who was ever helped by reading a novel? It's the entertainment business. Who, after all, is the greatest of the novelists? Tolstoy, I would say. And he understood there was very little solid thought in his own.'

'It's what Bernard has been doing, though,' said his wife phlegmatically.

Nell and Theo took their places before the white plates and began to help themselves to bread. Their eyes met briefly, and Theo gave her a quick half smile, as if to let Nell know he saw the Bronsteins' relationship as she did. Nell was sorry for Bernard Bronstein. One of the finest minds of his generation, Brian had said. But she didn't want to think of Brian.

'The fat of the land,' Bronstein said reflectively, watching Nell. She found her knife too blunt to make it easy to carve a slice through the hardened carcass of dried sausage, cased in a powdery rind.

'Yes. Aubergines. And courgettes and figs and olives. That's what I dreamed of when I came here first. Actually the frost got the olives in eighty-six but the peasants are richer. I'm not sure what the money comes from, but we can't get anyone to pick the olives on our little plot, so they can't need the money,' Bronstein concluded.

'Will you need one bed or two?' asked his wife abruptly, so that Nell was suddenly jolted into an embarrassed alertness. To her relief Theo replied.

'Two,' he said placidly. 'Can I use your phone for a quick call to London? Our expense, of course.'

'We don't have a phone,' said Bronstein. 'Horrible machine. Never use one unless I absolutely have to. Probably best to go into Gaioli and use the one at the bar. He'll give you some *jetons*.'

'For England?' Theo looked doubtful.

'Very cheap. Promise you. Especially after eight.'

'Six,' said his wife.

Bronstein glared.

'Tomorrow will do,' said Theo.

'If you need a bath,' said Bronstein's wife, 'you'd better tell me. It's never easy, and you'll need help to get the water downstairs. Turn off the fridge, will you, before you go to bed?'

When she had gone, Theo asked Bronstein: 'Are you by any chance really working on a novel? That would be quite remarkable, and if you wanted some help in getting it published, I can think of a great many publishers who would be interested.'

'Really?' Bronstein brightened for a moment. 'Trouble is, I'm not, actually. Don't read them: can't write them. She likes to believe I'm doing something more productive than just thinking, you know, so I let her believe I am. Why don't you tell her how interested you think people would be? It would cheer her up.'

Nell wondered if she should begin to clear the table, but was stilled by a warning glance from Theo. Bronstein seemed to feel nothing but friendship for his wife since she left the room. His tone became wry and sad and gentle.

'I'm afraid there won't be much chance to talk tomorrow,' said Bronstein apologetically. 'We have several neighbours and their appalling children coming to lunch and we have to shop and cook for them. It is possible my wife will go to bed.' Turning to Nell he asked abruptly: 'Can you cook?'

Nell shot a startled glance at Theo.

'Simple food,' she temporized.

'All food in Tuscany is simple to the point of brutality,' said Bronstein. 'That's agreed then. What a blessing you turned up.'

Nell stood outside in the soft white Tuscan moonlight, and saw the stillness of the hills, and their bushy serenity. She could hear the sound of cicadas and smell wild mint and basil. Why had Theo brought her? He was downstairs cleaning his teeth, and would no doubt find his way upstairs as soon as he decently could.

With some disgust she decided that he had seen nothing more in her than a good research assistant. So when she heard him at her side, she was irritated to find her heart begin to beat rapidly. She was afraid he would be able to hear it.

'Lovely night,' she said, staring up at the stars and taking deep tranquil breaths.

He put a hand at the back of her neck and they stared together.

'I can usually find the Plough,' he said, perplexed.

'Isn't that it?'

He ruffled her hair.

'Nothing like. How would you like to live here?'

'Beautiful,' she said, rather breathily.

He put both hands in his pockets and executed a little jig.

'Can't think of anything I'd like less. A nightmare. Whole area is like an extension of Belsize Park and Notting Hill. Johnnie Farrago has a palace over the hill, and Liza Thynne comes here every summer. All the circles overlap. Penny Simon's cousin's going to be here tomorrow. You know? The actor. And a shrink called Irving Stoneman who's always after me to put his family therapy programmes on the box.'

Nell was stung with disappointment that he had taken his hand away from her neck and she wasn't looking forward to renewing her acquaintance with Irving Stoneman.

'From the point of view of overlapping circles,' she said, a little pettishly, 'London is hardly an improvement. And at least you can look at the moon on the hills here.'

He laughed and came back to stand in front of her. She stared at him.

'What a very bad temper you have,' he mused, putting a friendly hand on her breast, and kissing her lightly on the lips. Then he put an arm round her waist. 'Come on,' he said gently, 'let's go to bed.'

As he guided her into his room instead of the one that had been allocated to her, he said thoughtfully: 'Incomparably better mattress. I checked it out.'

The next day, Nell found herself with the responsibility of preparing lunch for nine adults, three children and a stray cat that wandered in and out of the kitchen. Through the window the hillside flickered with olives and cypress; the sun sat at the rim of the hill behind the ash trees; the toy fields were in perfect array.

She peeled the purple-skinned onions, popped the white bean

pods, and began putting the beans to soak for the minestrone. Then she sliced the bulbous aubergines.

Somewhere in the olive patch, she knew, Theo was sorting out his interview with Bronstein. She had hardly spoken to him this morning; Theo had jumped out of bed with the intention of talking to Bronstein; and Nell had gone on lying where she was, guiltily taking pleasure in the scent of his head on the pillow and the memory of their bodies together. She only had to think of their lovemaking the previous night to find her body re-living the paroxysms of pleasure, and so she came down much later than she should.

Every so often she thought of Brian, and had to put the memory ruthlessly away. Not that she felt overcome with guilt. She had decided that Brian would have approved of Theo. It was Brian's injuries that troubled her.

At about eleven o'clock, Bronstein's wife came down from her own bed.

'I shall spend the next hour trying to recover,' she announced. 'If I don't, it doesn't matter. None of these people have the slightest interest in seeing me, and I don't like them.'

'Why have you invited them then,' risked Nell, 'if neither of you has the slightest interest in entertaining them?'

'If I could answer that question, my dear, I should understand why we bother to live at all. I need some hot water for a cup of tea.'

Nell said the kettle had just boiled.

'When you are young and in love,' sniffed the woman, 'nothing seems pointless. When all you have left to occupy your mind is the impression you will leave behind you, it is quite another matter.'

'Do you long to go back to Moscow still?' risked Nell.

'I must have my spectacles,' grumbled Mrs Bronstein. 'It's all right for Bernard, he has long sight and can see the expressions on people's faces. It's only for maps and circulars he needs glasses: but I can see nothing without them. Ah. There they are. Let me look at you.'

'Yes,' she said, after looking until Nell's colour came up into her face.

'In love, are you?' Vera Bronstein asked sharply.

'In a way.'

Mrs Bronstein sniffed. 'I was in love once,' she said. 'Didn't have much to do with fucking. Can't expect anyone from your generation to understand that.'

Nell began to crush the shiny white nuts of garlic.

'I never married the man I loved,' said Vera. 'Very few people do. But Bronstein and I make a life together.'

Nell added the sliced aubergines to a great iron pan. She found that, as Vera began to expand her thoughts, her own attention wandered back to Theo. She remembered the pressure of his body. The way he had said, 'Keep still a minute, can you?' and his gasp of pleasure. But she continued to cook industriously, nodding from time to time, and occasionally filling up Vera's mug with more hot water. Vera showed no disposition to retire to bed.

What did Theo imagine would happen next? Nell wondered. Her own intentions were certainly imprecise. She knew nothing about him. She wasn't even sure she liked him. None of that seemed relevant to the pleasure of making love with him.

'What a pleasant morning,' said Mrs Bronstein, as her husband and Theo walked into the kitchen. 'I was just telling this artless little girl some of our life story, Bernard my love.'

'Some vin santo would be nice,' said Bronstein indifferently. 'I wonder where it's gone? Can't stand those tooth-breaking little biscuits they always serve with it, but the stuff itself is all right. I'm glad you feel better, Vera. Ah. There it is.'

Theo came over to Nell and whispered: 'Good girl. I hope you can remember the sentimental bits. The theatrical celebrity isn't coming, by the way.'

'Good,' said Mrs Bronstein, who seemed to have very sharp ears.

Not all the expected guests showed up for lunch, but some that were not expected took their place.

Among these, shiny and blue in gossamer silk, was Liza Thynne, who had come down to her house on the other side of Gaioli.

'Bernard darling, I just looked in to see if you'd like to come

136

to supper tomorrow night. And here you are, having a feast without me. Good heavens, Theo, what are *you* doing here? Is there no-one I know who doesn't know everyone else I know? Tuscany gets more and more supernatural.'

Bernard enveloped Liza in a huge bear hug and they exchanged kisses. He was delighted to see her.

'Are you taking a spring break?' he inquired.

'A few days. Things are rather boring at the moment. Vera darling, how are you?'

'Not particularly well,' said Mrs Bronstein.

Theo met Liza's eyes and made an ironic bow.

'I'm here professionally.'

'And Nell?'

Liza's shrewd eyes took in Nell's situation without comment.

'Well, can I stay? Or shall I get back into my little white Fiat and drive off?' she inquired.

'Of course you must stay,' said Bronstein. 'Tell us all your news.'

'The only news I have is we're transferring Caroline's *Queen of the Amazons* to the West End. I had to call her in Seoul and tell her. I asked her what she was doing in Korea but she wouldn't tell me. Can it be something to do with the Games?'

'Shall I change?' Nell whispered to Theo, as Bronstein continued to purr over Liza Thynne.

Theo looked at her sharply for the first time that morning, and took in the neat white blouse and new short skirt.

'What for?' he asked.

Theo was wearing an immaculate cream shirt and Nell had to fight off an embarrassing temptation to put a hand underneath it.

'Well, this is quite splendid. A real country farmhouse,' said an American voice.

The next guest to arrive was a Californian, who had rented a mansion on the hill across from Bronstein's vines. Short and bouncy, and dressed in loose-fitting trousers with elasticated tops, he looked as tough as a bullet.

'This is Dr Ian Williams,' said Bronstein, with enthusiasm. 'You'll like him, Vera. Nothing literary about him. I recommend

137

his conversation, as being as mysterious and marvellous as Columbus' tales of the New World. What is your field again?'

'Molecular biology,' said Dr Williams gravely. 'It is true I have not had a great deal to do with literature.'

He was quite amused at the thought; indeed he looked as if he might begin to get a little exercise by jogging as he stood.

Irving Stoneman arrived next. His girlfriend had skin like a pale rose and eyes like the sea and she looked no more than eighteen. After a little hesitation, he recognized Nell.

'I know,' he said. 'The brilliant cousin. Mark's party. This is René and she has something to do with commodities in the City.'

'How fashionable,' said Theo. 'Isn't that the kind of work where you burn out at twenty-five?'

'By then you're so rich you don't have to work,' said Irving. 'That's the theory, anyway. I'm studying the phenomenon professionally. I reckon these people are going to need a great deal of therapy as they grow up.'

Nell laughed and went to test the soup.

The vin santo, made on a local farm, tasted as if it had been fortified and the conversation turned on the legality of local stills for a while, and then took off dizzily in the glow of alcohol. Every so often Theo's eyes met Nell's and she felt a little echo of that miraculously sharp pleasure she had experienced the night before. She hoped it didn't show on her face. I don't like the way he eats, she thought defensively. What am I up to? I've never even asked him whether he has a wife and, anyway, what about Brian?

'I'm going to sit next to Bernard,' said Liza.

Bernard welcomed the placing. And Vera, putting aside her intention of retreating upstairs, sat down too, so that Nell had hastily to lay another place further down the table. She really didn't care where she sat herself. She was amazingly hungry, as though the piquant spices she had used in preparing the meal had set all her juices flowing. She felt preternaturally awake. It came to her that she had not wanted a tablet of Valium for several days.

The soup provoked a chorus of approval.

'That's a great minestrone.'

'Classical.'

'Better than last night at the Dolphin.'

'Did you make it, Vera?' asked Liza.

The true cook was unmasked and Nell was congratulated. Her eyes met those of Liza Thynne, who looked amused.

'All the feminine virtues, Nell,' she said. 'Who would have guessed it?'

'I don't . . .' began Nell.

'Don't defend yourself, my dear,' said Bronstein mildly. 'It is a pattern that is always likely to reassert itself. I don't claim predictive power, but I should think there's likely to be some kind of swingback in that direction.'

'Impossible, Bernard,' said Liza comfortably. 'There have been too many changes.'

'But clocks can be put back,' mused Bronstein. 'Take the Jews as a metaphor. Through the nineteenth century they gradually won their equality. Then look what happened in the twentieth.'

Liza was undisturbed.

'It's a question of economics. Men can't pay the mortgage unless their wives go out to work, so they'll have to make it possible.'

'I'm very sorry for this new generation,' said Vera. 'They have to try so hard at every end, so to speak. At least I've led a comparatively peaceful life.'

Liza twinkled, her blue eyes steely.

'Women are always oppressed by their need to please,' she said calmly.

'And how are you so oppressed?' said Bronstein.

'Oh, I'm too nimble these days,' she said airily.

Nell caught Theo's eye and he gave her a conspiratorial wink.

Ian Williams began to explain his exercise schedule and Nell lost track of the general conversation.

'We expect to live till we're in our eighties and possibly longer in California,' he confided.

'Seems rather unfair, doesn't it?' said Nell. 'Is it even desirable?'

'Well, I want it. Don't you? I don't happen to buy the idea there's anything waiting after you're dead. Don't you imagine a California full of cripples in chairs either. We intend to keep the quality of life. That's been the real breakthrough. Wait and see.

139

Health. Fitness. Long life. The ideas will catch on in your country soon enough. Always do. Like serial monogamy. Has to come.'

She was reminded of Bob and Jolly at Television Centre.

'Do you know England?'

'I'm spending the year in Cambridge.'

'Are you? What fun. Which college are you attached to?'

He stared.

'I ate in the one with a big Elizabethan wooden roof the other day. Decent guy there said I could come in once a week. But I haven't the time, as I told him. I spend my days in Molecular Biology.'

'The food is better in College, though,' she suggested.

'Pretty unhealthy in both. Great slabs of meat, as if there'd been no research into diet at all. Amazing what this country serves up to its best brains. It would be regarded as murder on the West Coast.'

'Where is Molecular Biology?'

'Hills Road.'

'I didn't know much about science when I was at Cambridge.'

He stared at her incredulously.

'But Cambridge *is* science. What else is there?'

'Libraries, scholarship, students?' she suggested.

'I guess it is a teaching place, too,' he admitted. 'I haven't time to be involved.'

'What do you do in the States?'

'I have a laboratory on the West Coast and we look at molecules. It's pretty big business.'

'Business?' she echoed incredulously. 'You sound like Mrs Thatcher.'

'What actually is wrong with Mrs Thatcher? Seems like she's turned your country round pretty well.'

Nell thought about that and then said frostily: 'A strong pound doesn't really help the people lying about under the arches on the South Bank.'

'It isn't supposed to. You English liberals are so sentimental. Do you suppose this age invented poverty? Anyway, most people in your country are better off than they've ever been.'

Nell saw Theo was looking across at her with a mixture of amusement and irritation, and she hung her head.

'I'm not interested in politics,' she said, for convenience.

'Nor am I,' said the scientist promptly. 'That's why I don't want politicians nosing their way into my affairs. All I need is the freedom to do what I want. I enjoy hustling. I don't want the state giving me money.'

'How are you funded?' asked Nell then, not because she was really interested but because she very much wanted to have Theo stop frowning at her.

Williams began to explain at length.

The lunch seemed likely to continue for a long time. There was a pasta with basil sauce, bought from the local shop, and a huge casserole of beef and aubergines; and all the time people were pouring chianti wine and talking. Nell's head ached with both the wine and the talk.

And then Bronstein leaned over the table and began to speak, his face glowing almost as if there was a light inside a lantern. He had a pale flat moon of a face, almost ugly, animated by passion. Nell woke up to listen.

'We don't respect the artist, we employ him. And we *sell* him. That's what happened this last half of the century. Our best talents go into selling goods now, that's what this society is about, the way Florence was about discovery.'

'That may not be so much of a loss,' said Irving Stoneman.'I see too much of the artist as a narcissist on my couch.'

'Would you sacrifice the narcissism of Cellini's David, in love with his own poise?' asked Theo.

'Like a shot,' said Irving Stoneman.

Nell's attention quickened, as much at Theo's voice as what he said; until the conversation splintered again.

'Art isn't wise, it isn't curative, except for the artist. It's deception. So why should we care about it at all?' argued Irving Stoneman.

'We don't,' said Bronstein bitterly. 'Except as dead product for buying and selling or teaching, which is another kind of marketing.'

Nell woke up to the fact that Ian Williams had been speaking to her for at least ten minutes while she had been thinking of Theo and failing to attend. Williams didn't seem to have noticed.

'So I have to raise something of the order of twenty million pounds every two years or the whole place shuts down,' he concluded.

Nell was startled.

'And that's *peanuts* to what we'll need if our AIDS work takes off. Of course our sponsors will get it back. That's the point. We aren't a charity.'

'How impressive,' said Nell, and smiled dutifully.

She caught Liza's eye across the table at this point. It came to her that the smile was part of an old habit of trying to please, a piece of old-fashioned female trickery, and that without any particular effort the trick was successful. Ian Williams had no idea she might be faking close attention. On the contrary, he seemed delighted with her half an ear.

'You must come and visit me,' he was saying. 'There's a lot you would find really interesting.'

'I'd like a chance to visit Cambridge,' she said, still amazed at the ease of her duplicity.

And in a moment he was taking out his address book and scribbling away.

Theo was all attention at the other end of the table. If he noticed the exchanged addresses, he gave no sign. Not his business anyway, she told herself, aware of the anomalies in wishing him to care what she did.

Nell wondered for a moment about the little American. Underneath the bullet-like brutality, there was a teddy bear quality.

'Give them all some of that plum brandy,' said Bronstein coming next to Nell and hissing conspiratorily in her ear.

The lunch had animated him, she saw. She now understood its purpose. It was not superficial hosting, it was an opportunity for him to exist. He needed these people to make him into the person he was at his most alive. 'He only exists in conversation, of course,' Nell remembered Brian saying, when he spoke of the difficulty Bronstein had in writing books. She still had Brian's voice in her head. She couldn't really imagine the process of her mind without it.

As Liza began to put on her grey silk wrap in preparation for her drive over the hills, she stopped to say her first word directly to Nell.

'How's Brian?' she asked coolly.

Nell decided it was a friendly question.

'He's recovering from surgery. Everything going normally.'

'A nightmare,' said Liza. 'All of it.'

Nell stared. It was almost the first sympathy anybody had so far expressed for Brian's injuries; the first time anyone had come close to discussing the situation openly.

Emboldened by the plum brandy, Nell determined to take advantage of the situation. 'Liza, I've never asked you this before, but how exactly did your Nicky come to kill himself?' she asked urgently. She met a flash of cold blue steel, which she forced herself to parry. 'Did it have anything to do with Brian?'

'Silly girl. Of course.'

'How? Were they in some kind of racket together?' she hazarded.

'I don't know that Brian could ever be said to be *in* anything. Too bewildered, poor dear. But you are as bad,' said Liza energetically. 'It's taken you a long while to ask the obvious questions.'

'Wait a *minute*,' said Nell slowly.

'Must go,' said Liza, assembling her car key, silk wrap and an umbrella which had no obvious function. 'You can't expect encouragement all your life.'

'That's not *fair*,' said Nell, stung.

'And you *certainly* can't expect fairness.'

As Theo came up to her, Liza offered her cheek.

'Bye, bye, Theo. Look after Nell. She has a lot to learn.'

That night there were too many clouds for the moon to shine into their bedroom. Nell stood for a long while at the window, while Theo sat up in bed making notes on his conversation with Bronstein.

'How did it go?' she asked at one point. 'When will you bring in a crew?'

'Sorry to be so slow about this, but there's nothing worse than trying to find where you are on a tape if you don't make a few notes as you go. Are you in a hurry to get back to England?'

'I said I'd be a week,' said Nell.

'No problem,' said Theo. 'Do you want to call and see how your kid is doing?'

'Yes.'

Nell hesitated. He knew so much about her, and she knew so little about him.

'Do you have any children yourself?' she asked in a voice which she tried to make casual.

'Two,' he said, looking up briefly and grinning. 'Broken marriage. Live with their mother in Canada. I don't mind as much as I thought I would when the divorce came through. See them once or twice a year.'

He went back to his notes, and Nell continued to stare out of the window. If anything, it made her feel even more precarious to discover that Theo was unattached. She realized she had been assuming there were no consequences of this adventure, because it meant she did not have to confront how she felt about Brian.

'Now come here,' said Theo, putting his notes on one side and beckoning.

She went without questions.

'How are things back home?' she asked Millie the next morning, ringing at peak time because Theo said it could go on expenses.

'Absolutely fine,' said Millie.

Her voice sounded a bit odd.

'Is Becky going to school?'

'Not today, she's in bed actually. Don't worry. Have a good time,' said Millie.

Nell felt a prickle of alarm.

'*Why* is she in bed?'

'The doctor said it was a good idea.'

'She never goes to bed,' said Nell. 'She must be really *ill*. What

is it? Measles? I never gave her that new shot,' she remembered.
'Has she got a temperature?'

'No, no,'said Millie. 'It's nothing like that. She's just very tired.
There was a letter from Brian, by the way.'

'For Becky?'

'Yes. It seems to have upset her a bit.'

'Is he worse?' shouted Nell.

'Nothing like that. Thing is, perhaps you should have *told* her
he'd been hurt.'

'But doesn't she realize I was trying to protect her? I didn't
want her upset,' cried Nell wildly, sure now that Becky in bed
meant Becky in one kind of trouble or another, and probably
angry.

'She doesn't see it like that,' said Millie.

Nell saw at once that she would not.

'You're enjoying yourself, aren't you?' asked Millie hopefully.
'With your Theo Walloon?'

'Yes,' said Nell. Anything else would have sounded ungrateful.

'I've got a great part,' said Millie. 'Television. Pays well.'

When Theo finished his own call, he didn't seem to notice Nell's
dismay.

'Look, I'm sorry about this,' he said. 'There's some bad news,
I'm afraid.'

'Bad news,' she agreed with him, lost in her own anxiety.

'Mellonhead. He's gone.'

'Just like that?'

'Yesterday. Been replaced. Isn't that amazing?'

Nell was still too shattered by the thought of Becky's misery
and wondering what on earth Brian had said in his letter to attend
properly to what Theo was saying.

'It means we'll be going home without making the programme,'
he explained. 'I'm very sorry.'

'It doesn't matter,' she said woodenly.

He looked at her crossly.

'You don't seem to understand. The whole series has been
junked.'

145

'I'm sorry,' said Nell again. 'I know it meant a great deal to you.'

'The whole *series. And* the programme. *And* Mellonhead. That's a pretty big chopper at work,' said Theo. 'We'd better get a plane back tonight.'

She saw he was apprehensive and suddenly realized that more might be at risk.

'You mean lots of other people are being put out of a job?' she asked.

'How would you feel,' asked Theo, 'about joining a newly formed independent film company?'

THIRTEEN

On the plane home, Theo seemed preoccupied.

'What did you think of Bronstein, finally?' he asked Nell.

Nell pulled her scattered thoughts together.

'He's stopped thinking of anything new, hasn't he? That's what's making him so bitter. Not what's happened to *society*, he isn't really *in* society. He just hates what's happened to him. Maybe since he stopped teaching? Or since he left England. Maybe the whole trouble is Tuscany. He'd do more work if he didn't have all the ex-pats to sustain him. I have a feeling we got to him too late.'

He stared at her for a moment.

'You're very surprising, Nell,' he said. 'You see so much more than it seems you see.'

This unexpected approbation cheered her, but she was too worried about Becky to do more than smile wanly.

At Heathrow they parted with a quick kiss.

'I'll phone,' said Theo.

'Thanks for the trip,' said Nell.

'I'll be in touch. There are lots of new possibilities,' he said. 'I'm thinking very hard. How about Wednesday?'

'Yes.'

He saw her absentmindedness at last.

'Anything wrong?'

'Yes. But I don't know how wrong until I get back,' she said tensely.

'Don't worry too much,' he said, lifting her chin for a moment.

He hadn't shaved, she saw, focusing on his face as he examined hers. It was part of his arrogance.

And why was that so damned sexy?

147

'Tell me exactly what's been happening,' she demanded of Millie as soon as she opened the front door.

'Hold on, idiot,' said Millie. 'I'd have told you if Becky was in any danger. Did you rush straight back?'

'Someone else's crisis brought me back. Never mind that. Let's have a few details.'

'She took a lot of your old pills,' said Millie. 'The two-milligram Valium.'

'For God's sake! Why would she do that?' cried Nell. She calculated rapidly. 'But there were hardly any left. A dolly dose, not more.'

'Not enough to damage her,' agreed Millie soothingly. 'It wouldn't even put *you* out for the night. But she's thinner and younger, and I'm afraid she had a lot of Scotch too. So they washed her out to be sure.'

Nell bit her hand in horror.

'She'll have hated that.'

'Yes.'

'Did she say why she took the pills?'

'She thought they'd make her feel better, I suppose.'

Nell was suddenly afraid.

'Is she in bed?'

'No. She's sitting out in the garden under the pear tree. We're going to have a good crop this year, did you know that? I love pears,' said Millie.

The light coming in through the glass was a piercing, brilliant white.

'A cry for help,' said Nell.

'Yes.'

'I don't know how to help.'

'It'll help if you ask.'

'I wish I knew the right questions.'

She closed her eyes for a moment, as if to shut out the image of her daughter with a tube down her throat.

'Caroline phoned,' said Millie, uncertainly.

'I thought she was in Korea.'

'She's back, evidently. I told her you were in Tuscany with Theo Walloon.'

Nell shrugged. Everything but Becky seemed remote.

Becky looked thin, vulnerable and pretty in one of Millie's dressing gowns, her bare feet on the grass. She looked up briefly as Nell walked towards her, and then turned back to painting her toenails: ها splashes of scarlet on perfect, childish feet, the paint making the white toes look more soft and vulnerable.

'At least your generation never buggered their feet with high heels,' said Nell shakily.

She put her arms round the child, feeling tautness and hostility in the body that pulled away.

'I thought you were away for another four days,' said Becky.

Nell thought desperately for the right thing to say, and instead blurted out: 'Oh, Becky, what were you trying to do?'

'Sleep,' said Becky.

Her face was closed, and she would have gone back to painting her nails if Nell had not snatched at her wrist.

'Can't that wait? I just want to *help* you, Becky. I must *know*, don't you see?'

'There's nothing to know.'

'Is it a boy?'

Becky laughed.

'Is it me? Are you angry with me?' asked Nell wildly. 'Perhaps you think I don't care about you, because I go to work all day, and because I've been happier recently. Or because I went away. Is that it?'

'You put yourself at the centre of everything,' said Becky.

Nell released her wrist, unreasonably shocked by the flatness of tone, and the judgement in the voice.

'You *are* angry with me,' she said.

'Why didn't you tell me a gang of thugs beat Daddy up?'

'I'm sorry. I thought you'd be frightened.'

'I was. I still am. Aren't you?'

'Wait a minute,' said Nell. 'How do you mean, "gang"? I thought it was a prison brawl.'

'How can you be so silly? Can you imagine Daddy in a prison brawl?' cried Becky.

'Of course, I know there's some kind of horrible underworld

tie-up,' said Nell slowly. 'I just don't know where to start finding out what it is. And your father keeps trying to stop me doing any such thing.'

'Does he? That's a load off your mind then,' said Becky.

As Nell felt the blood beat up on to her forehead, she heard Millie shout from the other end of the garden.

'The doctor is here, Nell.'

The doctor was not Nell's usual GP. He was a sandy-haired man with a small moustache; his very pale eyes looked at Nell as though her short skirt and bristly hair confirmed some earlier diagnosis.

'Ah, the mother has returned,' he said.

Nell saw he was expecting her to defend herself, and resisted the temptation to do so.

He listened to Becky's pulse, and took her temperature.

'Colour's better today,' he said. 'Keep an eye on the weather, though. And put some stockings on.'

Nell walked him back down the garden to let him in through Millie's French windows and, as she did so, inquired whether there were likely to be any medical complications.

'Nothing much physically wrong with the girl,' he said, stopping to look her in the eyes.

'That's good.'

'Not so good. Not so easy to cure, the mind. She's very disturbed, Mrs Bolton.'

'Yes. I suppose she must be.'

'I've made an appointment for you both to go and see a good family therapist.'

'You might have asked me first,' said Nell.

'It will help both of you,' he said. 'In my experience there are few families where there is a child as disturbed as Becky where the mother is not also in need of help.'

'Of course I'm in need of help,' said Nell. 'But I'm not sure whether clinics like that are the place I want to go for it.'

He looked supercilious.

'Mothers never like it.'

'I suppose *fathers* are less guilt-ridden, are they?' asked Nell, stung.

'Well,' he said pityingly, 'little as you may like to recognize it, Mrs Bolton, psychic health depends much more on the mother than the father. Centuries of cultural development lie behind my opinion, and nothing in my experience of North London has altered it. Now, about those pills. Do you still use them yourself?'

'I'm off them now,' said Nell.

'Completely?'

'Yes,' said Nell, swallowing because just at that moment she had a craving for their aid. 'I was down to two milligrams a day last month, and now I only take them intermittently.'

'Then I'll take these with me,' he said, pulling another long-lost bottle out of his pocket.

She hesitated and he looked at her pityingly.

'It always pays to be honest, you know, Mrs Bolton.'

Nell stumbled back into her flat in time to pick up the receiver on the telephone.

It was Theo.

'The Beeb aren't expecting you back til next Monday. I checked,' he said. 'So, what are you doing for lunch tomorrow?'

'Nursing,' said Nell, and explained briefly.

'Pity,' he said. 'I've got a few things to discuss with you. My own plans mainly. What about Thursday?'

She agreed to Thursday.

'May as well sound you out now, though. I'm setting up my own company. I mentioned it in Tuscany . . .'

'I remember,' said Nell.

'I'll be able to do the kind of programmes I want that way. I'm going to need people with good ideas.'

'I suppose you will.'

'Off the top of your head, do you have any ideas for programmes you'd like to see? As a viewer?'

'Maybe something about mothers and daughters,' she said rapidly. 'Or something that tells you how to deal with doctors in the house. Or . . .'

'Wait a minute,' he said. 'That's rather what I thought. Listen,

151

would you be prepared to take a risk with me? I have to say I can't see your job at the Beeb is in any danger.'

She thought about it for no more than a moment.

'I'll need to be paid, though,' she said.

'Would twenty grand suit?' he asked.

When she didn't reply, he added: 'And could you give notice, because I'd like to get the show on the road some time in the next month.'

Caroline phoned at the weekend.

'What's all this I hear about setting up on your own?' she asked.

'Not entirely on my own.'

'Will you work from home or have an office somewhere?'

'St Martin's Lane,' said Nell.

Theo had rung in to tell her as much only an hour previously.

There was a pause.

'Well, I wonder . . .' said Caroline. 'I have a very good idea for a programme. I was going to take it along to Bob and Jolly but that department seems to have lost all sense of direction.'

'You must come in and explain it to us,' said Nell. 'Just as soon as we get started.'

Caroline hesitated.

'By the way,' she said, 'I'm having some people in for dinner next week. Are you free on Thursday?'

'I'll look,' said Nell.

But she was not.

'I'll tell you what,' said Caroline. 'I'll see if I can re-jig the dates. There are some very interesting people I want you to meet.'

FOURTEEN

It was heaven in St Martin's Lane. Not just the desk, and Theo just across it; not just the cafe across the road with its sweet onion soup and croutons and dripping gruyère cheese, and the little Greek restaurant with pale, home-made taramasalata that tasted of real fish eggs. It wasn't even the bustle in the streets, the sense of excited people eager to find out what was on at the opera. The work itself was fun. Some of the time Nell answered the telephone and made appointments, as she had at the BBC. But now she made decisions too, and had ideas of her own, and when Theo was there he listened to her.

Theo wasn't always there, however.

'Where do you go?' she asked him.

'I'm the hustling end of this enterprise,' he said, with a slow grin. 'We need European money. And I still have a few friends in New York. How's Becky?'

'Recovering. Back at school,' said Nell absently.

It was lunchtime, and he had a hand underneath her sweater at the back.

'I'd like to meet her,' he said, giving her a friendly squeeze and drawing away.

'I don't think I'm ready for that yet,' she said.

'Am I a guilty secret, then?' he asked.

Nell was silent.

'I'll be in Zürich again at the weekend.'

'Doing what?' she asked.

'Conference.'

She bit back her desire to ask more searching questions. About where he would be and with whom, for instance, and precisely where he would be spending the night. Sometimes he left the phone number of his hotel, but she schooled herself not to ask for it.

153

When he was in London, they made love in his Notting Hill flat. Whatever hour Nell left, she made sure to get back into her own bed for Becky to wake her up. At first, Becky pried into where she had been every time she came back after midnight, but now she just looked up with sharp, knowing eyes, and made no comment. Nell would have liked to be more direct, but she was afraid.

'I'm a coward,' she admitted to herself.

Emboldened by her first pay cheque she used her Barclaycard to buy a carpet, new curtains and some new clothes.

'What do you think?' she asked Becky, who was still looking peaky. 'You can change the woollies on Saturday if you like. I know I should have waited for you to come in and choose, but I was buying for myself and it seemed impossible not to bring something back for you.'

She really hadn't been sure she was doing the right thing. The jeans were easy, but the thick-knit woollies, with their cheeky, raised patterns, were not. Nell always liked tawny colours herself: golds and warm browns and greys, so that she looked now like a tree that autumn had coloured; for Becky she had risked sharp clashes, and she wasn't sure of her reaction.

'I like the colours,' admitted Becky, almost grudgingly.

'The curtains, too. I'll give you a hand putting them up. Unless you plan to be going out?'

'You got back very late yesterday,' said Becky. 'Where did you go?'

Nell hesitated.

'I went out to supper after the show,' she said at last.

It was true enough in outline.

'What show?' asked Becky.

'South African play at the Almeida,' said Nell promptly. 'You ought to see it. You'd like it.'

'Maybe I will. You're going to Bleakwood this weekend, aren't you?'

'Yes, I am,' said Nell.

She hoped Becky was not going to ask to come.

'You know that Kit Martin?' said Becky.

Nell bent over and attended very carefully to the necessary ruffling.

'Yes.'

'Saw quite a bit of him while you were in Tuscany.'

'Did you?' Nell wondered about that for a moment. 'Did he take you out on the town?'

'Of course not,' Becky laughed. 'Kit and Millie have something going. Didn't you know?'

Nell had occasionally thought about it.

'Have they?'

'When he's here. He can be fun, sometimes.'

'Yes,' said Nell.

She lifted the curtains in her arms.

'I'll need Millie's ladder for this.'

'I'll do it,' said Becky, kicking off her shoes and jumping on a stool like an agile young animal. 'Don't they make a difference!'

It was spring as Nell walked up the path to the gates of Bleakwood. She could hear birdsong; the leaves were still the light tender green of their first exposure to the air; the air itself had a kind of moist radiance. It was one of those days when just being conscious and not in pain seems enough happiness for a sentient creature. Perhaps to respond to such miracles, it is also necessary to be free. The clanking doors, the double-locking, the green-painted corridors of Bleakwood made another comment on the miracle of spring.

Brian sat up in bed, his face expressionless, his eyes black and beady. There was still a bruise on one cheekbone. And he looked much thinner.

'Darling,' said Nell, helplessly. For all her excitement in knowing Theo, the line of Brian's shoulder and rib brought back painfully old memories of love and need. 'Does your face hurt?'

'Not much. Not importantly.'

Nell glared at the nurse who sat impassively on the only stool. 'Couldn't we have a bit of privacy?' she asked.

The nurse looked unlikely to respond; indeed, she folded her mouth into an obstinately straight line. Nell took out her wallet and brought out four crisp five-pound notes. 'Just for a while,' she said, smiling, and making no reference to the money. 'We haven't been alone for so long.'

The nurse folded the notes away.

'Ten minutes,' she said. 'No more, mind. I'll be in the loo if anyone asks.'

When she left, Nell and Brian grinned at one another awkwardly.

'You look different. I don't know why,' said Brian.

Nell blushed.

'New clothes?' she suggested.

'I can see that. Expensive, by the look of them.'

'I've got a new job. I told you. It pays much better.'

'I can see,' he said. 'How's Becky?'

'Can we come on to that in a minute? It's not straightforward. Brian, I want to talk to you.'

'What's not straightforward about Becky?' Brian demanded. 'I can tell something is wrong; she wrote me a miserable letter.'

'Did she?'

'And she sent me a book. *The Master and Margarita.* Did you lend her that?'

'Well, yes I did,' said Nell slowly.

'I can't imagine what she makes of it. Stalin, Writers Union perks. What's any of that to Becky?'

'Well . . .' said Nell.

'The saving power of love. I hope she isn't turning into a religious nut.'

'That at least not,' said Nell incautiously.

He didn't take her up on the implications of that.

'She seems to feel I'm in need of affection, anyway. I was moved, if you want to know.'

'Were you? I wonder,' said Nell. 'Can I see what she wrote?'

'I don't think she'd like that.'

'I see,' said Nell. 'And are you? In need of affection, I mean.'

'Why all the sudden interest?' asked Brian bitterly.

Nell was struck by the tone of longstanding grievance.

'I want to help. I want to understand. That's why I'm here.'

He laughed.

156

'All that concern would have been more useful about five years ago when I needed to make decisions.'

'What decisions?'

'Exactly. You didn't want to know anything about them.'

'That's not fair. I didn't know what I wanted. We never talked about what I wanted, did we? It never came up. You know that. It was your life that had to be got right.'

'We didn't manage that very well, did we?'

Nell breathed carefully, deeply. This was going badly. She had intended to ask about the mysterious Babar. Not out of jealousy, and not indignantly either, since she was no longer in any position to be indignant. She wanted to ask about Babar because, in some way she didn't yet understand, she linked back to what had gone wrong in City Trust.

She wanted Brian to understand that, to see she was on his side, but clearly that was not his concern at the moment.

'Plumrose Crescent,' he said reflectively.

She was incredulous, but relieved to hear the direction of his musing.

'It wasn't much fun,' she agreed. 'Not what we planned, I know.'

'Imagine for a moment what it was like to get off that sodding Royston train and drive back to somewhere nothing happened. It's all right for you. You were always lost in your own world. I don't suppose you'd have behaved very differently if we'd had a house in Chelsea.'

'Don't you be so sure,' she said, stung.

He was launched now into his own thoughts, but the trouble was he had wrongfooted her. If she asked about Babar now, he would be bound to misunderstand. She spoke more brusquely than she intended.

'Never mind five years ago. What about two years ago, when you got into all this trouble? Brian, if I'm going to help you, I'll have to find out what happened.'

Brian looked sceptical. 'Nell, you'll never grasp any of it . . .'

She wanted to say: I will, I'll understand, because of Theo. But how could she explain that to Brian? And in any case, it turned

157

out that what Brian meant was rather different. He didn't think she could understand the details of the case against him.

'Technical,' she nodded. 'I see that. However, Brian . . .'

She shifted her gaze way from his face.

'There was a girl called Babar working for City Trust,' she made herself say firmly. 'Do you happen to know where she is working now?'

There was a silence from his bed.

'I'm sorry,' she said faintly. 'She was a secretary, I know that much.'

'Who told you about Babar?' he asked. 'Never mind. Not her fault, exactly.'

'Tell me about her,' she asked in as neutral a voice as possible. In all the time she had know Brian he had never lied to her.

'Pathetic little creature,' he said.

He sounded indulgent, as if he were talking about Becky.

'I really had to help her.'

'How did you?'

'Signed a few things. She needed a work permit.'

'Where is she now?'

'I've lost touch.'

She felt a wave of relief, which, in the circumstance, was inappropriate.

'Do you think she is still working for City Trust?'

'I don't know. They've moved offices anyway,' he said.

'Where to?' asked Nell. 'I'm going to find out. And I'm going to do something about it.'

Brian watched her scribble the new address into a dark leather filofax.

'That's new,' he said.

'Yes,' said Nell, colouring a little, because it was a present from Theo.

Fortunately the nurse came back at that moment, looking brisk. Nell stood up.

'You didn't say much about the kind of work you're doing or who you're working with,' said Brian querulously.

He'd picked up the difference in her. He wasn't stupid. It didn't seem the moment to explain.

A row of invitations stood on Theo's mantelpiece just under the heavy Victorian gilt mirror, and he picked up one or two and looked at them.

'The Arts Club,' he said. 'That'll be five hundred people bouncing around, and noisy. Then there's the Escargot. What do you think?'

'I'm not sure I can go to any party tonight,' said Nell hesitantly. Becky was having friends in to supper.

He put a hand on her hip and gave her a short hot kiss with open lips and no deeper inquiry.

'What kind of parties are they?' she asked, weakening.

'Publishers' parties. Promoting books. Hard to predict which will be fun. Sometimes they're just for the publicity department, a few reviewers, literary agents, that kind of thing.'

'Sound horrible,' said Nell.

'The Arts Club might be more interesting. There'll be people there I don't see often these days. If you don't see people you forget they're there unless you bump into them. As if they'd dropped out of the mental address book. Don't you find that?'

'I don't have that wide an acquaintance,' said Nell.

'When you're marketing ideas,' said Theo, 'acquaintance is business. Feel like having a look?'

'All right,' said Nell.

There was a long dark hot room, and a noise from an enormous number of people, none of whom Nell could recognize.

'There's Malcolm Bradbury,' said Theo, pointing.

'Where?'

'And Angela Carter.'

Nell looked about desperately from clump to clump of people turned inward towards one another.

'And Melvyn Bragg.

She recognized Bragg.

Theo brought her a glass of white wine. It was bubbling half-heartedly and not very cold, but she swallowed it anyway; it tasted acid underneath the sweetness, like lemonade left over from a children's party. Theo saw her face, and laughed.

'Publisher's plonk. Perhaps the red would have been a better

159

idea. I always stick to Perrier. People who go to these things every day of the week would die if they drank this muck all the time. Ah. There's Carmen. I need to talk to her.'

Theo darted away from her across the room.

Nell simply stood where she was, and waited to see what the party would bring her. She knew she was looking rather striking in black and white, but for a time nothing happened. There was a youngish man with a beard at her side who stared gloomily round the room without seeming to see her. So she spoke first.

'These huge parties. Do you know many people here?'

'Somewhere in this room there *may* be about twenty people I know,' he said, with a self-deprecating grin. There was an American buzz to his voice, and his eyes went on flickering hopefully over her shoulder looking for some of those intimate friends.

'What do you do?' she asked him.

'I have a magazine,' he said, pleased with the usual question. 'The best new writing. In prose. I don't touch poetry.'

Nell knew the magazine, liked it, and said so.

'Why no poetry?' she inquired.

'The horrors of the poetry scene in England,' he said. 'Too many people writing it and not enough people reading it. What do you do?'

She said she worked as a commissioning editor in a television company, and watched his darting gaze swivel from a point over her left shoulder to meet her own with attention. She was emboldened by this to take him up on his reasons for not wanting poetry in his magazine.

'Poetry is an *indicator* of something, isn't it? At least it's nothing to do with getting and spending. It's a *sign*.'

'You mean, a sign that the spirit lives, okay?'

'Something like that.'

Nell was beginning to enjoy herself.

From across the room Liza Thynne, resplendent in green shiny silk, and looking a little like a pantomime dame balanced on minutely-waisted high heels, recognized her and tripped across eagerly.

'Nell, how wonderful you look.'

'And you,' said Nell politely, turning to introduce the young magazine editor.

But they already knew one another.

'Love your work,' said Liza Thynne absentmindedly, being much more interested in Nell. 'I've been phoning and phoning you, Nell, but you are always busy.'

This was true.

'I've been thinking. Feminist Arts are branching out. Are you free on Wednesday for lunch?'

'I have to say we aren't looking for plays, Liza,' said Nell without fuss. 'We want to do documentaries. Theo hates fiction. He thinks it tells lies.'

'Fiction has its uses, but drama isn't all fiction. Do you like Groucho's?' asked Liza.

'Never been there,' said Nell.

'Small portions, nice food,' said Liza. 'Maybe you should join. See what you think of Wednesday. I've a great many new ideas to exchange with you. Documentary ideas.'

Nell yielded to a flash of opportunism, as she recalled that Liza knew everyone. And more than she'd said about Brian. Maybe she could be persuaded to help? Especially since her own husband was involved.

'Yes,' she said. 'Let's meet.'

As abruptly as he had left, Theo was once again back at Nell's side, looking dark and restless.

'I want to get to Farrago,' he murmured in her ear. 'I rather hoped he'd be here. His autobiography is one of the books they're celebrating after all.'

'There he is,' pointed Nell. 'I want to talk to him, too, as it happens.'

'I didn't know you knew him,' said Theo, surprised.

'He's a kind of relation,' she said. 'By marriage. You remember I told you about my cousin Mark?'

'But surely Farrago isn't Jewish?'

'Through his wife,' explained Nell. 'She's a relation of Mark's wife. German refugee. Czech, really. That sort of thing anyway.'

161

'Wonderful,' said Theo. 'You can introduce me. I always knew you were a useful girl.'

Across the room, Nell met Johnnie Farrago's bright blue eyes. Their blueness was so lazily, so insolently visible, she had a hallucinatory moment of feeling convinced it couldn't be natural. Then he smiled. It gave him an oddly sheepish expression. She couldn't be sure he recognized her, but he drooped his lids over that blue gaze and turned away, letting the crowd close behind him as he did so, while Theo began strenuously to propel Nell towards the place where he had disappeared in the crowd.

'Don't,' said Nell, uncomfortably.

She was trying to decide about the expression in those blue eyes. People only looked like that, she decided, when they had damaged you. She and Theo forged their way across, but Farrago was nowhere to be seen on the other side of the room.

The following Monday Nell took the morning off after coffee and picked up a taxi to 97c Portland Place. It was a tall building which had once been exceedingly grand, and was now made over into a series of baffleboarded offices. City Trust itself was supposedly on the fourth floor, and the lift, a narrow, old-fashioned brass cage, failed to respond to her finger. A warren of narrow staircases led into the back of the building. At last, she found a blank navy-blue door with a brass plate which read: City Trust.

The buzzer was answered by a discouraging voice.

'City Trust? No, they aren't here. Packed up a month ago and took everything away, right down to the lino. Are you an investor?'

'No. I'm looking for someone who used to work here.'

'We're renting from another bloke altogether now. Piss off.'

Nell saw that a little craft was needed.

'It's terribly important,' she said. Then she sobbed into the telephone. 'I have to find him. I just have to. Or I don't know what will become of me.'

There was a further crackling, but the navy-blue door remained shut.

'Like that, is it? No excuse, these days, not in my view. Still. Who was it you were wanting then?'

'He said his name was Merchant,' Nell lied swiftly.

'No one of that name here.'

'Brian Merchant?' she cried out wildly.

'Looks like he didn't give you the right surname. Poor little thing. I think there *was* a Brian once. Anyone remember a Brian?'

Someone called out: 'There were two Brians. Neither were called Merchant, though.'

'Can't you please help me to find them?'

'We can give you a contact number, but I shouldn't think it works.'

Nell listened to the number and wrote it into her filofax under the address Brian had given her. She stood where she was, trying to recall why the number seemed familiar.

She had taken longer than she expected. She had a meeting at three with the man who wanted to do a series based on live encounter groups. Even more pressing was the fact that Theo, who had spent the previous five days in New York, was going to be in at twelve and had suggested a lunchtime drink. His voice had been warm and alive, and she longed to see him. She longed even more to feel his warm, casual hand at the back of her neck. To know that he was still interested in her, still found her attractive; not to be too finicky, that he hadn't found some compellingly beautiful woman in New York. She would know at a glance when she saw him.

She wanted to go back, but she knew she had to proceed with her investigations.

And suddenly she knew why she recognized the telephone number.

It was Geoffrey's office number.

The recognition sent a chill along her spine.

'Theo?' she said, ringing to tell him how to deal with the man who wanted to make the live encounter programmes.

'What are you up to?' he asked a little truculently. 'And when are you getting back? There's a stack of stuff to talk about. You sound odd. You aren't ill, are you?'

'I'm playing detective,' she said. 'Tell you when I see you.'

FIFTEEN

The family therapy clinic was in central London, but its premises were far from grand. Little mean stairs. Broken lino. A receptionist with Dame Edna spectacles sitting behind her glass window.

'Boltons, are you? How many? Where's Father?'

'He isn't coming,' said Nell.

'Oh, we *do* like fathers to come too. We must try and persuade him next time. It's most important.'

'I don't think it's possible,' said Nell grimly. 'Her Majesty wouldn't allow it.'

'Army, is he? We can usually arrange things, you know. People understand these days.'

Becky sat down and studied her feet, which were stuck into broken sandals. Her skin still looked sallow and there was just a hint of perspiration on her cheeks, which gave her skin a cheesy pallor. Nell's heart contracted with a mixture of guilt and anger. She would have liked to take out a brush and restore some kind of life to the scuffed-looking hair.

'This way please.'

They went upstairs after a man with a beard and a very young face Nell did not altogether trust. She followed him nevertheless. Soon they were seated on plastic stacking chairs facing a wall which appeared to be a long glass mirror.

'Let me explain how we work,' said the bearded young man, tucking a receiver into one ear as if he were wired up like a newscaster for instructions. 'My name is Dr Halpern. You have agreed to the video already, I understand. Nothing sinister about it. Just very helpful to the team when we come to discuss your case.'

'Team?' asked Nell.

Becky said nothing.

'A group of my colleagues,' explained Dr Halpern. 'Behind that glass window. It's a two-way mirror, you see. Together we form a team that is going to work on your case. From time to time they will stop what is happening in here and suggest on this gadget in my ear some question or other they would like answered. So I may break off for a moment. Then, after about half an hour, I'll leave you, join the others and discuss our thoughts on your case. Then I'll come back with our suggestions. Shall we proceed?'

Nell nodded and Becky gave a little grimace and a shrug which Nell took to be consent.

'Shall we begin with you, Mrs Bolton?'

Nell was surprised at the surge of pleasure the invitation gave her. She put it down to her need to put her own case and nodded vigorously.

Becky looked sullen.

'Let me begin by asking you what seems the most troubling feature of the situation from the daughter's point of view.'

Nell was momentarily nonplussed.

'I think she's been disturbed by many things,' she began. 'Moving to London, of course; moving schools. But mainly, I have to say, because of her father. It's embarrassing, but the fact is . . .' She stopped. 'Last autumn he was sent to gaol.'

The man did not bat an eyelid. Perhaps he saw the wives of criminals every day, perhaps he knew the story already from the school; conceivably he did not believe her.

'And now, Becky. We'd like you to do the same thing. Tell us what you think is mainly troubling your mother.'

Becky stared at him scornfully and Nell felt a clutch of panic: this was a monstrous trick. Apparently Becky felt the same.

'Why should we be talking about *her* problems? That's all everyone thinks about. It's what she makes *sure* people think about. She always presents herself as a victim.'

Nell flinched.

'Why do you think that is, Becky? Tell us what you think makes her want to do that?' the man suggested seductively.

'She'd like to believe everything that happens is someone else's fault. And everything that goes wrong is something that happens to her. I bet she thinks that everything that goes wrong with *me* is something happening to her.'

165

'What do you think of what your daughter says, Mrs Bolton?'
Nell tried to breathe normally, but she was choking with indignation.

'It's totally unfair. Everything *has* gone wrong for me too. I had to leave my home, and move to London, and try to keep the show on the road with no help from anyone. Of course, I'm sorry things haven't worked out so well, but I can't see what else I could have done. I'm sorry she's been so unhappy. I tried to encourage her friends. I did the best I could.'

'Then you can't see *any* force in what she is saying?' asked Dr Halpern gently.

'There are ways I've behaved badly,' admitted Nell.

Becky made a rude noise. Oh God, thought Nell, feeling the colour come up in her face and throat. Ought I to confess about Theo? Could that help?

'I'm not a saint,' she began. 'What she doesn't know is . . .'

She stopped. She had never admitted to Becky what she believed about Brian.

'Yes?' he tempted her.

'Her father made mistakes too,' said Nell. 'He's the one in gaol after all. Why doesn't she blame him? I'd have gone on perfectly happily without grumbling if it hadn't been for that.'

Damn, I'm going to cry, she realized.

There were packets of tissues on the table for the purpose. Dr Halpern motioned her towards them. She was furious at falling in so readily with his expectations, but the tears came nevertheless.

At this point the proceedings were interrupted, as the voice which had been buzzing advice into Dr Halpern's left ear began to squawk passionately.

'Just a moment.'

He listened, with an increasingly sheepish expression.

'I'm afraid the equipment is faulty . . .'

The buzzing began again, even more urgently.

He sighed.

'I'm afraid the equipment in this consulting room is very old, and sometimes this does happen. Excuse me. I shall have to go next door and make out what they are saying.'

'Perhaps we should donate an extra few pounds to improve the wiring,' suggested Nell, amused, and forgetful for the moment that their consultation had been arranged at a specially reduced fee. She tried to catch Becky's eye to share the absurdity of the situation but the girl refused.

Dr Halpern returned, all twinkles and apologies, with notes of questions supplied by his invisible mentors. Nell wondered what they looked like and whether they were male or female. Were they old and wise or could they be, in fact, those very hurried young people she had watched from the waiting room running up the stairs as if late for work?

'We'd like you to try and act out how you feel,' said Dr Halpern. 'In mime. Let me explain. Nell?' She nodded mutely. 'We'd like you to think of some action to express the way you thought of your daughter before these troubles began.' Becky made another contemptuous little noise. 'There's a doll that might help,' suggested Dr Halpern.

Nell picked up the doll, and the shawl conveniently lying on the ground next to it. And her heart contracted with the memory of the love she had once felt for her first and only child. She lifted the doll into her arms and cradled it close to her face. She remembered how she had looked down into Becky's cot at night, and how she had told herself: I don't want anything more than this. If I see her grown up I shall have had as much as life can offer.

'I see. Now Becky,' said Dr Halpern, while Nell's tears ran down her cheeks uncontrollably.

To her astonishment, Becky huddled into a chair, put her thumb in her mouth and looked angrily out into the room.

'That's me, waiting,' she said. 'I'm waiting for Daddy and Mummy to come in from a dinner party and I'm lying awake listening for the car. And they aren't coming back.'

'Becky!' protested Nell.

Becky said: 'They're late. They were *always* late. They never cared about me.'

'There,' said Dr Halpern with great satisfaction. 'Now I'll just confer with my colleagues for a while. If you don't mind . . .' And he went ostentatiously to the screen at the left of the two-way mirror and moved a switch to another position so that the little red light went out.

'You can talk freely now,' he said. 'The video won't be recording.'

'Oh dear,' said Nell.

In his absence there was a deep silence. She would have liked to laugh about the whole business with someone, but Becky fixed her with a hostile gaze that made it impossible.

When Dr Halpern returned he said: 'We think both of you had better come back next week at the same time.' Nell agreed, with a sinking sense of dependence and hopelessness. 'And we also think, Mrs Bolton, that we should arrange a few therapy sessions for you.'

She cleared her throat.

'I have to work, you know. If you think it will help Becky . . . I'm not sure I can afford it anyway.'

'Well, we appreciate your situation. Absolutely. And that's what we've been talking about. A colleague has begun a little research programme and, if you were agreeable, we think you could take part.' Nell said nothing. 'It would involve your being willing to let your videos be seen by a research class, of course – only doctors and student analysts. And we should also ask you to fill in a questionnaire at the end of the sessions, which could take a little of your time. But there would be no cost. And in addition – and perhaps this is the most important carrot – you would be consulting one of the best brains in contemporary psychoanalysis in this country. What do you feel about that?'

Nell asked what kind of research she would be contributing to.

'Ah. Problems in the second half of life,' said Dr Halpern.

'The second half?' asked Nell, digesting the thought.

'Your own insights will offer you help in this troubled mother-daughter relationship,' he said, flashing a companionable smile at Becky.

Rather to Nell's chagrin, Becky smiled back.

Mark telephoned just as she got in.

'I hear you're getting on your feet.'

'I wouldn't go as far as that,' said Nell drily. She was still shaken by her experience at the family therapy clinic.

'Still worried about Becky?'

Nell was startled by this prescience.

'How do you mean?'

'Don't you remember? You wanted to get hold of Johnnie so he could find her a job over the vacation.'

'That was Easter,' she said. 'Things have changed.'

'Well, it's up to you. We're having him and his wife over to Sunday lunch, that's all. Do you feel like coming? He expressed an interest the other day. Said you and this man Walloon were part of some kind of telly boom. Can't say I really like all that high-powered intellectual stuff on the box myself, but there must be something in it if Johnnie's interested. He's astute, whatever else.'

'That's very convenient,' said Nell. 'I'll be over.'

SIXTEEN

That Sunday was cold and wet. The streets smelled of winter. Nell felt lower than she could altogether explain. The family therapy clinic had undermined her confidence, she decided; the struggle to keep Becky and herself afloat felt tainted now, narcissistic. She was too weary to argue when Becky refused to go over to Mark for lunch. Too much homework, she'd said, and Nell tried to believe her.

Nell took a taxi, rebelliously using some of her newly earned money for herself. It made her feel better. The sunshine helped too. There was a misty radiance in trees with their last few yellow leaves as the car flew by Whitestone Pond towards the Spaniards. 'That time of yeare, thou mayest in me behold,' she mused to herself, thinking of the Shakespeare sonnet.

'Nice leather,' said Mark approvingly, taking Nell's coat and hanging it up carefully on a hanger in the cloakroom. The approval lifted her spirits a little. At least Mark found her outward signs of increased prosperity praiseworthy. At least he wouldn't think she was only serving her own ends while neglecting her deepest responsibilities. He wouldn't have trusted the shrink either, she knew. They'd had the argument years ago, when he'd come up on a visit to her in Cambridge. She remembered them walking along the Backs behind the Wren Library together.

'I couldn't work here,' he'd said. 'Too pretty. I'd be walking around all the time in the sun. Much better to live where I do in Kilburn. I can't quite trust all this.'

She hadn't understood and he'd tried to explain.

'I like things to be what they *look* as if they are,' was the closest he had managed to get to it. 'I'm a straightforward fellow. I don't like things to be too fancy.'

That was the day they'd talked about Freud and Klein, and he'd shaken his head with a similar truculence.

'Well, everyone knows the right way to behave, don't they?' he'd appealed to her. 'Everyone knows what is approved of, and what is respected. It's not complicated. People like hard work and kindness and gentleness. People don't like men who loaf around, or women who don't bother to give their kids hot food. Everyone knows how to bring children up. The obvious is usually true. Rare things are rare.'

Just at this moment she would have welcomed some of that wry dismissive scepticism. But Mark had something on his own mind, and beckoned her into another room to tell her about it.

'Afraid Farrago isn't here,' he said.

Nell waited to hear why, sure that something important was wrong, because of the earnest way he was looking at her.

'His wife Jana rang to explain. Distressed, rather . . . Decent woman.'

Nell agreed she had always seemed very fine.

'They're divorcing.'

'Really?'

Nell wondered guiltily if Caroline had anything to do with it.

'Her idea and about time too. She's been a skivvy for fifteen years to that man. Emotional skivvy I mean, of course,' said Mark. 'Wasted on him. Wonderful, creative woman.'

Nell said: 'I suppose I always knew he was a womanizer.'

'Fucking around,' Mark said, with unexpected savagery.

'I don't recall you were so opposed to sexual freedom in our youth,' said Nell.

She felt defensive, because of Theo.

'That's not what I'm talking about. People forget about what hurts.'

Oh Lord, she thought. He knows something about the way I'm carrying on. Perhaps *everyone* knows. Who have I talked to about it? He doesn't know Caroline. Perhaps Theo talks about it?

'You don't sound as if you like him at all,' she said shakily.

'I don't. I don't like people who play around the way he does. I don't feel as indulgent to adultery as your lot.'

Nell felt a little colour coming into her cheeks. It was hard to shrug off this criticism, coming as it did less than twenty-four hours after rolling so greedily towards Theo on his silky-sheeted double bed.

'Is that mainly what you have against him?'

'It all goes together,' said Mark, 'in my view. I know it's not what you think. I don't want to talk morality with you, Nell. In my view, if people want to pack a marriage in, that's one thing. Painful but perfectly acceptable. I'm not bloodyminded about divorce. But all this hopping around with one girl after another just to keep lechery alive . . . Well, I've no time for it. Come along in, let's not talk about it,' he said, and it came to Nell that he didn't want the gossip to spoil the atmosphere of his own table. She decided his remarks were not aimed at her directly and felt a flood of relief.

It was particularly silly, therefore, to enter a political argument over the splendid roast. She had begun to talk about the guilt she felt walking past people in cardboard boxes down at the Embankment, and he had snorted his impatience with her sentiments.

'All very nice for your soul, guilt, but it doesn't help *them* much, does it?'

She stared in her turn, because he was right, it did not.

'Your lot!' he said, with what she felt as contempt.

'What lot am I part of? Writers are beginning to think seriously about these things, if that's what you mean,' she said, truthfully.

'Will that make much difference?' asked Mark.

'What *does* make a difference? At least it's a sincere effort.'

'I don't think sincerity really matters,' he said. 'I just want a bit of utilitarian effect. A few people with organizational energies.'

'Good works,' she said.

'I know,' he said. 'Your lot want to change the whole of society so there doesn't *have* to be any charity.'

'I do want that,' she agreed, 'and for that you have to change a great many people's hearts and not just have a few people about with charitable intentions.'

He made a rude noise like a schoolboy, and she was furious.

'You're a natural Thatcherite,' she shouted at him. 'Don't tell me again you don't vote Conservative. I know what you really think. People just have to pull themselves together, and the whole world improves for them. But it doesn't. Let's suppose you're living in Newcastle. Single parent, three kids, unemployment running at about twenty-one per cent. No transport except for buses out of your council estate. Now the Gas Board has decided to put you on a card system so you have to decide what time of day you can afford to have the gas on. What exactly are you supposed to do?'

'I didn't say *anything* about pulling yourself together. I was suggesting money and organization were a damn sight more useful than having the right feelings,' he pointed out. 'Where do you get all this Newcastle stuff?'

'A programme,' she said. 'Theo and I are doing a programme about Newcastle.'

In spite of the political argument, Mark seemed friendly again as she was putting on her coat, and she turned to him on impulse.

'Never mind all that,' she said. 'Listen, Mark, I'm pretty sure Brian's been framed.'

Mark's eyebrows rose, and his mouth twitched, and she pressed on quickly before he could interrupt.

'I *know* that's a funny B-feature word and I can just see your scepticism, but all the same it's what I think.'

'Rare things are rare,' said Mark again with a sigh. He spoke now as a general practitioner might, counselling a young woman afraid of AIDS unreasonably, or convinced she had a secret cancer.

'People *are* put in gaol mistakenly,' Nell argued.

'Yes. They are. I'm not surprised when you look at the jury system,' said Mark. 'How can you expect twelve perfectly decent ordinary people without the slightest grasp of money markets or computers to understand intricate bits of the law on fraud? The wonder is they ever get it right. All the same, I'd like to hear your evidence.'

She hesitated.

'How can I actually discover what evidence there was against Brian?' she asked instead.

'He must have had a barrister,' Mark replied promptly. 'Notes will have been kept. I don't know whether the lawyer would be willing, or indeed empowered, to open them to you. But I'm afraid you're going to be disappointed, Nell.'

'Rare things are rare, you mean?'

'Exactly.'

Seeing Nell's gloom, Mark was suddenly fired to be helpful.

'Look, there must be a transcript of the trial. Law reports. You can look in those. It might help, just to see the names of the witnesses. I mean, then you'd have names and addresses and could go and ask questions.'

'Mark,' she said softly, 'will you help? I've not wanted to ask because it makes me feel ashamed to be in this mess. I'm not sure I can handle it alone.'

She'd never confessed to any such thing: it had seemed too alarming to admit as much.

Mark looked very serious.

'It's something to do with Johnnie. And he's powerful,' she added slowly.

'Well,' said Mark immediately, 'at least I don't have to be frightened of Johnnie Farrago. I don't need his money and I don't love him. All right.'

'It's a question of worldly common sense,' said Nell, shaking her head.

'You never had much of that,' he said tolerantly.

'No,' agreed Nell.

'I'll help,' said Mark.

'Here's my little team,' said Geoffrey.

Nell took in the PCWs, Fax terminals and telephones. A girl with punk hair, looking hardly older than Becky, said: 'The pre-tax profits on Leisure Club ventures are up fifty-seven per cent, Geoffrey. What about that? They still have a lot of chips on the gaming table.'

Geoffrey smiled.

'Look into their new acquisitions, will you? They may have bitten off more than they can chew. This is Nell Bolton, by the way. Lucy Hyde-White. You probably remember my old friend Brian, Lucy?'

Was it Nell's imagination, or did a shade of caution come into

174

Lucy's eyes. Perhaps not. She could hardly have been out of school when Brian was working with City Trust.

'Their casinos are doing well,' Lucy said.

'Their discotheques?'

'They're really living it up in South Shields.'

'How many?' asked Geoffrey.

'They have thirty,' said Lucy, 'if you take those new acquisitions into account. Ten-pin bowling is making a come-back, incidentally.'

'All part of the democratic Thatcherite Revolution,' said Geoffrey. 'Nell, this is Charles.'

A boy with soft Asiatic features turned his blandly handsome face away from the screen and smiled.

'He knows everything there is to know about the Far East,' said Geoffrey.

'Bensons look pretty sound, Geoffrey,' said Charles. 'But Lucy says there aren't any exit routes.'

'There aren't,' said Lucy. 'Sorry to spoil your fun. Very nice IRR, but five years to get your money out, so forget it.'

Geoffrey led Nell into his office, which was appointed in a marvellous combination of charcoal grey and dark brown leather.

Bemused, and for the moment forgetful of her determination to play detective, Nell asked: 'What are you all doing, actually?'

'What do we do?' Geoffrey hesitated. 'We analyse companies, Nell, and decide which will make good investments. We use about fifty million pounds of other people's money. Insurance funds. Pension investments. That kind of thing.'

Nell was startled. 'Fifty million!' she said.

'For over here, I mean,' he said. 'Charles uses a further twenty-five in Tokyo and Hong Kong. Let me give you a sherry.'

'No thanks,' said Nell.

'I'd like to help in any way I can,' said Geoffrey.

He looked unhappy and she believed him.

'There is a way you can help,' said Nell. 'I think you have a secretary here who once worked with Brian. I want to have a word with her.'

'I don't think so,' said Geoffrey. 'You've got that wrong. What was her name?'

'I only know her nickname,' said Nell. 'Babar.'

Geoffrey blinked and shook his head. Nell frowned.

'You *must* know about her. She used to work for Johnnie Farrago. He told me that Brian got into trouble partly because of her. Come on, you've hinted at it often enough, so for goodness' sake don't suddenly start pretending to behave like Brian's loyal friend. The important thing is, I want to ask her what happened. Because I think something pretty spectacularly unfair has been going on and I think she knows something about it.'

'What makes you think she works here?' asked Geoffrey.

'I traced her from City Trust,' said Nell.

'I'm sorry I can't help,' he said.

She could tell he was lying: the tone of his voice gave it away. But she couldn't see how to push him further.

In the silence he got up restlessly and said: 'Are you suggesting there are things I know about Brian's troubles that he isn't telling you?'

'Yes,' said Nell. 'Will you please explain about fraud?'

'Most fraud is small scale,' said Geoffrey. 'Multiple share applications, mortgage frauds. That kind of thing.'

'I mean, of course,' said Nell evenly, 'whatever it was that has taken Brian to Bleakwood. I want to understand. Are there any papers relating to the case?'

'Hopeless. Too technical. You won't make any sense of it,' said Geoffrey, 'not without reading law for a year.'

'Try,' said Nell softly. 'Start at the beginning. Write it down if you think it will help. Give me a book so I can get it straight in my head.'

'There are terms of art.'

'Let's just have a narrative,' said Nell.

Geoffrey tapped his teeth with his elegant forties Waterman fountain pen.

'I introduced Brian to City Trust through Nicky Thynne. That's my only connection. Old friendship. Staircase in common in Trinity days. What are you getting at?'

'I want to know what happened.'

'Well, one of the firms they dealt with was a big merchant bank with their own fraud squad. Basically they were looking out for false payments of funds. Payments engineered to several offshore banking centres. That kind of thing. They found a document for a fifty-thousand-pound banker's draft, and handed it over to the Serious Frauds Office, and City Trust was implicated. Clear so far?'

'Explain implicated.'

'Someone at City Trust was involved in a rather elaborate piece of trickery. The court ruled that there was a prima facie case of faking.'

'And Thynne,' guessed Nell, 'was involved with some of that.'

Geoffrey stood up, and pressed a buzzer on his desk.

'Thynne was never charged,' he said.

In response to the buzzer, Lucy Hyde-White came in with a sheaf of papers.

'Here are the printouts you wanted,' she said. Her voice had an attractive, unplaceable twang. She had brown eyes and her hair was a quarter-inch-long fuzz of silvery blonde, except for a single strand that fell in a quiff over her forehead. She had a lively, monkey-shaped face and her grin was impudent. Her eyes were direct and open.

There were two oddities however; a single jewel pinned through her left nostril in the style of Asian girls from the subcontinent, and a flash of gold in her mouth which on first sight appeared to be an orthodontic brace, but which Nell saw now were two gold fillings in her eye teeth. 'It's all going good,' she said brightly to Geoffrey.

Geoffrey's red mouth closed shut, and he jumped to his feet precipitately.

'That's all I'll need for today,' he said, with a hand under Lucy's elbow. 'You can go home now if you like.'

'But I still have to sort through the Renbros account,' she queried.

'All for today,' he hissed at her, and their eyes met.

Something in Geoffrey's intensity made Nell speak impulsively: 'Babar?'

The girl turned, in the way people do when their name is called. Nell's eyes fastened on her face.

'Ah,' she said. 'Miss Hyde-White. What an attractive nickname.'

The girl turned, left the papers on Geoffrey's desk and hurried from the room.

'Geoffrey,' cried Nell, 'I must speak to that girl.'

'Too late,' said Geoffrey, with his reddest smile. 'She's already gone home.'

Nell sprang from her seat, opened the door into the next room and stared. The clatter of computer keys was indeed quiet, though the Asian boy was still putting things together on his desk.

'We start very early in the morning,' said Geoffrey apologetically.

'If she's really gone, give me her home address.'

'I don't have it.'

'Why should I believe that when you were lying to me before?'

'Ask Charles,' he sighed.

'Do you know where Lucy lives?' she demanded.

'Sorry.' Geoffrey's assistant shook his head. 'She's changing men again.'

'I'll find out for you by the weekend,' said Geoffrey.

He seemed well intentioned but Nell had a hunch that he needed a chance to consult someone else.

SEVENTEEN

'I hope you're free this evening,' said Theo, coming in at teatime with a sheaf of papers which he flung on the desk in a whirl of untidiness.

Nell looked up hopefully.

'Gürrelieder,' he said. 'Festival Hall.'

Schoenberg would not ordinarily have attracted her, and she admitted as much.

'Massed choirs in black? Heroes called Waldemar?' she questioned.

'Perfectly good name. Don't be so suspicious,' said Theo comfortably. 'The audience loved it the first time it was played in Vienna. As a matter of fact, they applauded so much it made Schoenberg angry.'

Nell had always disliked Schoenberg's bitter face, though she knew, as a refugee from Vienna, he had much to be bitter about.

'Why is that excusable?' she asked.

'I'll tell you,' said Theo, trailing his hand through her hair, and pulling her down on his lap.

Nell closed her eyes. It was a long time since they had been together, and there was no one in the office.

'The audience liked it so much they called out for him again and again,' said Theo. 'But when he came out, he only bowed to the conductor. And the performers. He deliberately ignored the audience.

'Why was that?' asked Nell.

His fingers were exploring the roundness of her left hip.

'You know what he said? "For years these people have refused to recognize me. Why should I thank them for appreciating me now?" Well? Do you find that monstrous?'

'No,' said Nell, since he seemed to expect a reply even with his hand cupping her buttock. 'Just unwise.'

179

He laughed and stood up.

'Tactical, like all women. Did you make notes on the encounter group programme for me?'

'Yes. I thought it was poisonous.'

'Now don't you be a prig,' said Theo, wagging his finger.

'Mark phoned,' said Becky, the very second Nell pushed her way in through the door.

'Did he say what he wanted?'

'He said he had a lead.'

'Really?' Nell looked at her watch. 'I have to be at the Festival Hall at seven thirty.'

'What *kind* of lead?' asked Becky.

'I don't know till I phone, do I?' said Nell.

They stared at one another.

Careful, thought Nell. I *must* avoid confrontation. She smiled, and to her surprise Becky smiled back.

'He's helping me to play detective,' said Nell.

'You've been working very hard at it, haven't you?' said Becky approvingly.

Nell rang Mark while waiting for the taxi.

'I've got some addresses for you. Lucy Hyde-White for instance. Would you like to write them down?'

Nell steeled herself to face Theo's grumpiness if she made them too late to be let into the hall.

'Go on,' she said.

She had them all in her filofax when she set out, ten minutes later than she should, to join the traffic jam at Eversholt. She also had her mind full of Mark's last thought:

'I've seen most of the small fry. Tell you what though, nobody seems to want to talk about Nicky Thynne. Didn't you work for his wife once?'

The Festival Hall was alive with buzzing enthusiasm and they had only a minute to find their seats before the orchestra received the conductor. Covertly, she studied Theo's face.

The first surprise was that she enjoyed the music, the easy tunes,

180

the singers' voices. The next was the enthusiasm in the audience. Then afterwards in the bar there was a further surprise.

Theo was explaining how much he wanted to mount a series on composers, and how ruinous it would be to buy the orchestral illustrations, when Nell became aware of Jana Farrago sitting at a table on her own.

'Who's that elegant woman waving at you?' asked Theo.

Jana was once again a figure in black wool, which her glowing, red-lipped face made glamorous. Her wave was a ballet dancer's gesture, at once graceful and peremptory.

'It's Johnnie Farrago's wife,' Nell said.

'Marvellous,' he said, beginning to urge her forward as he had at the Arts Club party.

'I hardly know her,' said Nell doubtfully. 'Why are you so interested in Johnnie Farrago, anyway?'

'I've a kind of hunch. And power is always interesting,' said Theo, with his hand under her elbow.

'Farrago won't be with her. They've split,' Nell explained, obscurely aware of other reasons for her reluctance to approach and yielding to the firm pressure of his hand at the same time.

'I heard that. Never mind,' said Theo.

Jana looked magnificent, her fine head moulded by black sleek hair. She was all gold and black, thought Nell, accepting the outstretched hand, and perceiving the single gold wristwatch with a minute clock face which was the only ornament on the ringless hand.

'How marvellous to see you,' Jana said.

For all her charm and finery, she looked a little jumpy.

'Surely you aren't here alone?' asked Nell.

'My son was going to keep me company. But then he had a party. Never mind. What did you think of the performance?'

'Brilliant,' said Theo.

And suddenly he and Jana were talking with enormous animation, in a way that excluded Nell completely. And not only because she didn't know about the music. These two shared something else, which at first she could not put her finger on. A kind of weariness? A kind of staleness even? It was something she

181

had seen in Theo the first time they met. As she reflected, the conversation switched to television.

'And what did you think of the Bielenberg series?' Theo was asking.

Jana frowned her dislike.

'I thought it was wonderful,' said Nell, surprised.

'I'm afraid English Jews have no feel of Europe so *you* can't tell. Natural enough, since the whole of England is at a remove from that experience,' said Theo, though she knew he himself had been born in Hendon.

Nell was too angry for a moment to know what to say. It was as if, in Jana's presence, the bond between herself and Theo had been snapped. She felt excluded from another grouping she had not absolutely identified, a feeling she remembered in Brian when they had visited Jerusalem, and she could hear him saying: 'I've never felt more hopelessly alien.'

Nell woke up out of the memory to find the conversation had moved on.

'Shall I tell you what frightens me about there being so many Jews in Mrs Thatcher's cabinet?' asked Jana.

'I know already,' Theo nodded.

'Like Hungary under Rakosi. A very characteristic Stalin trick,' Jana laughed. 'Notoriously, among those trained in Moscow to take over with great brutality, were four Jews.'

It did not seem to Nell altogether appropriate to compare Thatcher's England with a Stalinist regime, but Theo did not resist the comparison.

'How did that come about?'

'Natural enough. Think who ran to Moscow most eagerly in the thirties.'

It seemed a pretty absurd comparison to Nell.

'Surely,' she began, but Theo interrupted her.

'So you think when Mrs Thatcher's policies fail there will be a similar revulsion?'

'I am afraid so. I know it's unfair, but I expect it will happen.'

'But England isn't really such an antisemitic country historically as Central Europe,' said Nell.

They turned surprised eyes on her. It was almost the first sentence she had uttered since they had joined Jana, and they had almost forgotten she was there.

'Is it?' she concluded lamely, with the colour coming up into her cheeks.

She saw the way their eyes met.

They fancy each other, she thought.

Something clutched her heart with a bony hand.

'The mashed potatoes and onion are absolutely delicious,' said Liza Thynne, looking at Groucho's menu. 'But I think I'll have a warm salad. Do have whatever you feel like, Nell.'

'I wish I were hungrier,' said Nell.

'The portions are very small,' said the waitress encouragingly. 'Any wine?'

'I don't know,' said Nell. 'I have such a lot to do this afternoon.'

'All the same,' said Liza, one tiny rounded finger going down the wine list. 'This marvellous new idea I was talking about, Nell, let me explain it to you. I'm sure you'll love it. Fact not fiction. People are just beginning to wake up in this country to the need for a new Feminist intellectual discipline. Courses in all the universities, Feminist studies, you know the kind of thing. And television has made no contribution to the debate. A few programmes about whether women are yet given equal pay and that's about it. Whereas in France and the States Feminism is a way of reading the world, a whole new interest in psychoanalysis, Lacan, linguistics . . .'

'Doesn't sound like mainstream television to me,' said Nell shortly.

'I thought Theo loved doing high-powered think programmes. How are you two getting on, by the way?'

'The company is prospering,' said Nell evasively.

Her voice was a little sombre. She had found it more difficult to bear Theo's unpredictable absences since watching him visibly under the spell of another woman.

'Well, you aren't married to him,' said Liza comfortably, picking up what was not being said with rapidity. 'And how *is* Brian?'

Nell said: 'That's really what I wanted to talk to you about.'

Liza's blue eyes flickered.

'Forgive me if it's painful. But you told me in Italy your husband Nicky had something to do with what happened to him.'

Liza's eyebrows rose.

'Tell me about your husband,' said Nell. 'I know he killed himself, and I know there's never an easy answer to why someone does that. But it's relevant to why Brian is in gaol. Isn't it? Will you explain how?'

Liza sighed.

'I'll tell you what I know of the story, but I don't think it *will* help Brian get out of gaol. It *is* painful. First of all, you'll have to try and understand Nicky. It wasn't easy for Nicky being married to me.'

'Why not exactly?'

'I'd better go right back to the beginning. Coming down from Cambridge.'

'Yes,' Nell encouraged her.

'We didn't exactly marry for sexual passion,' said Liza. 'I was spotty and I ate my own weight in junk food every week. So I had to be needed for something else, like devotion, loyalty, hard work. You know the pattern? Well, they always find us out. Unerringly.'

'They?' queried Nell.

'Alcoholics, depressives, layabouts. They use us, we use them. And Nicky was perfect for me, terribly flattering actually because he was absolutely hopeless and rather beautiful at the same time. Nicky was always much more interested in young men, of course.'

'Ah,' said Nell. 'That must have been a problem.'

'Not really.'

Nell drew a deep breath.

'Is any of that why Nicky killed himself?'

'It's connected,' said Liza. 'I mean, I always knew he needed looking after. And then I stopped looking after him, and started looking after *me*. Something like that. Nicky came from a wealthy family, though his elder brother got most of it. And I didn't have a bean when we married. That was okay. I knew how to handle that. But when Nicky started to get into trouble, I coped badly.'

'Did he get into trouble because of young men?' asked Nell cautiously.

'No. Because of gambling. *Any* kind of gambling, before you ask. Cards, horses, roulette. He wasn't really passionately interested in sex.'

'So he was in money trouble before he died?' asked Nell.

'He'd been in money trouble for ten years,' said Liza. 'The whole period I spent floating my first successful company, he was in money trouble.'

'But if you were doing so *well*,' asked Nell slowly, 'couldn't you have bailed him out?

'I *kept* bailing him out, as you put it. The snag was, my help made him hate me. He began to say it was all because of *me* he had to gamble. So he started to lie and cover up, and I really hardly knew what was happening towards the end.'

'I see.'

'I blame myself for being so easily deceived. I thought he'd pulled himself together when he stopped coming for help. I didn't guess that he'd just found another source of cash.'

'What was that?'

'Client account,' said Liza succinctly.

'Explain.'

'He started borrowing clients' money. You know how solicitors have monies travelling through a separate account? So do brokers.'

'I see,' said Nell. 'But how did that affect Brian?'

'That's what I don't know exactly,' said Liza.

'I can't believe Brian put his hand in the till,' said Nell.

'What I think – ' said Liza, and stopped.

Nell looked behind her and watched two people she did not know sit down at the table next to theirs.

'Someone,' said Liza, drying her lips carefully with her napkin, 'someone covered up that shortfall in the client account. In return for a bit of fiddling of another kind.'

'Fiddling?' Nell's own voice dropped to a whisper.

Liza bent across the table and hissed: 'A good deal of money was laundered at City Trust. I know that much.'

Liza beckoned Nell to come closer.

'Gangster money. Drugs. Sexual services. That kind of money. The kind of money that has to be in a form that won't attract enormous attention. A lot of money, Nell. Nicky helped it pass through several different accounts until it looked legal.'

'*Whose* money?' asked Nell urgently, grasping the whole thing in a flash.

'Ah,' said Liza. 'That I don't know.'

Caroline was wearing a black hat centred on her forehead, and her black hair fell on either side so that she looked rather like a young photograph of Colette. She and Nell were sitting in the Café Penguin in St Martin's Lane, having lunch.

The meeting was Caroline's idea. She had sounded rather low on the telephone, but there was no sign of any emotion now.

'How's Becky?' asked Caroline.

The words slipped between Nell's ribs like a knife.

'Have you ever had any dealings with therapists?' she asked Caroline abruptly.

'Used to be so American, all that,' said Caroline. 'Now everyone has a little shrink in NW3.'

She spoke pettishly, her mind evidently on other matters.

'Well, Becky is enjoying it,' said Nell.

Against her will, the words came pouring out. Disloyal, angry words, filled with a resentment she hadn't quite admitted to herself.

'She sets me up. I fall into the trap every time. She wants them all to see how badly I run my life. She enjoys that.'

'Hold on,' said Caroline. 'Are you being fair?'

'Is she?' snapped Nell. 'I'm doing my best. I always did.'

'Let's have a few specifics,' suggested Caroline. 'How often do you go?'

'Every fortnight. We're supposed to be going tomorrow. At the *moment* she seems pleased with me, but by tomorrow she'll be playing the same game.'

'Everyone plays games,' said Caroline.

'I'm not trying to trick *her*,' said Nell hotly.

'No. But you know how it is between mothers and daughters.'

'It leaves me feeling so defeated.'

'If it's as bad as that, why bother to go?' asked Caroline.

'Because I'm scared,' said Nell. 'I'm scared to damage her.'

'What about damaging yourself?'

'Exactly. No-one seems to be afraid for me. I wish I knew what I was doing.' Nell felt a little prickle of tears in her throat.

'Theo Walloon?' Caroline nodded understandingly.

'Or what he wants from me,' said Nell.

'You've been a good girl for too long. That's all it is,' said Caroline.

'Is it? It seems to matter more than that.'

'It can be quite hard to keep going. I know,' said Caroline. 'There have been a few things in the last few days that nearly finished me off, I can tell you.'

'What *does* keep me going?' Nell murmured, more to herself than to Caroline. 'It isn't Theo. And it isn't exactly the job, either. I just need to believe things are worth the effort.'

'What things?'

'Getting up in the morning, all that,' said Nell. 'Trying to do things right. Sometimes I feel mine isn't the *right* kind of trying . . .'

'You should go to a shrink of your own,' said Caroline practically. 'Someone who has *your* needs in mind, I mean, if you have to ask questions like that. A woman, for choice. That lot have to think about Becky. It's their job.'

'I don't trust the whole profession,' muttered Nell.

The pale sun came in through the glass warmly, and touched Nell's cheek. The world outside was sill beautiful; she could feel the silvery sunshine like a warm hand on her cheek.

'You said *you* had things to talk over,' Nell remembered. 'You sounded low on the phone yourself.'

Caroline waited until the waitress had removed the soup bowls and then leant forward.

'What do you think of this?'

She held out a delicate little hand, displaying a huge green stone supported by tiny gold claws, between which rubies had been set perfectly.

'Very nice,' said Nell. 'What is it?'

'It's an emerald, silly.'

'No,' said Nell patiently. 'I mean why are you wearing it? Who gave it to you?'

187

'It isn't my ring finger,' said Caroline. 'It was a present. If things get too bad, I'll sell it.'

Her voice rose into a giggle.

'It cheers me up.'

Nell looked at the ring again: it was very fine.

'I hope someone good goes along with it,' she said. 'Was that your news?'

'Not exactly. In a way.'

Caroline stubbed out a rare cigarette.

'I suppose you know Johnnie Farrago has separated from his wife?' she said.

'Yes, I know. His wife is really managing *very* nicely,' said Nell.

Against her will, and entirely because of Theo's behaviour, a kind of waspishness had come into her voice.

'He's gone to South America, I hear. With his latest girlfriend. I haven't quite got through all that,' admitted Caroline. 'It's humiliating, isn't it? I mean, she can't be *eighteen*. She's nobody special, not even really pretty. With gold in her teeth, imagine, and a diamond in her nose.'

'Gold teeth?' asked Nell slowly. 'Must be this year's fashion. What's her name?'

'Lucy something. I forget. I tell you, she's just a little girl. I think she used to work for Geoffrey.'

'*Babar*,' said Nell. 'I *knew* it! Where have they gone?'

Caroline said moodily: 'You haven't usually shown this kind of curiosity about Johnnie's affairs. Or mine, come to that.'

'I know,' Nell admitted, unsure whether to trust Caroline with any more information.

'Have you seen much of Geoffrey?' she asked instead.

Caroline shrugged.

To distract Caroline from the importance of what she had just told her about Johnnie, Nell described the incident with Jana at the Festival Hall. At first Caroline refused to believe she had anything to worry about. That, thought Nell, was because Caroline imagined Jana scraggy and defeated, and Jana didn't look scraggy and defeated. It was only when she began to describe Jana's ballet-style black and gold looks that Caroline looked thoughtful in a different way.

188

With a flash of that prescience which often afflicts the jealous, Nell seized on a hunch with irrational certainty.

'Where did you see her with Theo?' she asked gaily, as if it were a matter of only marginal interest.

'Well,' said Caroline, 'last night at a party, I think. I'm not sure. Nell, I don't know that I'd recognize Johnnie's wife. It was what you said about the black and gold that made me wonder.'

'It's not important,' said Nell grimly.

She felt sick with the apprehension of loss.

'Are you still enjoying life in St Martin's Lane?'

'Yes,' said Nell dubiously. 'But I've taken to writing guiltily under the desk like a schoolgirl.'

'Plays?' asked Caroline.

'Poems,' said Nell glumly.

'Oh dear,' said Caroline. 'That's not very sensible, is it?'

'I *know*.' said Nell.

There was a great deal of work to be done when Nell got back to the office, but she felt too restless to tackle it. She was hurt, and alone, and what she found herself doing was as instinctive as licking a wound is for an animal. She took up paper and pencil, not to make businesslike comments for Theo on the treatments which lay on her desk but to add a new line to her notepad.

'The lonely cannot love solitude,' she wrote.

And then her mind filled with the words of a lonely Russian poet, writing New Year's greetings to Rainer Maria Rilke; writing out of poverty and rejection and much deeper isolation than anything Nell had seen. And so in all humility she worked on for about two hours on lines that jagged across the page, and had to be hauled back, with words that she moved about and threw away, looking for an elusive rhythm that missed the iambic by only one beat and was awkward and ugly and, just for that reason, exactly what she needed.

She was left at last with twenty pages or so of false starts and single words like blocks for a building not yet designed. Then she wrote out about eleven lines that said something of what she meant as clearly as possible, and stared down at them. It wasn't yet a poem, maybe not even the opening verse of a poem, but she was happy about the way the words had stopped slipping about.

Two hours later she woke to find Theo standing over her.

'What are you up to?'

'Nothing much,' she said, furtively pushing the note pad under the table. And then on an impulse she added: 'Have a good party last night?'

Theo stared at her and she felt the colour coming up into her face.

'Caroline mentioned it,' she mumbled.

She was already ashamed of herself.

'Listen, I want to talk to you,' he said.

'Go on.'

'There's a problem I want to talk out with you. Finance mainly.'

'Don't see how I can help you there,' said Nell.

'There's an idea I'd like you to agree.'

'Why do you need my agreement?' she asked.

He sighed patiently.

'You've been in this company from the beginning. It matters how you feel. I wouldn't want to do anything over your head. There's a personal angle.'

'Go on,' she said.

It's something to do with Jana Farrago, she thought, gritting her teeth silently.

But the telephone rang and the moment passed. She was too cowardly to press him further.

At the end of the day he said: 'Are you busy tonight?'

'Yes,' she said, which was untrue.

He shrugged lightly.

'Tomorrow then?'

She weakened. Maybe after all she was imagining what he had been going to say.

EIGHTEEN

Family therapy had been very insistent she take up the consultation with Dr Hirsch, but Nell approached that appointment with mixed feelings for all Caroline's encouragement to seek out a therapist of her own. She didn't like the fact that she wasn't paying or, more exactly, that she was paying by offering her experience to research. Walking up the long tree-lined road towards his Joint Psychiatric Services, she brooded about the ethics of such a relationship.

Dr Hirsch had a greying, wispy beard and tobacco-stained teeth: he had a kindly, knobbly ugliness. He didn't look like someone who was going to take her life into capable hands and remould it closer to the heart's desire.

His consulting room was a small box room, furnished in light green; the chairs badly scuffed, the pine table scratched. As Nell sat down, she saw her own face appear in the video monitor like a small TV set, an unflattering mirror which pointed up the flaws in her skin, and the lines of anxiety at the mouth. Out of habit, Nell pulled her hair into a more disciplined shape and smiled at herself rather nervously in an attempt to correct that worried expression. The smile looked sickly and forced, and her heart was beating with a dull, unhappy thudding. It wasn't the leather-seated, button-backed room of her imagination. There was no couch, either; it would have been difficult to photograph her for further study had she been lying down.

As Dr Hirsch bent to fix the monitor for the session, his shirt rode up out of his trousers, like a little boy's.

'Now then, let's begin at the beginning,' he said.

'Where is that?' Nell wondered.

'The source of your depression,' he smiled agreeably.

She did not like to hear her feelings called *depression*, as if she had a disease.

'My husband,' she began.

His sigh was close to a yawn, as if the predictability of all women over a certain age was in danger of sending him to sleep.

'Unfaithful,' he nodded.

She shook her head.

'Abusive? Unjust?'

'In gaol,' she said succinctly.

She was pleased to see his blink, but he controlled any surprise.

'You must be having a great deal of difficulty controlling your anger,' he suggested.

'I'm worried rather than angry at the moment,' she said.

He lay back and closed his eyes, waiting for her to go on, and, rather to her own surprise, she did so.

'I've been a rotten mother,' she said.

She expected Dr Hirsch to deny that. There was a lot she could have said in her own defence, and she was rather expecting him to say some of it. Hadn't she struggled on in extremely adverse circumstances? Hadn't she done her best? A lot of women would have collapsed, and she hadn't collapsed. Dr Hirsch didn't seem disposed to notice any of that. He just sat there, waiting.

She explained about her new job, what she did, how much she liked it.

'The male side of your life is prospering,' he said, nodding as if unsurprised.

In the silence, while he waited for her to speak, she had a sudden pang of longing for another kind of happiness. When had she last felt happy? Reading poetry, she remembered, in a garden with pear trees. The sunshine just warm, the words as chosen as sea-washed stones on a white ledge. She tried to explain some of this to him.

'Writing and poetry?' He shook his head. 'Displacement activities. People who don't get their life straight put far too much emphasis on things like that. Remember Bobby Fischer, and chess?'

She thought of the scribbled note pad and the lines there, the sense of beauty and order it had given her to set them down.

'How can you help me?' she asked boldly.

'I can make you less passive.'

'How am I passive?' she raged at him. 'I've done my best to

make my life work again. It's not my fault if Theo has gone off with that silky foreigner. Of course I don't have that kind of chic. How could I, born in the Midlands? She's from Prague, she has style.'

She stopped, since clearly he could understand none of this.

'Your husband prefers someone else?' he nodded, however.

'*Not* my husband,' she said through clenched teeth. 'My lover.'

'I see,' he said. 'A pattern there. Your husband didn't encourage you, your new lover has let you down. How did you get on with your father?'

'You mean I'm choosing men who will treat me like my father?' asked Nell.

'Most women do,' he said.

She thought about that.

'I can't remember how my father treated me,' she said.

And then she did.

She remembered a bright autumn day, and a tree with few leaves; they were yellow with an intense, almost translucent pallor; and her father was looking up with a kind of reverence. The leaves had the colour of a Japanese pear, a kind of water yellow against the pale blue sky.

'He puts on a good show,' her father had said, looking up at the tree.

'He?' she asked him, a bewildered child.

She was dressed in a white coat, with curly hair like Shirley Temple.

'God,' he said, ruffling those curls with a big soft hand.

Did he really feel so intimate with God? She hadn't been sure. She'd asked her mother, who said crossly: 'Oh yes, he feels he has God in his pocket, with a special dispensation for the rules he breaks.'

'What rules does he break?' asked Nell.

'His God,' her mother had said furiously, 'doesn't like pork.'

This had seemed so absurd to the small child that she had burst out laughing. Why was she remembering that scene anyway?

'You see, it's marvellous, the world,' her father had explained to her. 'Watch the seasons, the beauty of the changes. That's what God is doing.'

'*Do* you talk to him?' she'd asked in a small, almost frightened voice.

'Often, but don't worry, I've never had a reply,' he'd said.

Some of this she told Dr Hirsch, though she couldn't help noticing his furtive little glances at the wristwatch that would tell him the time her session came to an end. And then she told him about her mother's divorce. Her mother, with her harsh tidiness and everything-in-its-place, and her tight rules: always living within your income, cutting your coat according to your cloth. She was such a sensible woman. And she told him about her father's love of splendour, the life in him; the way he danced and gleamed and showed off.

She talked about the day her father left home, the way he had come to see her in her bed to explain. 'Don't remember me this way, Nell, don't think of me badly. I have to go.' And the way she had clenched her own teeth: 'Daddy, Daddy.'

In telling Dr Hirsch the story, she began to sob lightly.

'And so this left you with a horror of abandonment?'

'Doesn't everyone hate to be abandoned?' she asked.

'We make the world conform to our expectations, because it is safer to deal with the problems we know. That's why I expect you feel safer with men you can help.'

'No,' she shouted. 'I want Theo. He doesn't need anybody's help. He is bright and black and wonderful and he's about to disappear with somebody else's chic lady wife.'

'Rather as your mother must have felt,' he pointed out.

This is a crash course, Nell thought to herself. It's as if he's trying to get to the point quickly so he can make something happen.

It wasn't the way her mother talked about it, her father either.

'He had been a pilot in the war,' she'd said to Nell. 'That was it. The uniform. And he was decorated in the Battle of Britain. Oh, it wasn't like marrying a Jew at all! And of course he loved shellfish.'

Dr Hirsch was rounding the session off now.

'More open to experience,' he was saying.

She knew the experience she wanted to be open to.

194

'You mean if I listen to you Theo will come back to me?'

He couldn't promise that, and said so.

'About your husband,' he said. 'You were married a long time. Your feelings seem curiously subdued.'

'I know,' she screamed at him. 'I subdued them long ago, when I saw he didn't love me as I wanted to be loved.'

She had never quite put it to herself like that.

'If you get your way and he is released, if he is innocent,' asked Dr Hirsch, 'what basically will you do?'

'I won't go back to Plumrose Crescent.' She shook her head. 'I want to go on working.'

He frowned.

'We must try and encourage more of your feminine side.'

'Why? I've suffered nothing but defeat on that side. And it isn't just me either,' she said, thinking of Caroline. 'Damn it. Women *are* defeated. Especially in the second half of life,' she said. 'I mean, *what do you imagine happening to me now?*' And she thought: It's all jiggery pokery, the latest magical religion. It will be as astonishing to the generations that come after us as Elizabethan ideas about chemistry.

Sitting afterwards in his secretary's room, she remembered her father again in the garden: the yellow leaves translucent as a Japanese pear, the flesh of a water chestnut. And doing so she felt a surprising flash of something like happiness, before settling to the mimeographed questionnaire.

There were six sheets filled with questions and boxes to fill in. The first question asked her to characterize the session by ticking squares set out between contrasting adjectives. Had her interview been Warm or Cool? Active or Passive? Agitated or Calm? Helpful or Useless? Nell did the best she could with these questions.

What had seemed to her the most useful insight the session had afforded her? More difficult, Nell decided, made cooperative and competitive by the old wish to do well in examinations. The bit about her mother, was it? Or remembering her father going away?

Puzzled to get it right, she decided to go on to the next question and come back, and read through to the last question.

'About when in the interview did your insight occur?' the sheet

195

demanded. Nell thought about that. In a flash, it occurred to her why it would be useful to know: it was in order for students to find the occasion easily on the video-tape.

The knowledge checked her. All that febrile, trembling self, which it may well be the whole point of such meetings to stir, settled into its old place. She picked an insight or two for the early questions: then neatly filled out the rest of the form speedily.

'You were quick,' said the typist, watching her, with something like disapproval in her voice.

NINETEEN

Theo and Nell lay naked beneath an Indian-patterned duvet. In Nell's half-sleep she was aware that Theo was staring up at the ceiling with wide open eyes. After a few moments he clicked on the wall lamps and they filled the room with a pleasant golden light which left the bed in darkness.

'Have you thought what's going to happen,' he said, 'if your sleuthing pays off?'

She was surprised into alertness.

'I mean about us,' he said. 'We haven't talked about it.'

Nell drew in her breath sharply. Careful, she told herself.

'You aren't in love with me, Nell,' he said, absently stroking her flank.

'Aren't I?'

'You know that, really.'

'I don't, actually,' said Nell.

Her voice shook, her mouth was dry, she felt as if she had suddenly found herself on an exposed mountain pass, too narrow to walk along or back, with no handhold and with steep drops beneath her.

'I suppose you think I'm still in love with Brian?'

'I don't know what's going on there. Do you?'

'Marriage,' she said shakily. 'A long marriage like ours. I can't get behind it somehow. It's like biology by now. Like being a parent. Or a child. Of course, in that way I'll always love Brian.'

'Those are the strongest passions.'

'Are they?' she said. 'Should they be? I'm not sure it's appropriate. Maybe that's what was always wrong.'

'Was something always wrong?'

'I'm not even sure about that. I couldn't ever, really turn away from Brian if he needed me.'

197

'Well, that about sums it up,' said Theo, putting both arms behind his neck.

'I don't know that I ever wanted him quite like this,' said Nell, putting a hand shamelessly on Theo's private parts.

Theo gave a loud snort, put her hand away, and moved to get out of bed.

'You've got everything very cosily arranged, haven't you?' he said. 'Sex with me. Love for him. Get dressed. I'll call you a taxi.'

'Come on,' she said, unable to move for panic. 'You've never said what you wanted either. I've never known where I was with you, have I?'

'I've been generally available,' he shrugged.

'To how many women?' she asked, far more shrewishly than she intended.

He stopped, in the act of pulling on his neat little underpants, and stood with his hands on his hips.

'I know why you're bitching. I make you feel guilty, don't I?'

'No.'

'It's true. And quite right. You *should* be. You play around here then rush off to get back home to little Becky. And when Brian comes out of gaol it will be Nell, Brian and Becky all over again. Now *won't* it?'

Nell could feel tears of panic coming up into her throat.

'What do *you* want?' she asked slowly. 'It would help to know that.'

He was in his trousers now, looking round for a shirt, his shoulders as always surprisingly powerful against his neat waist and hips.

'I certainly don't see myself sitting around waiting for your free afternoons. Are you going to go on working for me?'

'What kind of question is that?' She was angry now. 'Am I useful or not?' He looked pleased to see she was angry.

'Remember I left a perfectly good BBC desk for you,' she said, unintentionally aggressive.

'At twice the salary,' he pointed out. He was looking the other way now and she could not see his expression. 'By the way, the extra capital I said we needed for the psychodrama shows. It's no longer a problem.'

'Jana Farrago,' she guessed.

Theo smiled at her.

'Channel Four actually. You're quite right to think she could be useful though. I'm thinking of taking her in as partner. But I felt you'd like to be consulted first.

Nell was out of bed now. She looked at her reflection in Theo's long mirror. In the softly golden light she looked rounded and lovely, and she smiled at herself.

'I am not in the least jealous,' she said to Theo.

He raised his eyebrows innocently.

'And I never pretended anything,' he pointed out.

They were looking at one another with hate. For a moment she thought he would hit her, and unconsciously lifted her chin so as not to cringe.

'Damn you. Get dressed,' he said.

TWENTY

She woke at six. It was a wet morning; the sky dark blue, the pavement shining black, the street lights throwing pools of silver on to the metal of the parked cars. The growling noise of heavy lorries taking a short cut to the A1 disturbed the quiet with the early morning urgency of a holiday.

Nell didn't know quite why she was so excited but she felt sure something was going to happen.

Women with brisk steps, men with briefcases, all were making their way along the street to the tube, about their daily lives. She had looked at them and envied their normality often this year; longed to be one of them, as if normality were some kind of protection, as if she had been snatched from that condition, and exposed to an inclement world.

She felt now, and she couldn't have said why, that the shape of her life was coming right.

Nell knocked on Becky's door and, when there was no answering call, went in. Becky was still asleep. Her brown hair was soft and long over the pillow, the skin on her face poreless as a baby's, a sweet flush of colour in her cheeks, her breath coming and going easily through plump red lips.

The young are always beautiful, thought Nell.

'Do you feel like breakfast?' she asked Becky's sleeping form, and the girl's eyes fluttered as if in a dream, but didn't open. No need, really, for her to get up for another hour, thought Nell, wanting her company yet reluctant to wake her. She couldn't explain why she felt so happy.

The darkness had lifted in the bathroom window and she was just towelling herself dry when the telephone rang. It was Mark.

'Come over right away,' he said. 'I'm just back from New York and I think I've cracked it.'

'Now? Do you mean this *minute?*' asked Nell incredulously.

'Now,' said Mark. 'Get a cab. I'll tell you all about it when you get here.'

Mark had not yet been to bed, it seemed, but was looking unusually spry.

'What have you been up to?' she asked him. 'You look as pleased with yourself as a schoolboy.'

'Slept both ways,' he said, with a certain complacency. 'Didn't take a pill, either. Shall we have a coffee?'

'It smells wonderful,' said Nell. 'Mark, what were you doing in New York?'

'Business. Your business. What a ghastly place the Algonquin is. I can't think why Johnnie Farrago stays there. Terrible snobbery, in my view. Just because Dorothy Parker and her Round Table sat round there, I can't see why people should enjoy sitting around uncomfortably now, eating bits and pieces. I found Lucy Hyde-White, Nell, and talked to her.'

'How did you manage that?'

'A friend of mine. Business colleague. He spotted Johnnie, phoned me, and I jetted over by Concorde.'

'That was very decent.'

'A matter of curiosity by now,' said Mark.

He looked younger than when she had first seen him again in London, for all his fatigue, and kept getting up as he spoke to walk about the room.

'I tricked her. I sent her a little note, asked her would she like to try and help an old pal.'

'And she said she *would*?' inquired Nell incredulously. 'Just like that?'

'Yes. She's a remarkable girl. Hopelessly naive, for all her computing quick wits. Doesn't read. Listens to nothing but the latest bands. Doesn't believe in capitalism, she says, just using the system till it collapses. Do you recognize the kind of thing?'

'That's what she's doing with Farrago? Waiting for the revolution?'

'No. Using the system. She's got this weird idea that all ordinary morality is bound to disappear anyway, so villains are no worse than the rest of the citizenry. The revolution when it comes appar-

201

ently won't come from Russia, either, in case you think she has International Socialism in mind. No, it will be masterminded from Algiers as far as I can make her out. She reads the Koran, does Sufi exercises.'

'She was having you on,' said Nell, remembering the spruce, brisk girl in Geoffrey's office. 'I don't suppose Brian is the old pal she was willing to help?'

'I'm coming to that,' Mark temporized. 'Point is, she's a pretty sick girl.'

Nell guessed: 'Drugs?'

'Of course. I was quite sorry for her. I imagine that's how Brian felt,' added Mark, 'if you'll forgive my mentioning it. It's lucky she is quite sharp, but she still needs more money than she has. So she had to do what she was told.

'How does Brian come into that?'

'She does actually feel very guilty about Brian, Nell, because he was one of the few guys who tried to help her for no reason at all,' said Mark.

'You mean they *didn't* sleep together?' asked Nell.

'I didn't *say* that,' said Mark patiently. 'She has her own kind of honesty, which seems to include giving sexual returns for services rendered. I understood that much. I've an idea that's what happened. I don't think Brian is stupid, so he must have known what he was doing was rash, but he thought he was protecting her.'

'Well, who *was* he protecting?' demanded Nell.

'Farrago, of course.'

Nell stared.

'How?'

'Farrago's empire is built on drugs,' said Mark.

Nell was startled.

'Are you sure about that? He owns a lot of other things.'

'That's the point,' explained Mark patiently. 'He kept his hands very clean over here. He came to England from Hong Kong about fifteen years ago and set up all kinds of respectable ventures. But he has a house in Belgrave Place, and he likes to live in style. So a couple of years ago he wanted to bring in some of his ill-gotten gains, and he needed a firm to do it and that's where Nicky Thynne came in. Very helpful what you found out about Nicky Thynne.'

202

'I see,' said Nell slowly. 'It was Farrago's money.'

'Exactly. Farrago ran into Nicky in a gambling club and Nicky told him his troubles. There was a deficit in a City Trust current account, just like your friend Liza explained. When Johnnie lent him the money he was pathetically grateful. The same thing must have happened several times before Johnnie explained how Nicky could repay him, just by trailing Hong Kong money through the firm's accounts. Nicky must have been delighted. I mean, it can't have even seemed very wicked.'

'Who lost by that? The firm? Client?'

'Inland Revenue mainly. The trouble was there were a few people in the firm who began to notice something was going on. Brian was one of them. In fact, Brian became a genuine problem. He started to get very persistent about the figures of incoming and outgoing stock. Nicky got worried by his questions. Which is why Farrago arranged for Babar to set him up.'

'You call her Babar too?' asked Nell in astonishment.

'It seems to fit,' said Mark apologetically. 'Anyway, he sent her in with a sob story about her dependence on drugs, which would have moved a heart much less easy to touch than Brian's: that she was being *bullied*, she was being forced to do this and that, and would he help her. So he signed a few of Nicky's slips. One or two people from the DTI had already started asking questions. It was an extremely silly thing to do.'

'Wait a minute,' said Nell. 'Wasn't it Johnnie who told me about Babar and Brian? Why would he do that?'

'He thought you'd act like a jealous woman and put Brian out of your mind.'

'I suppose that's roughly what happened for a time,' said Nell slowly.

'He didn't allow for guilt,' said Mark, smiling brightly.

A little colour came into Nell's cheeks. Now she was convinced Mark knew about Theo.

She brought her mind back to Farrago's villainy.

'I don't understand why he would send in *Babar* anyway, if she belonged to him.'

'Oh, I don't think she did then. She wasn't much more than sixteen. He knew just what would appeal to Brian. Of course she was very sharp; Johnnie saw that later, and liked it. Hence the Latin American travels.'

'Why did she tell you all this?'

'I'm afraid I offered her the chance to stay out of trouble,' said Mark apologetically. 'It wasn't very moral, but there was something about her that appealed to me. And the fact is we couldn't do much without her evidence. She isn't frightened of Johnnie, unlike almost everyone else. That's largely because she doesn't really care whether she lives or dies, which is a pretty psychotic kind of courage. But when I put it to her, she gave me a statement and signed it. Not many people would want to risk that. There's no question in my mind that it will stand up in court. After which she said fine, and set off to find a boyfriend of hers who lives in Tunisia,' Mark concluded triumphantly.

'Does Johnnie know?'

'He knows she's gone to Tunisia, but he doesn't know she's shopped him. I've put a fair copy of her confession in the safe,' said Mark. 'You can have this xerox. Read it carefully. We'll get the case re-opened. It may be rather a slow business, my friends say. Unless of course . . .' He hesitated. 'Would you have the nerve to go and see Farrago yourself when he comes back next week?'

'If it will help,' she said. 'If you'll explain. I'm tougher than I look.'

He stared at her, struck by another thought.

'A funny thing happened on the way back. On the plane. I met a Russian poet fellow. You'd know the name. I didn't. We talked about *glasnost*, *perestroika*, all that kind of thing. He'd been living in the States for a while, and something was making him unhappy. It was poetry. He claimed that in the West you could write whatever poetry you liked because no one cared about it, and he said all the power had gone out of the poetry because of that. He was afraid the same might happen in Russia.'

'Well, it's an old argument,' said Nell.

She was tired, and she couldn't see why Mark felt concerned in this.

'Do you think it's true?' he insisted.

'Well, you know what Mandelstam said – that you can tell poetry is really important in Russia because they kill you for it.'

'Yes, this bloke quoted that. It's the next bit I mean. About the reason the power has gone out of literature here.'

She stared at him.

'Like religion. Nobody kills people in the West now for believing the wrong things either, and nobody believes much any more,' said Mark.

'Isn't that rather better?' she asked.

'Of course it's *better*. I know the gains. But what about these losses?'

'Do you care about poetry having any power?' she asked, surprised.

'I suppose I must.'

She could hear birdsong in her ears. A single bird somewhere, smelling an unexpected warmth in the air. Her head was aching.

'Mark, you've been so wonderful. I don't want to have a political argument now.'

'Is it about politics?'

'What makes people work well? Yes. Exactly it is. I thought in the England of Now it's supposed to be competition.'

'You've made me think more than I usually do about all that. Best thing about having you come back on my scene, actually.'

'Really? You showed no sign of any such pleasure.'

'I don't mean this Russian made me change my mind,' Mark pointed out.

'Well then?' she said weakly.

'It's just that he made me see what looks crackpot here isn't *necessarily* crackpot in itself. Very eloquent he was. *You* were always a nut, of course.'

'Thank you very much.'

'Unworldly, anyway. But you've found some kind of niche where your way of thinking pays off, haven't you? Very nice. I'm glad for you.'

'I'm not so sure I've got it right yet.'

'Wouldn't surprise me if you ended up writing poetry yourself.'

'You're very surprising, Mark,' said Nell slowly.

'What do you think Brian will want to do? Will he want to go back to the City?'

'I can't think about that,' said Nell. 'Explain what you want me to do. Now. About Farrago.'

TWENTY-ONE

Nell did not often dream. That night she went to bed early, without even waiting up to see Becky safely home, and fell asleep at once, feverishly, her eyelids streaked with confused images.

Her mother came into her first dream, her face tremulous as she turned to Nell and said: 'Don't *frighten* me, girl.'

'I suppose I could divorce him,' she had said wonderingly to this concerned, slender mother, so unlike herself. 'But how would that help me, or Becky? How would that make me less alone, or more protected?'

'People live alone,' this surprising mother said, shaking her head. 'They cope. You'd be all right.'

In the dream she didn't ask her mother what reason she had for thinking it was better to live alone.

Nell woke with a dry mouth a little after two, to the sound of crashing glass and quarrelling voices. Two voices. Kit's and Millie's. Mainly Kit. Drunk.

'You've been watching me go downhill for months now, haven't you, Millie? Saved by that wonderful inner soul of yours, or is it your common sense? You would say you have common sense, wouldn't you, Millie? Wouldn't you? Or don't you say anything definite? You want to say again I'm making fun of you? I have to allow for the fact you're probably not very bright. That's the trouble. That's why you don't hear the desperation.'

Nell couldn't hear Millie's reply.

'You just make gestures of help,' Kit went on. 'You don't intend or expect anything to happen. You don't expect *anything*. You'd rather talk about how I'm not speaking nicely to you.'

Now Nell could hear Millie's voice:

'I haven't said more than – '

'You'd rather talk then help, Millie. That's clear. The only person you want to help is yourself.'

207

'If you insist on – '

'Let's have no ifs, maybes and possiblys, shall we? Let's have something you think for a change, something you really *think*.'

'Leave me a space then.'

'Oh, I'll shut up. That's what you always ask for. You don't realize I only talk to fill the vacuum.'

'Kit, what do you want from me?'

Nell missed the reply, her body sweating.

'When you talk to the coroner, Millie, you'll be able to tell him you tried, won't you? He'll ask: "Didn't you think it was a bit odd, this and that about him." And you'll say: "No, he was just eccentric, he was so eccentric I never thought anything much about it." So you just naturally let him get on with the business of destroying himself until he'd made a job of it. What else? Just human. Human beings just think about themselves all the time, don't they, Millie? You're just a fly on the wall, aren't you? Don't like to *commit* yourself to thinking anything in particular. In fact, you don't think much at all, do you? I mean, you'd do anything rather than think.'

Millie's voice was muffled now.

'I only say this kind of thing because I'm sick, isn't that what you think? I mean, an ordinary healthy guy wouldn't find it was a bit unlucky to be turning to you for help, would he? There couldn't be anybody more caring, could there?'

Nell couldn't hear Millie's muffled reply, but she did hear something crash to the floor, the sound of angry sobbing and the slam of the front door.

Out of her depth, she sat up shakily and put her legs over the edge of the bed. She wanted to go and comfort Millie. But she sat where she was for a while, thinking bleakly about the savage quarrel she had overheard. Kit, she recognized, was very drunk. But there was more to it than that. Why had Millie chosen Kit and with that choice evidently chosen herself as a victim? Millie must have connived at this kind of battle for months. Just as she accepted that the rent would always be late. As if she didn't feel she deserved anything better.

Nell sat and thought. She didn't feel like crying; she felt harsh and dry. She had always been afraid of turning into her mother, with her petty bridge-playing concerns, her sweetness souring into disappointment at the terrible quiet of her life once her husband left. I'll *never* be like her, Nell had always vowed to herself. I won't be a victim. *Won't.* I'm going to be happy, not ill and frightened. That's why she had hardened up in the face of Brian's trouble. That's what pain did, wasn't it, unless you went under? If you survive, you harden up. What else was there to do?

Did all human beings have to be such separate little selves, looking after their own person, pleasing and gratifying their own little I? Was that the only way the modern city could be? There was no point denying it and pretending to something better if that was all there was: the only sense was to know the truth.

I'm unnerved, thought Nell. I've been keeping afloat, trying to define myself in this harsh city in the terms this city uses. It's all the fault of that damned Dr Hirsch, telling me to open up, have relationships, love. Very clever. And who loves me? Theo? Brian? I don't know what Brian thinks.

She put on her dressing gown and went out to see if Millie needed any help.

She found her in a Japanese kimono, brushing shards of broken vase and some dried flowers into a red dustpan.

'I'm sorry if you were woken,' said Millie.

She seemed composed enough.

'Are you all right?' asked Nell, a little embarrassed.

Millie stood upright from what she was doing.

'I rather liked that pot,' she said drily, 'but it might be worse.'

'I couldn't sleep,' lied Nell. 'I went to bed too early. Let's have a drink.'

'Fine.'

They went into Millie's sitting room and Millie hopped easily into her tub chair with her long legs tucked underneath it while Nell poured the drinks.

'I'm sorry,' Millie said again, clearly ashamed and angry at what Nell had overheard. 'I know all you're going to say so don't bother. Okay?'

'Millie, you mustn't put up with it. Get another lodger. Get another *man*,' pleaded Nell. 'You're not stupid; you must see you deserve much more.'

'I've been studying too hard at *deserving,*' said Millie, with a fake accent and a marvellous grin. 'And I need his rent.'

'Balls. You can *easily* let those rooms. You know that. It's just an excuse. Why can't you remember the advice you gave me?'

'He *can* be fun. Some days.'

'I know,' said Nell. 'Kind too. Some days. He was kind to Becky when I was away. Look at him tonight, though. How *often* is he like that?'

'Most men are shits,' said Millie equably.

She had recovered her composure. Both women sat with a glass, sipping.

'I'm not sure that's true,' said Nell.

She had begun to feel better herself.

'How is your Walloon man?' asked Millie.

She was just trying to be sociable.

'I'm trying to think that one out,' said Nell.

Millie didn't press her.

'Just at the moment, I don't have too much going on myself. I'm getting tired of tapping out other people's playscripts on the WPC,' said Millie.

Nell was suddenly illuminated by a surprising idea.

'Listen, Millie, I've got a job for you.'

'I word process quite nattily,' said Millie, pouring them both another drink.

'*Not* word processing,' said Nell firmly. 'Though don't think that isn't going to be useful. What I mean is this – we're going to be financing some fringe theatre. With Liza Thynne. Feminist plays. Black plays. You can help us choose them.'

'What would I do? Give you a black female voice?' asked Millie truculently.

'Would you rather we had black plays chosen by white editors?' demanded Nell. 'Be sensible. It's not a question of principle, it's common sense.'

'It's a favour. You don't know I'm any good.'

'Yes, I do. I read your track record when I was at Feminist Arts.'

'Where's the money coming from then?'

'We may be using some illgotten Farrago money,' said Nell.

Geoffrey's phone call the following morning caught her on the way out of the house. She was in two minds whether to take it.

'Your tenants,' said Geoffrey. 'They're going back to Canada.'

'Fine,' said Nell.

'Shall I try and find others? The East Anglian property market is very buoyant. You might well find you had a very pleasant surprise if you sold the house now. Did Caroline tell you our news, by the way?' asked Geoffrey.

Nell was surprised.

'We met for lunch last week. What news is that?'

'I'd feel safer if she'd told you herself,' mused Geoffrey.

Nell guessed that Geoffrey was the giver of the ring, but she had more on her mind in connection with Geoffrey than his matrimonial plans.

'Geoffrey,' said Nell, 'how well do you know Johnnie Farrago? You've always hinted at much more than you were willing to talk about and I wondered if you knew Brian was innocent.'

There was a pause at the other end of the telephone.

'Innocent?' queried Geoffrey. 'I never thought that. I mean, I didn't actually see him as the mastermind but that's not quite the same thing.' He sighed. 'You've always been suspicious of me, Nell. I don't know why. Haven't I tried to help?'

'I don't know what you've been up to,' muttered Nell.

'Then perhaps it's time I explained. I meant Brian very well, introducing him into Nicky's firm. Thought he'd have fun.'

'I know all that,' said Nell, annoyed. 'That was a long time ago.'

'Oh no, you don't know all that,' said Geoffrey energetically. 'Absolutely you never realized.'

'The commuting,' said Nell dully. 'Plumrose Crescent. I don't mean I knew about it at the time, but Brian described it to me.'

'Did he mention the boredom? The five days a week, tooth-grinding boredom of the job itself? Brian wasn't a natural computer man, he had to keep his mind on what he was doing. And all his expenses were geared to his salary, so he was more or less trapped. I didn't know how to help. Tried, of course. Provided a few diversions. But he wasn't interested. So when he took up with Babar I encouraged him.'

211

'Thank you very much.'

'You didn't seem to notice. Well, you didn't even notice when he spent huge sums from your joint account. I don't know what you were dreaming of, some Russian masterpiece or other, you were always out of this world. I was on his side. I admit that.'

'Very frank.'

'And, of course, Babar dropped him in trouble. I realize that. So there I am again. Responsible.'

'Yes. And that was why Farrago used you to offer me money?' Nell asked coolly.

'But that was *my* money,' said Geoffrey.

He sounded genuinely surprised.

'Didn't you *guess?* Caroline and I talked about it. I thought you needed it and wouldn't take it unless I made up some kind of story. But I thought you'd realize.'

'I see,' said Nell.

She thought about it.

'You were always difficult,' said Geoffrey. 'To be frank, I never altogether liked your style. Sorry for what happened, of course. Still. You should have known Brian better. Encouraged him.'

'People have to find their own courage,' said Nell wearily.

'Now then,' said Geoffrey, 'don't be pompous just because you've fallen on your feet.'

'There are still a few things that aren't clear to me,' said Nell, refusing to be diverted into a discourse on her own moral short-comings. 'Why did you give Babar a job in your own firm?'

'Because she was really smart,' said Geoffrey. 'And because Brian asked me to.'

Nell was startled.

'Did he say why?'

'Obvious, isn't it? There was a certain reluctance to employ her,' said Geoffrey. 'He thought she didn't have much of a chance.'

'How could he still be sorry for her after everything that had happened to him?'

'He thought of her as a victim. Which she was, of course. And he liked her. So do I,' said Geoffrey unexpectedly.

'I'm not sure she's quite what I mean by a victim,' said Nell, thinking of Millie and Kit, and the loneliness that London could mean if you didn't have Babar's knack of finding protectors.

'You've done quite well out of coming to town yourself, haven't you, Nell? said Geoffrey, with a sudden anger in his voice. 'Caroline tells me this and that. Did you know she sees you as some kind of heroine? Little Nell in Thatcherland. I liked you more when you were soft and bewildered. Less steely. Less shrewd about the main chance.'

'I'm still bewildered,' said Nell. 'And you *never* liked me much anyway.'

She was angry too.

'You'd like to see me punished, wouldn't you?' he said. 'Even if I've done nothing wrong.'

'You *are* the spirit of England Now,' she said.

'Enterprising? Self reliant? Individualist?' he teased her.

'You've never believed in anything but your own advantage.' she said wearily. 'There's just one last thing I want to know from you. Why was Brian beaten up in gaol?'

'Don't know the details of that. I think Brian got a bit lonely in prison. Started talking in the tea breaks or whatever they have. Very foolish,' said Geoffrey.

'I wish he'd talked to me instead,' said Nell.

'I don't think he was convinced,' said Geoffrey gently, 'that it would *possibly* have been any help.'

TWENTY-TWO

Nell passed the Saudi embassy with Babar's xeroxed confession in her pocket. Two heavily bearded, elegantly dressed young men lounged against the pillars in front of it.

Farrago's house was near Belgrave Square. A splendidly dressed African with greying nappy hair stood on the porch of Farrago's house. The door was open and a carpet stretched into the huge interior. As Nell approached, she realized that there was some kind of tea-party going on. When she entered the hallway a woman dressed in maid's black, with a frilly white apron, took her coat and ushered her into a room with chandeliers whose bulbs were shaped like candles, and huge curving windows that opened on to a magical garden. There were a few women sitting on velvet chairs in neat hats; their skins glowing with more than youth. *Money,* thought Nell, apprehensive and amused at the same time.

And then, suddenly, there was Johnnie Farrago himself; large, handsome and cool as a stranger.

'So glad you could come,' he said, and introduced Nell to an ambassador's wife. 'This is our regular Wednesday gathering, but Jana is away.'

Nell smiled politely. It was a decided relief to have other people about. In her fantasy, she had imagined a deserted dark house, with a sinister butler from some thirties gangster movie.

Nell said: 'I want to talk in private.'

'So you said. No problem,' said Johnnie and, putting a hand under her arm, steered her away from the room where most of his guests were congregated. On the way an elegant gentleman in tails offered her a silver platter of bread smeared with black caviare.

'There,' said Johnnie, when they were seated together on a cosy window seat far from the noise of party conversation. 'Now we are private enough.'

Nervously, she ate her round of caviare.

'Is this real?' she asked involuntarily, her tongue delighting in the way the grey eggs broke open and released their savour.

He laughed.

'You don't seem very afraid to beard the monster in his den, little Nell.'

'I'm not,' she said.

But it wasn't true – she could feel her lips drying with the knowledge that everything now depended on how she handled herself in this room.

'If you really have evidence of criminal deeds, as you said on the phone, aren't you afraid I will do something criminal to you?'

His eyes were cold and blue. She could see them in the mirror they were facing.

'I would be,' she said, 'but I've taken a few precautions. Before I came here I lodged everything with my cousin Mark, who is incorruptible. And Geoffrey, who is sharp enough to look after it.'

'And then again,' said Johnnie, 'what evidence is that exactly?'

'Signed affidavits on the City Trust fraud,' said Nell promptly. 'Properly witnessed. A barrister put them together. There's no question but that they'll stand up in court.'

'Your cousin Mark again,' he said, nodding. 'Yes. Bright fellow. I assume there is some reason you are coming to see me. What actually is the point of tipping me off, as it were, if you already have all the evidence you need?'

'I want to get Brian out of gaol,' she said, 'a great deal more than I want to send you into it. If you help me to do that, you'll be putting right one of the nastiest tricks you ever played.'

'And what on earth makes you think that I'll just collapse, and fold up my tent?' inquired Johnnie politely. 'Am I thought of as a pushover?'

His blue eyes looked sharp and dangerous, and Nell took a deep breath because this was the difficult bit. This was exactly the point Mark had stressed was crucial. And Mark wasn't even sure, he was only guessing.

'You're selling up anyway. Aren't you? I'm only suggesting you advance your plans a few months.'

He frowned now.

'Explain.'

She hesitated.

'Something to do with your father. The war. Rumours.'

'That old story,' he said. 'Nothing was ever proved. What is it to do with me what my father did? The Americans didn't care.'

'Well, I don't care what you're running from either,' she said, as if wearily. 'My point is you've already started to move out, haven't you?'

Now he was angry his eyes looked like chips of steel.

'That's a tale could wipe millions off my shares.'

'Exactly,' she said.

She was home and dry.

'But there's no need for it to get about.'

He stared at her to see if he had understood her correctly.

'I see. And if I do what you say, you will quietly let me skip the country?'

'You could go anywhere you liked,' she said.

'I might believe that of *you*. But not of the incorruptible Mark.'

'He seems very fond of your wife,' she pointed out. 'There seems no reason why she should be put through the whole trial.'

'And how about all my business concerns?'

'They will flourish without you, I'm sure.'

'I seem fated,' said Johnnie, with a flicker of humour at his lips, 'to be separated from part of my money. Very well. I am persuaded. Will I have about twenty-four hours?'

'Yes.'

'And will you and Brian be happy?' said Johnnie, appending his signature without further argument.

'I don't know,' said Nell. 'We used to be.'

TWENTY-THREE

'How do you mean, I can leave?' asked Brian.

He didn't seem as absolutely delighted as Nell had imagined.

'Don't you want to go?'

'Depends on what is out there,' he said. 'If it's more of the same, I'm not sure I do.'

'Well, I've sold Plumrose Crescent,' said Nell.

She hadn't meant to break it quite like that, and in fact it wasn't absolutely true; she would need Brian's signature when the contracts were exchanged the following week.

He stared.

'We can't move Becky again, can we?' she persisted. 'Not just before O levels. And there's nothing holding us in Royston now, whatever job you get. Is there?'

'Very assertive,' he grunted. 'But we'll need a mortgage. And what kind of job are you thinking I'll get?'

She didn't quite know how to put it.

'You could wait and see,' she temporized. 'What have you been doing?'

'I've been reading Pindar,' he said.

She stared at him.

'My Greek was quite rusty when I came in. I've just about got it back. It's the best thing I ever did. It's made me happy, for the first time since – '

'Since we got married,' she finished for him glumly.

'Since we had Becky,' he corrected. 'That was the turning point, wasn't it?'

'You don't want to go back into the City?' she asked. 'Mark said there wouldn't be a problem.'

'I hope you aren't going to keep on running things,' he said.

'I *had* to run things, didn't I?' she said, stung. 'What was I supposed to do, not do anything at *all*? Just go under?'

'Little Nell,' he said moodily.

'I was an idiot when you married me,' she admitted, eager to throw off any claim to bossiness. 'Brian, listen, there are one or two things I want to sort out. Have you heard what happened to Babar?'

'South America, wasn't it? Or Mexico. With the great Farrago himself.' He laughed bitterly. 'And I was sorry for *her*.'

'Her statement is what saved you. She was touchingly grateful, apparently.'

'Is that what you wanted to talk about?'

'No.'

'It's about Theo Walloon, isn't it? Becky hinted this and that last time she came.'

Nell let that go.

'I don't think I want to know any more about it, really,' said Brian.

'You may not *care* now,' she said cautiously, 'but I think you might later on.'

Brian smiled. It was such a complacent smile that Nell found herself telling the truth, in a rush and without worrying whether he would be hurt or not.

'I'm not absolutely sure it's right for us to go back together, you and I, anyway,' she concluded.

He looked extremely surprised.

'Becky said there wasn't a problem now. You and Theo had quarrelled, or something.'

'We have.'

'So?'

'I have to feel there's something still there between *us*,' she said. She wanted him to say: Nell, you've been wonderful, you've saved me, there's never been anyone but you. I love you.'

He didn't say any of it. Instead he leaned forward and kissed her lightly on the forehead.

'I suppose it makes most sense to stay together,' he said.

A flood of anger rushed up to her hairline. His half-grudging, surly manner seemed no way to start a new life. It came to her that she had often been angry in just that way in Plumrose Crescent and expressed none of it. What on earth was the point of not being angry now?

They would be a family again. Becky would be happy. That was something, she told herself. But it wasn't enough. It wasn't.

'Look,' said Brian, 'you and I were apart for a long time. Long before City Trust and the legal trouble. For years, almost all the while in Plumrose Crescent, our lives were miles apart. You can't just expect us to fall into one another's arms now.'

'I do, though,' she said. 'I insist on it, actually.'

He looked surprised by her new vehemence.

'I've been going back too,' she said. 'Reading and thinking. And writing.'

'Scripts,' he nodded. 'Becky said.'

'Not only,' she said. 'There are things I want to show you.'

She wanted to say: It's not just the salary and the job in St Martin's Lane; it's my sense of self that has changed this year. She went on looking straight into his eyes instead.

'More,' she said. 'I want more than just making do.'

On the way out of Bleakwood, she passed a public telephone box and went to it impulsively.

'Theo?' she asked gruffly.

Theo sounded as surprised to hear her voice as she was to find him at home on a weekend.

'I'm at Bleakwood,' she said. 'Don't interrupt. I thought you were in New York, but since you aren't, let me ask. Could I move in with you for a while?'

There was a pause.

'What about Becky?' he asked finally.

'Brian can look after Becky,' she said.

She didn't mention Jana Farrago.

There was another pause.

'What's happened?' he asked.

'Nothing's happened,' she said drily. 'That's rather the point. Brian's packing up and taking a later train. I'm coming back now.'

'Good,' he said. 'I'll wait for you at Paddington.'

219